I0671055

The Music of Chaos

BY

P. KIRBY

ભ

Decadent Publishing
www.decadentpublishing.com

This book is a work of fiction. Names, characters, places, and incidents are the products of the author's imagination or used fictitiously. Any resemblance to actual events, locales or persons, living or dead, is entirely coincidental.

The Music of Chaos
Copyright 2011 by P. Kirby
ISBN: 978-1-61333-060-9
Cover design by Dara England

All rights reserved. Except for use in any review, the reproduction or utilization of this work, in whole or in part, in any form by any electronic, mechanical or other means now known or hereafter invented, is forbidden without the written permission of the publisher.

Published by Decadent Publishing Company
www.decadentpublishing.com

Printed in the United States of America

~DEDICATION~

For Justin, the love of my life.

In loving memory of Gheri, my forever love and muse.

Chapter One

There is nothing hellish about the world of the Sh'ree demons. If humans could get past their understandable aversion to seven-foot tall, blue-skinned, yellow-eyed demons, the Sh'ree homeland might easily bypass Hawaii in tourism. The summers are hot, but no hotter than Phoenix, Arizona. With its mild winter, and a spring and fall best described as idyllic, the Sh'ree plane has the added potential to attract retirees in droves.

Of course, most humans have no idea such a place exists, and the Sh'ree aren't about to start passing out travel brochures.

Humans are banned from the Sh'ree plane.

Given that I owed half my existence to a human mother, I should have been honored by my admittance to the Sh'ree world and the finest magic school in all the known planes—the Sh'ree College of the Arcane. I should have been on-my-knees-grateful, because what I really deserved was the type of institution whose name included the words "School for Incorrigible Girls."

I was not honored and, in fact, was rather peeved by what I felt was an egregious miscarriage of justice. This particular day, I was four hours into an adolescent snit.

I couldn't have picked a nicer day to be miserable.

The sun and breeze had reached that perfect state of balance, each politely deferring to the other, neither taking the lead. The result was the kind of day that drives everyone out into the fresh air.

I had the picnic table to myself, a consequence of the ambiance created by an abundance of sulky energy. Little angry doodles—stick figures with either pointed ears or sharp fangs—covered the piece of parchment before me. As soon as I finished a figure, I would obliterate it with a dense weaving of sharp, crosshatched lines.

I was completing another drawing, the toothy variety, when a long shadow fell across my work. I dipped the pen in an inkwell and started to annihilate the stick-figure vampire. The shadow shrank as its caster sat down across from me.

After a minute, Talis, the shadow's owner, spoke. "The elves, I understand." He pointed at one of the stick elves. "But vampires? Why are you so angry with vampires?"

I looked up at the brave soul who had dared the displeasure of my company. Imagine the stereotypical elf, tall, blond and blue-eyed, and then stuff that image into a toaster with the setting on "dark." What pops out would look a lot like Talis. He had skin the color of a Hershey bar. His straight black hair was short, scruffy and uneven, bangs falling over canted pale blue eyes.

Talis, like myself, wasn't a native of the Sh'ree plane. He hailed from the Fey plane, a place where you are nothing if you are not an elf, and less than nothing if you are a *dark* elf. Talis didn't venture home too often.

In lieu of an explanation, I drew another elf, this one with its skinny arm held straight out to the side. The next figure had no fangs or ears, and I drew it lying at the elf's feet. I added a handful of drops that fell from the elf's arm and down to the human stick figure's mouth.

"There was an elf." I pointed at the drawing. "This elf came across a dying human. The elf thought he might save the human by giving him Blood Gift." I turned the human's eyes into little Xs. "But it didn't work. The human died and his soul went...wherever souls go when they escape their earthly bonds." I sketched a vampire. "Except, with all that magical elf blood in his system, the human didn't take dying lying down." I drew an arrow from the dead human to the vampire. "He became a vampire."

Talis, who knew the story already, listened with indulgent patience.

I drew a second vampire. "And, the first vampire created another vampire." I drew the new vampire's mouth so that he appeared to be smirking.

6

"If it weren't for *that* elf and the vampire he created, I'd have never met *this* vampire." I jabbed the pen in the approximate location of the vampire's heart.

"Ah," said Talis. "So it's not all elves or vampires. Just those three." He pointed at Vampire Two. "So what did he do?" Talis leaned over the table. "It is a 'he,' right? You didn't draw any anatomical details."

"Talis!" My voice cracked with embarrassment. "Yes. He."

The version of the story I told Talis was accurate but somewhat abridged.

Four years before, I had been a happy-go-lucky drain on my father's resources—eating, sleeping, and dodging schooling when possible. Up until that point, I had largely escaped Dad's attention.

Playing tonsil hockey with one of Dad's business associates, a.k.a. the smirking vampire from my drawing, got me noticed—fast. Dad came to the logical conclusion that his daughter suffered from a lack of constructive activities and the time had come for her to join the family business. I was packed off to the Brethren's Paris headquarters for four years of strategy and combat training. The study of all things magical was the current leg in my career journey.

What I didn't tell Talis was that *that* vampire had the notable distinction of being, to date, the first and only person I had ever kissed. At the time of the fateful kiss, I had been sixteen; currently, I was twenty going on twelve. Any semblance of maturity was a good century away.

"And on account of that one kiss, I got banished to a demon plane," I said, reaching for the tones of a Shakespearean actress, and falling far short.

"Wow," said Talis, "Does this fellow have a name? Or should we just call him 'Wonder Lips'?"

I covered my face with my hands to hide the blush that simmered up to the surface. "Nobody," I answered, peeking between my fingers.

"Nobody?" He set his bony elbows on the table and propped his thin face in his palms. "Oh, yeah. 'Nobody.' I know him."

I tried not to laugh and failed. Talis laughed too, humor warming his ice blue eyes.

"On account of Nobody, I'm here." I thumbed though the book in front of me.

"This isn't that bad." Talis gestured around the park with one loose-jointed elegant hand. "It's kinda..." he paused, searching for the word, "picturesque."

Conservationists as well as powerful sorcerers, Sh'ree demons took pride in their spectacular landscapes. The late afternoon sun, filtered through a permanent cloudbank in the western sky, was always a warm murky orange. Thick-trunked trees with gnarled alligator bark flanked the western edge of the campus park, blocking out most of the sun's rays.

"I suppose. If I were here on holiday," I replied, pushing out a sigh. I'd spent the morning feeding my angst generous spoonfuls of self-pity and wasn't quite ready to send it away.

"This is part of your Wolfe training, right? And being a Wolfe brings prestige among your people, doesn't it?" Talis stretched long legs under the table and nudged my feet with his.

"Perhaps," I said with a shrug. My notion of "a people" was, and still is, a bit nebulous. I'm the improbable outcome of human and vampire hanky-panky. My irises are dark opaque green, an indication of a pinch of elf in the wacky genetic mix. I'm not immortal, but I'll probably give Methuselah a run for his money.

The Grey Brethren, a sort of old boy's vampire business club, financed my training. Think of the Masons, with all the ritual, and very little of the charity work. In me, the Brethren thought they'd found the perfect operative: a daywalker with girl-next-door looks, almost indistinguishable from a human, right down to my soul.

I flipped open the textbook—*Techniques of Sorcery I*—and started my homework. A lock of black hair, which had somehow squirmed its way loose of my braid, fell over my eyes. I shoved it behind an ear and tried to concentrate. Out of the corner of my eye, I saw Talis's slender fingers close around another book. He slid the text over to his side of the table, opened it and studied the loose sheet of paper tucked within its pages.

"An interesting approach."

I lifted my head. "What'd you mean? Math is the one subject I'm any good at."

His angled eyebrows climbed upward. "You're very good. The way you solved this problem. It's clever and obvious, but I'd reckon everybody else will do it the hard way."

"Thanks." Most of the classes were taught in formal Elvish. I could speak passable Common Elvish, but the more sophisticated version of the language translated into meaningless pretty chatter. My inability to communicate didn't matter in mathematically-based classes, but everything else was a sticky morass of audio confusion.

"Something the matter?" he asked.

"I'm failing...everything," I said, surprised by my candor. "Especially, this stupid sorcery class."

"Really? I hear you always take the top score on the practicals."

I winced. "Practicals, yes. Written? I've failed every test to date." I scowled at the homework problem before me. "I just don't get it." The question posed was as follows: "Provide the correct word/syllable sequence required to lift two freshly cut wooden dowels and twist them together into a spiral."

The correct response should have been a sequence of words in any language. The language itself didn't matter. Only that the cadence and rhythm of the words create a sympathetic vibration with the user's innate magic and thus craft the spell form. I could hear the musical tune that would accomplish the task, but *words?* Even when I got the right ones, it usually didn't work.

Early on in the class, I had asked if music was an allowable substitute for words. The instructor's answer had been an abrupt "No." I hid my disability, but I think the instructor knew I relied on "a tune in my head" to get through the practicals. Oddly enough, I was never marked down.

Talis grasped the edge of the sorcery book, dragging it and my homework away. He spun the text around and studied the problem. A group of passing fairy girls took advantage of his distraction to study him with tittering awe. Despite being the member of a discredited Fey race, Talis was an effective playboy, his bedpost about one notch away from crumbling structural failure.

Attention still on the problem, he plucked the pen from my hand, and twirled it through his fingers, never spilling a drop of ink. After a minute, he glanced back at my math homework and then carefully wrote something down. He pushed everything back at me.

I stared at what he had written. The correct answer, in formal Elvish, and in a pretty good approximation of my handwriting.

"A bloody, playboy, polo player is smarter than me." I rubbed my eyes. "Sorry, I didn't mean...."

He shrugged. "I can get you the exams...ahead of time?"

"Get" must have meant "steal." Ironic, since I doubt he ever had to steal exams for himself. I met his eyes. Everything has a price.

"Thank you. But, I'm only given a small stipend. I can't afford—"

"I meant, free of charge." A wounded expression settled on his dark face.

"Oh. Sorry." I stared at the page before me, homework problems that would take all night. At least.

"What if I get caught? My father—"

"You won't get caught," he said with a lazy smile and a tone that melted women's undergarments. "Trust me."

I drew a deep breath. In my head, a nagging little voice said, "Don't do it, Regan. You'll regret it." That little voice had an incredible workload back then and was hoarse and inaudible most of the time. It was echoed by my father's: "Make me proud."

I couldn't make him proud by flunking out.

"All right. Just this once. Midterms," I said like a future dopehead buying her first hit.

Over the next five years, academic dishonesty would spread through my course work like a head cold in a preschool. I'd graduate and go to work at my awaiting job, convinced I'd gotten away with all that cheating. Even with regular challenges to my deficient job skills— bickering demons, trade wars, the fashions of the 1970s—I survived.

But Justice isn't blind. She's just overbooked.

More than a century later, I finally popped up on her docket.

Chapter Two

At the distinctive sound of her footfalls, my eyes widened and I searched my cubicle, wishing for an escape route or at least a hiding place. It was nine o'clock Thursday morning. That inglorious time when lunch is nothing more than a faint hope and quitting time just a fable.

In the ensuing century since completing Wolfe training, I had discovered that my mathematical abilities could add up to surprising success and even respect in the eight-to-five human workplace. So long as I avoid anything high profile—like astronaut—and it didn't interfere with my duties as Wolfe, the Grey Brethren tolerated my forays in a regular career.

Of course, traditional jobs are not without their irritants. My most recent degree, a doctorate in Computer Engineering, had earned me an only-slightly-larger-than-tiny cubicle at Koar Industries. I sighed and spun my chair around to face the doorway and one of that special breed of irritant—a coworker.

"Regan. Good morning," said Eva Osborne as she breezed into my cubicle, her eye shadow reflecting a silvery blue glare. Her hands rose to brush at hair far too red for her olive skin. Plump and gregarious, Eva was an eternal optimist. Despite being the divorced mother of two teenagers from hell and the unfortunate ex-wife of one Carl Osborne, Eva still believed in happy endings. Romantic, schmaltzy, happy endings.

"Oh, would you look at those...." Eva's voice trailed off, her gaze on the one place on my desk that wasn't covered in paper.

I glanced at the small swath of cleared desk space. Little origami cranes, fashioned out of paper that read, "While You Were Out," were lined up in a meandering row.

"It's my evil army of cranes, ready for world dominion and suchlike." A row of plastic green army men—a gift from a friend—stood valiantly between the wicked birds and an unprepared world.

Eva gave me a condescending smile. "They're pink, Regan."

"Unfortunately, these things don't come in black." I flapped the remains of the message pad at her. "Why do we have these, anyway?"

"They're for people who can't figure out how to use voice mail," said a toneless voice from behind Eva.

Eva startled and turned to face the newcomer. Joan Wallace stood in the tiny doorway of my cubicle, faded blue eyes magnified and expressionless behind Coke bottle thick glasses. The left corner of her mouth twitched upward—Joan's version of a smile—and she tilted her head toward our boss's office.

"Hey, Joan," I said.

"I'm going down to the warehouse," said Joan. "I'll be back around one." I was Joan's immediate supervisor, although I didn't care what she did as long as she finished my assignments on time.

Once Joan left, I fixed Eva with a solid stare. "No."

"No?" She sounded hurt. "But I haven't—"

"You sure you're Catholic? Because you'd have made a great Jewish *yenta*." I hummed a few bars of *Matchmaker*.

"Humph." She folded her arms over her large chest, then unfolded them and picked up one of the cranes. "Be nice or the birdie dies."

"Okay, okay." I hated to waste good minions. "Tell me about *him*." I shuddered and held out a hand.

She plopped the little pink bird on my palm. "He's very nice."

"Uh-oh. *Nice?*" I returned the crane to his companions.

"Nice. Sweet." She gave me a Mom look. "I think you two have a lot in common."

"Like what?" *He hasn't had sex in decades, either?*

"He's smart and cute in a nerdy kind of way. Like a professor."

"A professor?" I've spent too much time in institutions of higher learning for that to be a selling point. "As in dirty old man chasing twenty-something grad students? Or as in...'Nutty'?"

"You're so cynical."

"Uh-huh. Tonight's my hair washing night."

"Please, Regan." Her chest rose in a dramatic sigh and she fired off a stream of words. "He's a friend of Kyle's. Kyle's been working a lot. We've been having a hard time finding the time to see each other. Kyle and Jason have to work again, tonight. I was hoping to see him for dinner. But he doesn't think that would be fair to Jason. You know, three's a crowd?" Hope burned from her eyes. "But if you could come along, tonight?" She tried to smile and only succeeded in baring her teeth.

"Okay." Eva's desperation vibes were sapping my cranes of their will to plot dark and nefarious deeds. "But if this Jason character turns out to be creepy or weird or anything icky, I'm outta there."

"Thank you, Regan. Thank you so much!" Afraid she might hug me, I slid my chair back a few inches. She fluttered out of my cubicle.

I peeled another pink sheet off the message pad and began folding an addition to my army.

It was nearly six, the office quieter than a tomb, before I shut down my computer and started to leave. Five days a week was a little too much exposure to any one group of humans, so I preferred to work four, ten-hour days. Usually I came in at seven, had lunch at my desk, and stayed until five-thirty. Tonight, going home had been preempted by a blind date, so I wasn't in a hurry to leave.

Behind me, a door clicked as Edward Aguirre locked his office. His loafers padded across the carpet as he approached my cubicle. Still stalling, I was in the middle of arranging the cranes into a V-shaped attack formation. I looked up when he reached my doorway.

If not for his technology phobia, Edward might have made a good spy. He had a nondescript, forgettable quality—a middle-aged, portly man of average height and features too bland to be categorized as handsome or ugly. His scalp was downsizing, leaving a small troop of intrepid hairs to do the job of thousands.

"Go home, O'Connell. Get a life."

"I don't want a life. Lives are complicated."

"So true," Edward said, no doubt thinking about ex-wives and alimony. His ex-wife was a lover of cliché—literally. Two years before, he'd came home to find her playing a rousing game of hide the biscuit with the pool boy.

I gave him a sympathetic smile, in part because it was expected, but also because I genuinely felt sorry for him.

As a rule, I'm not fond of middle-management types, but Edward was okay. He was that familiar archetype in the information technology business: an MBA impersonating a skilled technical professional. Edward, however, had the good sense to realize his failings, and compensated by hiring competent staff and trusting them to get the job done.

"I got a call from Marcus Saiz from Roadrunner Prep School," he said.

"Uh oh."

Edward's smile bared teeth too small for his broad face. "He wanted to tell me how happy he was with the tracking system. Good job, O'Connell."

"I had a lot of help. Sean did a great job with the interface, and Joan turned their data into something useable."

"Joan Wallace." He twirled his car keys around a thick finger. "She's so strange. Sometimes I wonder how you can work with her."

I shrugged. "I'm used to strange."

He nodded and then his eyes lit up. "You ready for your blind date?"

"Ugh. Does the entire company know?"

"By now, most of the state knows." Edward's humor escaped as a low, rolling chuckle. "Who knows? Maybe this guy will be 'the one'?"

"'The *one?*' Edward, you old romantic." Edward's shoulders rose in a conciliatory shrug.

"Anyway," I said, "Blind dates are always a train wreck. Always."

Chapter Three

*D*riving is just a means of getting from one place to another. I try not to take it seriously and have never been one to spend the Gross National Product of Tunisia on a car. I'm fond of mid-size models with long warranties and my vehicles are always coated in an armor of protective filth.

If I believed in omens, I might have taken the sudden outbreak of inept drivers on Albuquerque's roads to be just that—a wicked bad omen—and gone home. Even under the worse circumstances, sandwiched bumper to bumper in the thickest, gooiest traffic jam, I can switch on the radio and keep my cool.

Tonight, traffic was making me homicidal. The car in front of me swerved from side to side, apparently under the influence of driver with cell phone. Another driver, in direct defiance of logic, accelerated while his brake lights gleamed brightly. And those were the sober drivers.

Albuquerque's West Side sprawls like an adolescent boy—awkward and pimply. The area's growing pains include cookie cutter housing and a road system that wouldn't adequately serve the horse-and-buggy transportation of the Amish. It took thirty minutes to drive a couple of miles to the pizza parlor Eva had chosen.

The restaurant was already hopping, filled with a mixture of families lured by easy kid-friendly food and the after-work crowd swilling cheap bear by the pitcher.

"Regan!" Eva waved her arms in the manner of an island castaway who'd just spotted a plane. The plane grimaced. Having my name yelled in a public place made me queasy, especially since this was the first time in about a century that I'd used my real name. After a quick appraisal of all possible exits, I made my way over to Eva and company.

Eva, Kyle and Jason stood up. Eva had described Kyle as well-built, but I think "neck disadvantaged" would have been more appropriate. Kyle was tall in a lumbering, brontosaurus kind of way, brown hair cut military short; his beady mud-brown eyes slid over me in an elevator stare. A snide smile sat on his face and seemed very much at home.

"Kyle Peterson," Eva chirped, "this is Regan O'Connell." His handshake was more squeeze than shake. Somewhere in the back of my mind, a little alarm began to go off. Kyle reminded me of someone or something....

"Jason. Jason Lake, this is Regan O'Connell."

"Hello," Jason said in the clipped tones of an Englishman. If it's possible for a mixture of boyish, nerdy and rugged to be cute, he was cute. His dark brown hair was short without being excessively so, and his smile reflected in his hazel eyes.

"Hi." An odd little shimmer of energy brushed my skin when we shook hands. The four of us stared at each other awkwardly for a couple of seconds before sitting down.

Eva had already ordered one large pizza with a variety of meat toppings and a small cheese and green chile pizza for me. After a few moments of uncomfortable silence, Eva started her matchmaker sales pitch, listing all my supposed best features with the practiced ease of a used car salesman. I stared at her with the numb horror of impending road kill mesmerized by an eighteen-wheeler's headlights. Jason smiled politely and nodded. Kyle looked bored.

When Eva's monologue finally ended, I bit back a sigh of relief. "Um. I'm gonna get an iced tea." I pushed my chair back to get up.

"You don't drink *either?*" Kyle asked. He had already ordered a pitcher of beer. I watched him, my expression neutral. Life, even my preternaturally long life, was too short to drink cheap beer.

"Eva says you don't eat meat," Kyle said, nudging Jason. "Don't drink, don't smoke, what do ya do?"

A ghost of irritation peeked through Jason's eyes. He stood up. "I'll get it. Ice tea?"

"Thanks."

When he returned a few minutes later, I gave the tea a furtive sniff. Jason didn't strike me as the kind of guy who'd slip something into a drink, but it didn't hurt to be careful. Thanks to my genetics, I have a sense of smell that bloodhounds envy.

Eva began to chatter, and I surreptitiously watched the two men. Brains and brawn. The alarm morphed into an air raid siren. *It couldn't be?*

The little spark of energy I had felt during the handshake was magic. While Jason gave off plenty of sexy beast magnetism, what I had sensed was the raw innate power that swam though the blood of all magical creatures, and the occasional human. Mr. Occasional Human sat across the table from me, brimming ninety-proof with magical energy. In humans, power of that magnitude was rare and had a nasty habit of coinciding with membership in the Holders of the True Light.

Jason and I made the usual small talk and my suspicion sprouted roots and grew. He explained he worked in the research division of a security company. Kyle handled the more "hands on aspects" of security.

Security, eh? My brain started shuffling around searching for any references to a Kyle Peterson or Jason Lake. I debated a trip to the bathroom, but Eva would take that as an invitation for girly chatter. Which would make my phone call impossible.

Temporarily out of anything meaningless to say, Jason and I exchanged uneasy grins.

"Cue the uncomfortable silence," Jason said, taking a sip of beer.

"A necessary component of any blind date." I twirled my straw around in the ice tea. "Often followed by, 'Whoa? Is that my cell phone? My beeper? Really, sorry, I'm needed in the operating room. To perform an emergency…rhinoplasty.'"

His face softened and the beginning of a relaxed smile revealed white even teeth. "A frequent occurrence for celebrity plastic surgeons, I imagine."

Wow. Apparently, the British had discovered good dentistry. "Mild-mannered project manager by day, celebrity plastic surgeon by night. That's me."

"Really? Do you have superpowers?"

"No. But I've got cool gadgets. Lightning scalpel. And a cape."

Jason's mouth curved in a full and charming crooked smile. "Keeping the world free of unsightly cellulite," he quipped and I nodded.

"And you?" I asked, staring straight into his eyes. "Any secret personas? Superpowers?"

"So, Regan? How old are you, anyway?" Kyle broke into our conversation, and I saw a hint of relief flash across Jason's face. "You look like jailbait."

"Kyyyyle!" Eva whined.

"What? She looks like a high school kid."

"So?" Eva's eyebrows marched upward. "Why is that a bad thing?" She frowned at Kyle. "Anyway, she doesn't look all *that* young."

Eva, who seemed to be related to everyone in the Metro area, seized on the opportunity to haul out a relative. "My Aunt Connie is the same way. Look at her and you'd swear she was still in her thirties, but the woman is fifty-six. *Fifty-six.*"

In my head, I grimaced at the comparison. I've seen her Aunt Connie. The woman resembled a Hispanic Yoda, short and wrinkled with wispy hair on her chin. The conversation got even duller after that, so I plastered on a listening face and paged through my mental files, searching for anything about the Holders of the True Light, or Holders.

Once upon a time, the Fey (elves and fairies) and other Non-Earth plane types owned a lot of Earth real estate. Some time around the eighth century B.C., humans discovered iron and sent the Fey and most demon species packing. Owing to their propensity for taking all the upper management positions (kings, gods) and demanding virgin sacrifices, the departure of the Fey and Company was met with relief and drunken revelry among humans. After the dust settled and everyone's hangover wore off, it was clear that despite the change of address, Non-Earth folk could and did continue to meddle in Earth's affairs. The Holders of the True Light—the True Light was the sun as it shined on Earth plane—were founded for the express purpose of keeping Earth a humans only, magic-free zone.

"Regan?" I startled at my name. *So much for staying on my guard.* Eva stared at me expectantly.

Realizing I hadn't been listening, she asked again, "How about a movie? The four of us?"

"Tonight?" I asked a little too fast. "I've got rehearsal."

"Regan plays violin," Eva explained. "I was talking about tomorrow night. Pay attention, girl." She made a fist and knocked on my forehead.

"I don't know. Wh-what movie?"

"What about that vampire movie?" She nudged Kyle. "What's it called?"

"Yeah, Let's see that. Because vampires are romantic and heroic." He sneered. "What a load of crap."

"All movies are predicated on a certain amount of crap," I replied. Kyle snorted.

"How to grow a movie. Fertilizer," said Jason. Our eyes met and then we were both smiling.

Marvelous, I thought. *The first guy I'm attracted to in years is human and worse yet, possibly the enemy.*

Eva cleared her throat, fussed with her hair and went on to list several other movies. Kyle proceeded to dismiss them as either chick flicks or simply boring. Despite agreeing with his assessments, I kept my mouth shut for Eva's sake.

"Hey," I said after a few minutes, "I really need to get going. Rehearsal." I stood up and turned to Eva. "I'll let you know about the movie, tomorrow."

"Thanks, Regan. I'll call you."

Jason cleared his throat and tilted his head toward the door. "Mind if I walk you to your car?"

I thought about it for a second. "Nope. Let's go." *Keep your friends close; keep your enemies even closer.*

Despite being midway through January, the night air was almost warm. Jason wore a light sport coat over a black sweater and blue jeans, the effect vaguely professorial. If your definition of professor was Indiana Jones with a class full of dewy-eyed co-eds. Separated from the dwarfing presence of Kyle, he acquired height and an athletic physique.

Holder operatives were dispatched in pairs—one person specializing in research and magic, and the other specializing in brute force. Since Kyle probably couldn't count to twenty-three without stripping naked, that left Jason with the spells and books and suchlike. Judging from the amount of energy that passed between us when we shook hands, he was a sorcerer of some power.

I shivered, suddenly aware of the strategic edge that gave him. Over the years, magic and I had come to an understanding. I didn't try to do much and it didn't pat me on the head and say, "Magic is for grownups, dear."

"How long have you been in Albuquerque?" I asked. The Holders didn't send out operatives for piddly concerns like killing the occasional mentally ill vampire or minor trade negotiations. Ironically, they expected the Brethren and its Wolfes to take care of the little stuff.

"Nearly..." he paused, thinking, "three weeks." *Holders in town for three weeks!* Something big was going on and I was out of the loop.

"You from New Mexico, originally?" he asked, pulling me out of my thoughts.

"No. Arizona." At least that was where my current alias graduated high school. "Tucson." I stopped at my car. "So, where in England?"

"England? Why England? Why not Wales or...Pakistan?"

"I know what a Welsh accent sounds like. And you're a tad pasty to be Pakistani." I was grinning at him despite myself. We looked at each other, and I felt the first real jolt of attraction for someone in years.

He looked away with a touch of attractive shyness, and his gaze passed over my car and onto the street beyond. "About the movie—"

"More time with the Sphincter-Man and his faithful whipping girl, Eva?" I pulled a face. "Nope, sorry."

The outside corners of his greenish eyes crinkled around future laugh lines, and he smiled. "Sphincter-Man? Not captivated by Kyle's all encompassing charisma?"

"And wit, don't forget his wit," I added. "You don't seem terribly offended."

"Kyle knows the business, but his personality—"

"He has one?" Feeling wicked, I said, "You know, Kyle told Eva that he couldn't possibly see her unless she arranged a date for you as well. Blind date blackmail."

"Really." Jason's expression hardened. "I'll have to thank him. Tell me. My etiquette is rusty. What is the appropriate way to say, 'Thank you for making a beautiful woman think I'm a loser'? A card? A gift?"

"Fruitcake, definitely fruitcake." My mouth started to crease into a grin again, which annoyed me. "Oh and use of the word 'beautiful'? Charm duly noted."

I realized I was flirting with a Holder. He had to be a Holder. My instincts were pretty sharp—compensation, I suppose, for a lack of magical ability and a smart mouth.

Which brought me back to the current dilemma. Why were they here?

"How about Eva's vampire movie?" He smiled, showing those pretty teeth. "No Kyle, no Eva?" he added.

"Vampires." I touched my tongue to blunt human teeth. It took a lot of concentration or anger, but I could shift my eyes to a nice sinister yellow and acquire small fangs. "Blood sucking gothic fun. Okay."

Jason would never tell me why he and Kyle were in Albuquerque. The Holder credo could be described as protectors of Mankind from the *knowledge* of the scourge of vampires, demons and other entities. Sort of like Men in Black, only replace bug-eyed aliens with the boogieman.

Around seven hundred years ago, the Brethren and the Holders went to war, each hoping to exterminate the other. After significant losses on both sides, each came to the distressing conclusion that destruction would be mutual. Since neither the Brethren nor the Holders were willing to go out in a blaze of martyred glory, the result was the Compact of Non-Aggression. Basically, the Holders and Brethren agreed not to go out of their way to kill each other. Naturally, that didn't rule out various forms of espionage.

"Saturday? A matinee?" Jason asked.

"Sounds good." After digging around in my purse, I produced one of my business cards and handed it to him. There was no harm in him having it. The only phone number listed was my cell, whose billing went to a post office box—that was opened under an alias and the trail ended up somewhere in Switzerland. I held out my hand. "It's been nice meeting you, Jason."

We shook hands and exchanged the usual parting pleasantries. He headed back, his pace slow, to the restaurant. Obviously, he didn't relish the prospect of returning to the Kyle and Eva Show. My dislike for Holders was rooted in something more personal than professional rivalry, but Holder or not, I felt sorry for Jason.

Chapter Four

*R*emember your first best friend? That childhood friend you shared everything with? Deepest, darkest secrets, your dream to be a superhero, chicken pox? You sat close together, whispering in the dark about boys who really weren't worth the oxygen, or maybe you shot little green army men out of homemade canons powered by firecrackers.

I never had a friend like that.

At least not until I was fifty-three. I met Cara while on assignment in Paris. 1926.

A prostitute by way of a failed attempt at an acting career, Cara Ryan had red hair and green eyes like my mother, a razor sharp wit, and somehow, deep down, a really big heart.

Cara was my first best friend.

I always figured her vocation would be the end of her. Instead it was me; I was the reason she died.

One winter night a Holder named Cyrus Purcell took her life, dragging it out of her body in a long bloody river. To get at me, Cyrus Purcell, researcher for Holders of the True Light, killed my best friend.

A few years later, when I finally faced what had happened that night, I discovered that Cara had been just one in a long gory list of experimental subjects.

His bio in Holder records describes Cyrus Purcell as "...a brilliant researcher whose innovative investigational methods took the study of the energy of the soul in new directions."

Brilliant researcher, indeed.

Since then, I have regarded all Holders with the same affection vampires carry for bright sunny days and wooden stakes.

I drove up my driveway, brooding.

Although I am currently based out of Albuquerque, I live just to the north in the semi-rural village of Corrales. Family farms once dominated Corrales, but as real estate prices have skyrocketed in Albuquerque, most of the farms are giving way to large homes for the rich and wishing-they-were famous.

My home is an eighty-year-old adobe house that has been in my family for about fifty years, cycling in ownership from alias to alias. Presently, it belongs to Andrew Romano, a.k.a. my "brother" Argus.

The original plot of land was probably several acres, but through various subdivisions had been winnowed down to about an acre. Enough to give me elbow room and space for Bill, the world's laziest horse.

As soon as I pulled into my driveway, Bill lifted his head and neighed, answering the inevitable question: "Is he alive or is he stuffed?" Bill came into my life seven years ago when a misguided friend rescued him from an abusive home and dumped him in my backyard. I tried to sell him, but since he was only two, ugly and untrained, I couldn't give him away. Time went by, he went from homely-horsy to coppery tan with a white-blond mane, and I got attached.

Since it was nearly eight o'clock, Bill burned a few calories by waddling closer to the fence, reminding me his dinner was late. If at all possible, he confined his daily activity to a walk over to the water trough and back to the feeder.

"Sorry." I wandered into the barn, pulled a chunk of hay off a bale, and heaved it over the fence into his feeder. "You wouldn't believe the evening I had." Bill peeped at me through blond horsy bangs. "Never mind, you don't want to know. A bloody Holder," I grumbled and started toward my house, giving the rest of the property a cursory look.

The landscaping was quintessential rural, laissez-faire. I.e., if it thrived on neglect, it was landscaping. Four enormous cottonwood trees—three up front and one that shaded Bill's paddock—dominated the lot. Sagebrush had won the battle of the weeds and saved me the trouble of dealing with its more mobile brethren, the tumbleweeds.

Redneck was the best way to describe my neighbors to the north. Landscaping on their property consisted of a powder blue mobile home, an assortment of immobile cars and trucks, and herds of winter-brown tumbleweeds. A horse farm bordered my property to the south, populated by high-strung Arabian horses that peered down their sloped noses at Bill and me.

I opened the back door, did the listen-and-sniff thing, and then stepped through the door. My sense of smell and hearing operated like nosy fingers, able to reach out and probe around corners and far beyond the usual human limits. Not that I expected any trouble. Vampires needed an invite into any mortal's residence, including mine, and I could smell demons and other Non-Earth-plane folks a mile away. Ditto for humans. But a girl can't be too careful.

I had been living there for eight months—a long time for me—and had pulled a lot of my stuff out of storage to make things homey. With proper restoration, a lot of my furniture might be worth something. Scratched-and-dull, however, hides my inattention to the task of dusting and it goes well with the brick floors. Flea market chic. Thanks to my new couch, the living room and kitchen were permeated with the morbid good smell of leather.

A little pin, shaped like a leaf, sat on my kitchen counter. Out of habit, I scooped it up and put it in my pocket. After a second or two I reached for my phone. *Who to call? Dad?*

The little leaf pin buzzed, its vibrations dampened by the surrounding cloth. *Huh?* I pulled it out of my pocket and stared at it, surprised. It hummed and shimmered in my hand.

I cleared my throat and spoke. "Sh'Tah."

A few feet away, the air shimmered and a fairy materialized in my kitchen. She was about five-feet tall, a few inches shorter than me, with a shaggy mane of bright burgundy hair and golden eyes. Pointy ears poked out of her wine-colored hair, and she was wearing a simple blue dress. If you looked closely you could see the vague outlines of nearly transparent wings.

"Hey, Lex."

"Regan," she chirped. "You seem surprised. Why?"

"You've been M.I.A. for months."

"Really? Oh, it hasn't been that long." She flounced out of the kitchen and into my living room. I heard a click, followed by the sound of the television. Strangling a sigh, I followed her.

When Lex and I first became friends, she had a nasty habit of dropping in uninvited. It took some time—fairies have no concept of privacy—to explain why this was a problem. Eventually we devised a solution. She gave me a small charm, fashioned into a pin, which allowed her to magically buzz me. A fairy beeper, if you will. Now, whenever she wants to visit, she signals via the charm and if I respond with "Sh'Tah," she materializes. The pin and accompanying magic were put together by a Sh'ree tempus mage.

She had last buzzed me about eight months ago.

As she had commandeered the comfy recliner, I flopped down on the couch. "So, Lex, whatcha been doin'?"

Her slim hand waved. "Oh, this and that."

Iron is like plutonium for Fey and demons. Prolonged exposure can cause potentially lethal iron sickness. Over time, some Fey develop varying degrees of resistance to iron and small electromagnetic fields, the other bane of their existence. Lex had been popping into my life for close to a century. So things like remote controls, televisions, and refrigerators were not a problem. Talis can even drive a car, although he hates small appliances.

"Trouble in paradise?" I asked.

"Oh, look! *I Love Lucy*."

"The *Chocolate Factory* episode. Cool," I said, leaning forward. *I love Lucy*; I can relate. My life was full of Ricky Ricardos, all shaking their fingers at me and saying, "Well, Lucy, what have you got to say?" *If I'm Lucy, who's Ethel?*

"What happened with Prince...Crom'Teal-something?" Pronouncing Fairy names required verbal acrobatics, hence Lex, versus whatever her real name was.

"Crehm'Teal is an abysmal bore." Lex put down the remote and sprawled on the recliner so she could face me. "He wants to get married!"

"Ew?" I tried.

"Exactly. Married. Me! And he wants children."

"Wow. What an ogre."

She missed my sarcasm. "And he expected me to," she lifted her hands to make quotation marks, "'confine my affections to him and him alone.' Who does he think I am? Some old, shriveled, fairy matron?"

I got a silly image of Lex, the fairy godmother, and grinned.

"I've got admirers, Regan. Far too many to incarcerate myself in marriage." Sitting up, she posed as though about to take flight, her wings reflecting images from the television, the ultimate fairy archetype. "There is a world of men out there."

She frowned. "It is really quite a pity, though. He was absolutely marvelous in bed. You would not believe the size of his—"

"Ew! I don't need a description of his fairy man part. Thanks."

"Tongue. I was going to say tongue, Regan."

"Yeah. That's worse."

Chastened, she turned to the television. Since Lex can only sulk for a short time, in a matter of seconds, she flipped around in my direction.

"And you? What have you been doing? Anyone interesting?" She giggled at her own wit. Unlike Eva, Lex wasn't after a mention in a wedding day speech—"If it weren't for Lex, we might never have met"—but she does believe celibacy is a sin.

"I've got a date with a Holder. Saturday afternoon."

An approximation of a serious expression made it to the fairy's face. "A Holder? But you hate Holders."

Something slimy crawled around in my stomach. "Yeah," I responded, trying to sound blasé.

"But, they...Cyrus Purcell...Cara. How could you?"

"I know what Cyrus Purcell did to Cara. I was there Lex, remember?" *I remember every detail. What he did; what I didn't do.* "You think I'll ever forget?"

My tone must have been really harsh because Lex shut up and that was extraordinary. I rubbed my forehead with the heel of my hands.

"Eva. One of my coworkers. She's dating one. A Holder. She set me up on a blind date with one of his friends, who, as it happens, is his partner in crime. Also a Holder. Of course, Eva didn't know this. Obviously, he's not going to tell her." Words tumbled out of my mouth.

Lex watched me, unblinking. "Why are Holders, here, in New Mexico?"

"That's what I'm trying to find out. I was about to call my father when you showed up."

Showing surprising insight, she asked, "What did you do this time? Another breach of diplomatic protocol? Or has this place had a surge in the population of Lesser vampire crazies?"

"No 'surge,'" I said. "More like an 'enthusiastic trickle.'"

Blood Gift is an elven emergency measure used to keep a dying comrade alive. The first elf to try it on a human was probably just trying to save a friend. Nevertheless, the majority of The First—those vampires turned by a drink of pure elf blood—were a plague unleashed by vengeful elves, annoyed by their exile from Earth.

Humans-turned-vampires by one of the First are known as Second Generation. Vampires created by Second Generation vampires are Third Generation and so forth.

Around the Fifth Generation, the influence of elf blood starts getting weak and the resulting vampires are often unstable, physically and mentally. Lesser is the term for Fifth, Sixth, Seventh and higher Generation vampires.

Somewhere in Albuquerque, a Lesser vampire was turning out more Lesser vampires with a persistent regularity. This vampire had been smart enough to stay out of my way, leaving me with the rather endless task of killing off his or her demented progeny. The Brethren had started to grumble about my lack of progress on the matter.

I'm good at killing, but I don't enjoy it. A small part of me wished the Holders *would* take care of the problem. No chance of that happening. Except in cases where vampires' activities affected the more affluent, the Holders never allocated resources to culling Lesser vampires.

Something else has to be going on. I watched Lex as she cackled at the television.

At the onset of their exile from Earth, elves, fairies, and demons put their best and brightest minds to work on the iron problem. Nothing worked. Even for those who could acquire a limited immunity to the metal, iron-wielding humans were just too great a foe. In time the elves gave up, having decided humans were more trouble than they were worth and bound to destroy Earth, anyway.

For fairies and demons, however, hope springs eternal. They continue to skulk around Earth plane, testing the defenses the way a coyote tests a chicken coop. Lex's reappearance in my living room—

now—may have been driven by something more than a yearning for 1950s sitcoms.

"So, what have you heard?" I asked Lex. "Any word from the Non-Earth plane types?"

Lex shook her head. "About New Mexico? Nobody cares about New Mexico." She scooped up the remote and tossed it toward the coffee table where it landed with a clack.

"I'll call Kadin," I announced. Kadin is another one of my "brothers." If there is even the slightest possibility that I might hear disappointment in my father's voice, I'm going to avoid it.

"Mmmm, Kadin." A dreamy haze filled the fairy's eyes.

"Ew." Kadin was cute, but we were related.

"I know." The fairy flew onto the sofa next to me. "You should call Breas." Her golden eyes slipped back into dreamy mode. "Mmmm, Breas." She licked her lips.

"Again. Ew." Breas was *turned* by a different bloodline, but *ew* anyway. I glowered at the television, willing the station to change, too lazy to retrieve the remote from the coffee table.

Lex bounced up and into my kitchen. "Got anything to eat?"

"No. I haven't been shopping."

"Wonderful. Let's go," Lex said. With just a little magic or a hat and sunglasses, Lex can pass as human.

"No. I don't like shopping with you. You put junk food in my cart when my back is turned. Potato chips, cheese puffs, cookies...."

Lex perched on the top of the sofa. "Mmmm, cookies," she purred.

"Ice cream's better." We smiled at each other.

"Mmmm...ice cream," we said together.

Lex was out the door before I had even picked up my car keys. The little voice in my head beat tiny fists against my skull, lambasting me for poor judgment and demanding that I immediately pursue the matter of the Holders. Naturally, I ignored it.

Grateful for any excuse to postpone calling Kadin, I followed Lex.

♫

BELFAST, IRELAND 1887

The stable boy's reaction was atypical to say the least.

"*You* ran him into the ground. Take care of him yourself," said the boy, who had just emerged from the shadows of a long row of horse stalls. The lad made no move toward the horse.

Ferociously aware of his hunger, Breas pulled his senses back from the *thud-thud-thud* of blood rushing through the child's heart. He stared at the brat through narrowed eyes, wondering if Cullan O'Connell would miss the little twit.

"I'm tired," Breas said, glancing back toward the manor. "Do you have any idea how long it's been since I've eaten?" In the employ of a vampire, it was possible that the boy understood the underlying threat in his words.

"So? The poor horse has much less choice in the matter, when he eats, than you do."

"You're paid to do a job, brat. Do it." Bored and anxious to be done with his business, he emphasized the command with a stream of Mesmer power. The boy spared Breas a dark look and turned to return to the confines of the stable. Surprised, Breas barked, "Hey! Boy!" His words covered in another layer of enchantment.

The boy paused in the dim light of an overhead lantern. Pulling the tired horse along, Breas marched up to the boy. The light revealed dark green eyes. Elf green. That explained why Cullan tolerated the little monster. Extending his senses gingerly, he felt the shimmer of innate magic. O'Connell must have been grooming the boy as a familiar or perhaps, a vampire.

Although, at the moment, it appeared no one had put much time into the boy's actual grooming. Much of his black hair, which had been tied back with a leather thong, had escaped its confines and fell around his dirt-smudged face. Brambles and hay interwove in his hair and his clothes were brown with stable dirt.

Moving with easy preternatural speed, Breas snapped his hand forward, grabbing at the collar on the boy's shirt.

And his fingers closed around nothing. Absolutely nothing. The boy, eyebrow cocked in outrage, backed a step farther from the vampire. Thinking he must have somehow—how?—misjudged the distance, Breas repeated the action, much quicker.

And the child evaded his grasp. "You sir, are presumptuous. You are on the lands of Cullan O'Connell and you cannot—"

"I know whose lands these are. I'm his guest." Suddenly curious, Breas focused his vampire senses tightly on the boy. "And you would be?" His check confirmed that the person before him had a beating heart. "You are a girl."

"You have a marvelous grasp of the obvious," the girl observed dryly.

Breas studied her. What he had mistaken for an angelic boy's face was actually the delicate featured countenance of a pretty girl. After several baths and a fortune in soap, perhaps. Trying a charming smile, he said, "I'm Breas. Breas Montrose. And you are?" She watched him, no words escaping her mouth. The magic in her bloodstream buzzed, clearly not controlled or likely used much.

Trying a different tact, he closed the distance between them, his movement slow and unthreatening. He closed his fingers on her shirt collar, pulling her languidly towards him. The ruse worked; she stared at his hand, dazed.

"What is your name?" he asked, lifting his other hand to her face and rubbing a smudge off her cheek. Tendrils of his innate magic intertwined with hers. Seeing that no one was likely to "take care of the horse," his equine wandered towards a nearby water trough.

"Morri...Regan." She was clearly thrown by his change in demeanor. "Morri Regan?"

"M-my name is Morrigan. B-but my father, he calls me Regan."

Morrigan. The name sent a reflexive shiver through his body. "Your father?"

Seeming to recover some of her bearing, she spoke the name, "Cullan O'Connell."

Breas's fingers quivered and nearly loosened his grip on her shirt. "Rumor becomes flesh. Cullan's improbable child."

Regan frowned down at his arm and then up at his face. "Unhand me." She had the commanding tone of an aristocrat's daughter.

"No," he answered, grinning. "How old are you?"

"Sixteen, yesterday." Anger gathered in her ivy green eyes. "Unhand me, now!"

Sixteen. Cullan had done a good job of keeping the girl hidden, sheltered from all interested parties.

He pulled her closer. "Regan O'Connell. You smell of sunlight, heather, and raspberries."

Faint disquiet emanated from the girl. "They—they are in season. And—and I smell mostly of horse."

Breas smiled. "I like horse." He touched his lips to hers, teasing her skin with magical energy. "A useful animal, the horse." He pressed a kiss against her lips, tasting berries.

Stunned, she didn't respond. He dropped his arm around her waist and pressed her to his body, running his tongue along her lower lip. Feeling her soften, he wove more of his magical energy with hers and was rewarded by her weight leaning limply against him.

Inexperienced women bored Breas, but kissing O'Connell's daughter was pleasant, more than pleasant. An odd sensation of connection sparked, and he felt an overwhelming sense of completion. Idle curiosity became real need; he tightened his hold on her body.

Suddenly overwhelmed, panic raced from the girl to him and she freed herself from his arms with astonishing speed. Almost disappointed by the end of the kiss, he stared at her in confusion.

Her fear turned to indignation; she lifted her hand and struck him. His head rang from the blow that was not an idle slap, but a hard-fisted punch crashing onto his mouth. Regan shook her hand in pain, knuckles bruised by his teeth.

Instinct drove his features to something fiercer and he glowered at her, sending her stumbling backwards, green eyes wide in astonishment. Natural rage still reigning preeminent in his system, his fist connected with her jaw.

And he felt her pain, felt the heat of tissue bruising under his knuckles and the dull concussion that reverberated through her skull.

Overcome, she swayed and fell, crumbling into a heap.

If someone were to ask what he felt at that moment, the most accurate word would be befuddled. He bent over the girl, his motives unclear even to himself.

As if understanding the very danger in his confusion, Regan's fingers slipped around the only available weapon. She pushed herself toward him, jabbing recklessly. The jagged end of a broken pitchfork handle raced toward him, and Breas twisted, trying to evade its point.

Splintered shards bit deep into his side and he staggered away, clutching at the makeshift stake. Ripping it from his flesh, he fell to his hands and knees and regarded Regan in dull shock. She met his gaze and a moment of shared pain passed between them.

Then her eyes rolled backward and she slumped in a dead faint.

"Montrose." The voice, sharp and angry, pushed aside some of his pain. He lifted his gaze from Regan and saw Kadin Farahani, Commander of Brethren Security, standing just a few feet away. Commander Farahani's eyes, normally dark brown, were angry yellow. Breas shuddered. The pitchfork handle must have been constructed of oak; the entry wound burned brightly. Too weak to exercise his preferred option to flee—he offered Kadin a wan grin and chased Regan into unconsciousness.

Chapter Five

"*F*arahani," the voice on the phone barked in a business-like manner.

"Kadin. It's Regan." I leaned on the kitchen counter, compensating for muscles that were not entirely awake.

Immediately, the speaker's tone changed. "Regan, love, how are you?"

My kitchen window looked eastward, out to the cottonwoods of the Rio Grande Bosque. The distant hulking mass of the Sandia Mountains loomed above the fingerlike outlines of the leafless trees. It was early Friday morning and little bits of frost clung to the edges of the window.

"Barely awake." This was the best time to reach Kadin, who was currently based out of Moscow. At around four in the afternoon—vampire early—Kadin was just getting up and probably not buried in business yet.

Vampires don't *have* to sleep during the day. In fact, vampires require a lot less sleep than humans or any other creatures, magical or otherwise. In the "old days" sleep was just the only thing to do when the sun was up. Now, with mass communication making working at home so easy, many Greater vampires were up all day—faxing, phoning, emailing, etc.

Kadin, like all vampires in my life, is a Greater vampire, as in falling into the category First through Fourth Generation. Kadin owes his vampirism to one of the most formidable Firsts, Cullan O'Connell, the guy I call dear old Dad.

"How's life in your little mud hut?" he asked.

"Adobe. It's adobe and people out here pay big money for little mud huts." Mankind, by Kadin's estimations, had come too far technologically to still be building homes out of dirt. "Adobe is a good investment," I said, appealing to his fiscal side.

"Again illustrating why we are the superior species," replied Kadin.

Kadin, like most Greater vampires, had no desire to devour all of mankind and take over the world. That would be akin to all meat eaters driving cattle and poultry into extinction. (I'm allergic to meat protein and blood, and thus a vegetarian.) Besides, when left to their own devices, humans are tremendous innovators, moving technology forward at an astonishing pace. Vampires love technology.

"So what news from the Land of Enchantment?" he asked.

"Ah, you know. The plague, hanta virus, drunk drivers and now...Holders."

"Holders?"

"So, this *is* news to you?" I puttered over to the refrigerator, opened the door, and rummaged around in search of anything to eat.

"Holders in Albuquerque? New Mexico?" he muttered, answering my question indirectly.

"Um, there's a Wolfe here. Why not Holders? It's where all the posh paranormal experts come for holiday."

I could feel Kadin's smile through the phone. "No offense, kid," he said.

Kadin Farahani was my favorite "brother." I had three, sired in the traditional blood exchanging way, by my father. Born somewhere in Persia in the twelfth century, Kadin had a deceptively easygoing personality. Deceptive, because frankly, he was one of the few vampires who was capable of scaring the shit out of me. Kadin had light olive skin, dark brown puppy dog eyes, a handsome boyish face, and fighting skills that alternately gave me fits of jealousy and a weak bladder. Commander of Brethren security force, Kadin was technically upper, upper management. Thanks to nepotism, I got away with a fairly informal relationship with him.

My search moved on to the pantry where I pulled out a bag of microwave popcorn.

"So what have you learned so far?" asked Kadin.

"They've been here," I paused to put the popcorn in the microwave and pushed the start button, "three weeks. Sorcerer's name is Jason Lake. Militia is Kyle Peterson." I stepped back from the noise of the microwave. "Kyle Peterson is dating Eva, the human resources specialist at Koar."

"And that's how you learned of their presence in the area?"

Knowing I'd never hear the end of it, I took a breath before speaking. "Eva set me up on a blind date with Jason Lake." I cringed in expectation of his reaction.

There was a moment of silence, followed by laughter that slowly built in intensity.

"Sorry," Kadin sputtered. "Did you say you were...set up with a Holder?"

"Uh-huh. It's love at first sight. We'll be getting married shortly. I'm choosing china patterns as we speak." The popcorn started to pop in earnest. "You know, Kadin, I think I'm gonna have to reconsider your status as favorite brother."

Kadin took a few seconds to compose himself. "I trust the Holder has no idea what or who you are. Because if he does—"

"No," I said, and then paused to let my brain catch up with my mouth. "I don't set off vampire detectors. But he is a strong innate, so he may have sensed I have some power."

"Anyone with significant power, with the exception of you, little sister, can sense another innate magic user. At any rate, he's more likely to mistake you for a human with elf ancestry." Kadin chuckled. "I'd wager he'll try to recruit you to the Holder ranks."

"Wager?" Kadin was fond of gambling. "You're gonna start a pool, aren't you?"

"'When will the Holder unknowingly attempt to recruit the Wolfe?' Pick a date, five dollars a chance."

"You're gonna tell everyone, aren't you?" I asked mournfully.

"Of course. You're great for morale, little sister."

I sighed and switched the microwave off before it scorched the popcorn.

"And you've heard nothing, no reason that would bring the Holders to New Mexico?" asked Kadin.

"No. All's quiet on this western front."

"I'll pass the Holders' names on to Cypher. In the meantime, keep a low profile. It wouldn't do to have the Holders take too much interest in you."

"Of course."

We said goodbye, I hung up the phone, and shuffled back to bed with popcorn cradled in my arm like a fragile child.

I had conveniently forgotten to tell Kadin about my date on Saturday.

Chapter Six

*N*ot that I'm an expert on sexuality now, but back when I attended the Sh'ree College of the Arcane, "virgin" was a valid way to describe my level of experience. Thanks to Talis, I got my first eye-popping introduction to sex.

Talis thinks human and vampire women have less sex appeal than old gum stuck under a table, so the education wasn't first hand. Elf polo is the sport of choice on the Fey plane and beyond, and a good player can transcend humble birth or species to become a cult hero. In his day, Talis was a phenomenal player. Dark elves may have been *persona non grata* on the Fey plane, but a good many elf women were willing to forget that little detail for a night of dishonored bliss with Talis. Falynn, my roommate during my time at the College of the Arcane, was one such female. I came home from class one day to find her and Talis making two-thirds of a moaning Oreo cookie.

For a sheltered Victorian era girl, it was pretty traumatic. Over the years, the image detail has faded, but I still try to avoid looking any lower than his chest.

Talis was a recurring player in my life, almost too conveniently showing up in the many places I've called home. As he had done in the past, he moved to Albuquerque before I even knew I had been assigned there.

At the moment, Talis was dead set on playing the part of tragic rock star. Sex and drugs, with a detour around the rock-and-roll. I don't know how somebody so smart can get so very stupid. I don't ask, he won't tell.

After my call to Kadin, I had hunkered down for another three hours of sleep before schlepping myself into the shower and then into blue jeans and a sweatshirt, and finally out of the house and into my car. I made my way across town, zipping south along I-25, heading for Nelly's restaurant where Talis and I met every Friday for breakfast.

Nelly's was located two blocks away from Central Avenue, in a neighborhood that was essentially a college student ghetto. The restaurant attracted an unusual mélange of patrons, ranging from local celebrities to college students and the homeless, the latter two being largely undistinguishable from one another.

Talis stood outside, waiting. Characteristics that screamed "Not human" were camouflaged by a glamour; the simple spell made him look like a nondescript dark-skinned man. Time and bad habits had taken a toll; much of his former dynamism had faded. His Earth native clothing—jeans, T-shirt, scuffed leather jacket—certainly contributed to his loss of Fey mojo. But when he smiled, a hint of the old Talis still shone through.

"Hey," I said.

"Hey," he responded. "You're late."

"I'm always late."

Talis stuck his hands in his jacket pockets and wiggled an elbow in my direction. I took his arm and we entered the restaurant.

Nobody stands on ceremony at Nelly's. You place your order at the counter, sit where ever you wish, and when your order number is bellowed over a loudspeaker, you pick up your meal at the counter. Simple and better yet, no tipping required.

The discordant sounds of pop music played at a low volume over the loudspeaker and in my head, I hummed a precisely in-tune version of the song. Nearly all music sounded out of tune to my ears. The curse of perfect pitch.

Talis and I stopped several feet from the counter and waited for the person ahead of us to place an order.

That person was a pencil thin middle-aged woman with a bird-like face. "Your beef tacos. I'd like to substitute tofu for the beef," she said to the unfortunate cashier.

I scowled first at the woman and then at the large menu that hung above the register. Reading had never been my forte. Letters have a nasty habit of flipping upside down and switching position, but even to my dyslectic brain, the words "No Substitutions" were clear. I closed my eyes, pushing back impatience.

"These people," I muttered, "humans. It's hard to believe they were able to chase the Fey and demons off Earth plane using only iron."

Talis's stomach growled. "No," he answered. "There was more to it than that."

I opened my eyes. "Really?"

"Yeah. Humans are short-lived but very, uh, fertile."

"So?"

"So with other races, demon or Fey, conquest is much easier." He paused. "Come in, kill everyone who resists, leave only the most compliant, the old, the weak."

"Oh," I said, after a few seconds. "With a long-lived species, the conqueror can sit back and rest on his laurels, because it'll be centuries before a new hot-blooded generation grows up. But with humans, a new crop of heroes arises every few years or so."

"Elves," Talis said, with a hint of distaste, "and fairies, and demons. They are all lazy. Humans are just too damn much work."

Bird-woman finally moved on, and Talis and I made our way to the counter. We each ordered a breakfast burrito, and Talis got a plate of *carne adovada*. He got coffee, and I, tea. I found us a booth against the back wall that afforded a good view of all the doorways, where we sat in the comfortable silence of old friendship. What, I wondered, would I do if Jason walked through one of those doorways? How would I explain my Fey breakfast companion?

Our order number was called over a loudspeaker and I stood. "Extra chile, right?" I asked, and Talis nodded.

"And a, uh, take-away box, please."

In New Mexico, chile is an indispensable ingredient in most foods. Nelly's keep a big crock pot full of chopped green chile and tomato sauce on a counter next to the sugar, catsup and other condiments. Because of Talis's aversion to electrical appliances, I did the honors—smothering the burritos in steaming spicy sauce.

While I was up picking up the order, Talis had gotten us knives and forks and a handful of napkins, so we got down to the business of shoveling in breakfast. Talis ate half of the *carne adovada* and scooped the rest into the Styrofoam box.

"Eithne likes that stuff?" I asked.

Talis smiled. "She loves it." Eithne, his cat, subsists on table scraps and takeout.

I let my bangs curtain down over my face, and I contemplated my companion. Little orangy vessels fingered out across the whites of his eyes, and dark circles under his large eyes made them more dramatic.

Talis's people are called kobolds. Kobold is derogatory, but apparently, preferable to "dark elf." The real kobolds were a lizard-like people who were wiped out by the elves. Talis's people were a lot harder to exterminate, so in frustration, the elves likened them to kobolds. The name stuck with a barnacle's tenacity and nobody knows what the politically correct moniker should be. Besides a dark complexion, the only notable difference between a kobold and elf is dentistry. Kobolds have wolfish grins due to slightly elongated canines.

Obviously feeling my scrutiny, Talis asked, "What's the matter?"

"Nothin'."

His attention moved past me, sparing us both the repetition of the recurring, When-are-you-going-to-quit-doing-drugs? Soon-I-promise conversation. "Hey, I know him," he said.

I turned in the direction Talis was looking, groaned, and turned back to my meal, trying to make myself as small as possible. A Teile demon had just picked up his breakfast and was making a beeline for the condiment counter. The demon was about four-feet tall and composed of hard blocky angles. His mottled green skin and buzz cut indigo hair were disguised with a glamour, so the human patrons of Nelly's, if they looked at him at all, saw a short man who apparently used his gym membership.

Unfortunately, the demon spotted me. "You!" he said. He changed direction and marched resolutely toward our table. Because of the afore mentioned variety of clientele at Nelly's and his glamour, the other restaurant patrons didn't pay much attention, mistaking him for just another angry weirdo of the Homo sapiens variety.

"I think he likes you," Talis said, rubbing the calf of my leg with his foot. Playing footsie was our version of platonic flirting.

"Right. What's his name?"

"His name?" Talis looked puzzled. "But he seems to know you."

"Yeah. We met two days ago. He introduced himself, but his name was a mile long. He wanted Brethren permission to start a dragon farm outside of Santa Fe. His business plan was longer than *War and Peace* and written in Teile. I denied his request."

"Oh," said Talis, in a tone that indicated he knew where this was going. I managed not to flunk Teile and several other language courses thanks to Talis's ethically flexible intervention.

"Naturally, I couldn't read the paperwork. So I winged it."

"You could have brought it to me—"

"There wasn't time. I was trying to be, you know, um, independent."

Talis's expression was mournful. "His name, the short version at least, is Angry."

"Angry?" This conversation was in danger of sliding into an Abbott and Costello *Who's on First?* kind of skit.

Talis's mouth nimbly said the demon's full name. "AngryAtthylMartrlrahct." His blue-eyed gaze moved from the approaching demon and back to me. "I take it you didn't compliment him."

"Not exactly." Teile social niceties dictate an exchange of compliments during negotiations, preferably the kind that likened the demon's masculinity to something on a par with a draft horse. "I bought him the most expensive meal on the menu. Figured that would make up for not discussing—"

Angry thumped his tray down on our table, sending little bits of lettuce garnish jumping off his plate of tacos. Talis and I shrank away from the vegetable shrapnel. "It is done. Thanks to you," he said, sliding into the seat next to Talis, forcing the kobold to move over.

"What'd she do?" prompted Talis.

"The Teile and Sharet are now at war."

Talis's eyebrows shot upward. "You started a war?" he asked me, grinning. "Congratulations."

I kicked Talis's foot. "No, no wars—" I gulped and shot a glance at the demon.

The demon nodded.

"Huh-how?" I asked.

"My prize bull-dragon impregnated a female from a nearby wing, a wing belonging to the Sharet cabinet minister. Had I been able to relocate my wing to Earth, war would have been avoided."

"Dragon sex? You're going to war over randy reptiles?" I asked.

"Shit," Talis said, and rolled his eyes. "The cause of the last war was dragon shit. The Sharet emperor's pet dragon defecated in the Teile ambassador's garden."

"Yeah, well, that's a frequent cause of conflict here on Earth. Suburban dog poop squabbles." I frowned. "But war means fighting and killing, limbs and torsos going their separate ways, right?"

"Yes," Angry replied.

Well, that's not good. I'm no stranger to war and I definitely don't want to be the cause.

"So what can we do to, um, end this?" I asked.

"End?" Angry said.

"Yeah. You know. Peace?"

Angry's broad nose wrinkled as though he'd just gotten a whiff of dragon poop. "Nothing. Our mutual honor, the honor of the Sharet and Teile, must be satisfied." With that he grabbed a taco and began to eat. Talis gave me a crooked grin and got to work on his burrito.

I picked at my meal, appetite gone, visions of battlefields strewn with green arms and legs in my head. The ravages of war forgotten, Angry began discussing chile with Talis.

"Listen to me, boyo." The demon nudged Talis. "I'm telling you, we could make a fortune." He reached across Talis and scooped a forkful of chile sauce off the Fey's plate. "The addictive power of this stuff far exceeds Elf Dust. Demons, Fey, we could get them all addicted and charge a king's ransom...."

I sighed. *My life is like a bad joke. "A dark elf and a demon walk into a restaurant...."*

Soon after, Angry finished his breakfast, left a business card with Talis and shuffled off to do whatever Teile demons do while on Earth.

Talis did the footsie thing again. "They fight all the time, you know."

"Yeah, but—"

"Wagering on Teile and Sharet warfare is kinda like a sport. There are betting houses in Tara devoted exclusively to the nuances of Teile/Sharet relations."

"That's awful." Noting the discomfort on his face, I added, "You placed a bet, didn't you?"

He looked pained. "You lost me two hundred in elf currency. I didn't reckon they'd go to war for at least another month."

"Serves you right." I slid out of the booth. "I'm going home. I'm gonna ride my horse, and afterwards, I'm eating a carton of ice cream and going to bed." *Isn't that how all successful warmongers finish off the day?*

We left the restaurant and Talis walked with me to my car.

"Oh, I forgot to tell you," Talis said. He shook his head. "Always forgetting."

I dug my keys out of my purse and unlocked my car. "Forgot what, Tal?"

"Marty. You know Marty, right?" I nodded and Talis continued, "Marty said a friend of his had an interesting conversation with a human. The human was asking about you."

"A human? A tall, dark-haired, kinda hot human?"

Talis blinked. "Huh?"

"What did the human look like?"

"Oh, uh, I don't know. Marty said the human was scary."

"A scary human. Not real specific."

Talis grimaced. "I got the impression he thought the human was dangerous, powerful."

Jason, maybe? "So who is Marty's 'friend'?"

Talis stuffed his hands in his coat pockets. "I'm not sure. Marty wouldn't say." He leaned toward me and continued in a low voice, "But, I think Marty meant Icarus."

"Icarus, his boss?"

Icarus was a demon and the proprietor of a rather successful interPlanar import/export business. He stood about three-feet tall and was strong enough to pull the legs off an elephant. I had a hard time believing he'd describe any human as "scary."

"Weird," I said.

"Yeah, nothing spooks Icarus." With a touch of his old grace, Talis lifted his hand and brushed my bangs out of my eyes. "Be careful, okay?"

"Always." We hugged goodbye and we each went on our way. The drive home took about thirty-five minutes, five of which I spent thinking about the mystery human, and the rest, I devoted to Talis and his memory lapses.

Chapter Seven

If the Brethren had a personnel department, it would generate the following description for the responsibilities of a Wolfe: "Duties to include, but not limited to, espionage, diplomacy, trade negotiations, security detail, and the control/elimination of Lesser vampires."

I was spending Friday night tackling the last item on the list.

Lesser vampires emanate a distinct magical signature which can be picked up with a locate spell. Before leaving my house, I ran a *locate* that narrowed my search down to an industrial area in the southwest part of Albuquerque.

The area was bleak and colorless—a place where motor vehicles came to die and the desperate bought mobile housing. This was the desert after all, so moody, blue, atmospheric lighting and glowing tendrils of fog were out of the question. Instead, the scene consisted of dusty lots cordoned off with chain link fencing; the air carried the dense reek of diesel and motor oil.

I cruised through the area a few times, before settling on a parking place several blocks from my target, a motorcycle junkyard. Before moving on, I paused by my car's rear bumper and hummed a few spell words, a simple *obscure* spell, over the license plate. It was bloody efficient, harmonic magic. With just three music notes, I cast a spell that normally took six or seven words. Too bad its use labeled me as some kind of freak.

A few years into my education at the Sh'ree College of the Arcane, I found out why the instructors tolerated but didn't encourage my use of musically-enhanced magic. Harmonic magic is a rare ability, revered and found only among the Sh'ree. Well, it *was* exclusively a Sh'ree power until I came along. I guess the Sh'ree instructors were dismayed to see the ability manifest outside their species, in a demi-human no less. I share their dismay. On the other hand, it's the only way I can reliably cast even basic spells—so I sing, hum, and whistle my way through magic whenever no one else is around.

Keeping to the shadows where possible, I made my way down the block. The motorcycle lot resembled the aftermath of a nuclear holocaust, the metal skeletons and entrails of Harleys and imports strewn across the property. A large brindle guard dog watched me, waving a tail that might have been long and fluffy, had half of it not been missing.

Jagged razor wire spiraled along the top of the fence. "You don't happen to have a key?" I asked the dog, who just wagged his stubby tail harder. My hunting outfit is always unremarkable: jeans, running shoes, a pullover with pockets, and leather gloves, all dark gray. I fumbled in my pocket and pulled out a doggie treat. "There's a whole box of these in my car if you can find me a key." Fluffy or Fang crunched away on the treat, obviously a food whore and not trusted with vital intelligence—like key locations.

After a moment's hesitation, I wedged my foot in the chain link fencing and prepared to climb. Just then someone cried out in pain only to be cut off abruptly. The dog and I both whirled around to look across the street toward a mobile home lot.

The guard dog made a startled whine-bark, jammed his truncated tail between his legs, and ran. The lights from a passing car hit the chain link fencing, flashing it into a silvery lattice. Once the vehicle had cruised on by and well out of sight, I hurried to the other side of the street.

"Lucky's Repo Depot," read the sign in front of the business. Like the motorcycle lot, the entire establishment was fenced with chain link and capped with razor wire. Since most of Lucky's inventory consisted of large doghouses very thinly disguised as human habitations, I guessed the fencing served as the Berlin Wall of sales, keeping in prospective customers until they signed on the dotted line.

The sound of coarse laughter and something else came from a close-knit cluster of especially ugly doublewides in the far corner of the lot. Keeping the majority of my senses focused on the noises, I crept along the fence line. Only a dozen feet along the boundary, someone had cut a hole, ragged and not terribly subtle, but preferable to razor wire.

After slipping through the gap, I jogged toward the far corner of the lot, giving each building I passed a cursory examination. All the action seemed to be confined to four mobile homes. Slowing to a walk, I stepped around the corner of the first building.

One figure crouched over another and the iron smell of fresh blood cut through the tang of petroleum. My stomach gave off an irrational hunger pang. In the darkness, the prone figure wasn't much more than a faint reddish outline. Residual heat. To my eyes, warm-blooded *living* things give off a bright infrared glow. The man—I sniffed and detected the aroma of human male—was twitching from nerves that labored on unaware of their impending pink slips.

The vampire glowed with a faint bluish halo. I watched, waiting to see what he would do. A smart, watchful vampire would have picked me up right away; instead, he just kept working on his gory snack.

One final squishy slurp later, the vampire stood up, wiping his mouth on his sleeve like a toddler. He took a couple of steps toward me, still ignorant of my presence.

"You're just gonna leave him there? Like that?" At the sound of my voice, he stopped, vacant eyes searching the darkness. He sported a brutal short haircut that always made me think of old-time lice treatments, and he wore a University of New Mexico jersey. In Albuquerque, even the undead support the home team.

"What the fu—?"

"It's considered good etiquette to dispose of the body. You know, cover your tracks?"

He squinted into the darkness. "Who the fuck are you, bitch?" he asked, taking another step in my direction. Cold-dimwitted eyes studied me. "Yeah. I bet you taste real good."

"There's only one way to find out, eh?"

Even in the dim light, I saw his dark eyes alter to yellow and the white flash of fangs as he lunged at me with preternatural speed. A dagger, responding to its magical summons, materialized in my left hand.

A fraction of a second before he reached me, I took a quick—quicker than he could move—step backwards and lifted the hand that held the dagger. Obligingly, he stepped into the weapon, driving it deep into his chest. The heat as he flashed to dust stung my hand.

Two daggers and a short sword, all three made of a nearly indestructible black wood and edged with titanium, are standard Wolfe equipment. I passed combat training, the part where a Wolfe and her weapons become one, with flying colors.

If vampires were cars, I would be the newest improved model. Sort of. I'm faster, have keener senses, and can make the most of a sunny holiday in Hawaii. There are some tradeoffs: I'm not strong, so the average human male can beat me at arm wrestling; and I tire quickly, so prolonged fights are out of the question. But against the average Lesser vampire, it's no contest.

After a dog-like sniff to clear my nose of vampire remains, I walked over to the body and crouched next to it. Something metallic glimmered on the man's chest. A badge. Security guard. I held my hand, palm down, over his heart and chant-sang a quick spell. Even as I straightened and pushed my *senses* toward the doublewide at the end of the row, the gash on his neck was starting to close and the blood fading from his clothes and surroundings. It would be easy enough to *vanish* his remains altogether, but he probably had a family, people who deserved better than a lifetime of wondering what happened to their loved one.

The vampire-infested mobile home had the usual poor facsimile of a porch. I heard around seven or eight vampires in the building and from the sounds of things they were doing nothing more extraordinary than sitting around, drinking booze.

I scooped up a handful of gravel and considered my options. Knock on the door like a paranormal Avon lady? Some of them sounded sane enough for conversation; I could try asking who turned them. There were a few too many, however, for a quiet little tête-à-tête.

Opting for a little caution, I hurled the rocks at the door and slid just out of view. Several long strings of cuss words later, the first vampire stomped out the door. Fully utilizing his enhanced senses, he detected me instantly and rushed around the corner. I ducked his careless grab and slashed a long line across his torso. Yellow eyes glowing with shock and anger, he stumbled back into the vampire who followed. Vampire Two staggered under the sudden weight of his companion. His eyes widened and altered to yellow when the first vampire collapsed into dust.

I *called* back the dagger before it hit the ground, and then sent it hurtling toward the next vampire. The dagger did its job and returned to my left hand. A matching dagger appeared in my right. More curses erupted from the porch, followed by the sound of running feet. The front door clanged shut.

Okay. Now I was left with the ones who were sane enough to recognize when they were outmatched. I took a breath and started up the stairs.

The problem with *easy* is that it tends to lead to cocky, which in turn leads to *sloppy*, and sloppy leads to inattentive. Feeling that the only threat, if you could call it that, was the vampire trailer trash, I let down my guard. In fact, part of my guard was already home eating a carton of ice cream.

Two distinct footsteps crunched gravel on either side of the mobile home behind me. *Damn!* A quick sniff confirmed my suspicions. *Humans. Uh-oh.*

Taking one deep breath, and hoping the vamps weren't armed with more conventional weapons, like...guns, I hopped on the porch and turned the doorknob. Locked.

Crunch. Crunch. Crunch. The footsteps' pace quickened. I took a step back and hoped the trailer was as poorly constructed as it appeared. My first kick only rattled the door, but with the second, I heard the gratifying sound of something cracking. Somewhere in the trailer, feet scurried furtively. The third time was indeed the charm and the door flew open.

I jumped out of the doorway. When no projectiles flew out from the opening, I jumped forward, flinging myself to the floor just in time. A small wooden bolt, from a standard issue Holder weapon, hissed over my head.

Guess who? Damn, damn, damn. The sound of booted feet echoed on the crappy porch. I scrambled up and headed in the direction of what I supposed were the bedrooms. Someone reached out and grabbed my arm and I slashed at a blue outline, rewarded with a shriek of pain.

I darted down the narrow hall and into one of the bedrooms. After shutting the door, I twisted the pitiful locking latch. If the front door was any indication of the structural integrity of this place, I didn't have much time. At least I was alone.

Just a few steps took me over to the outside wall. The vamps had boarded up the windows. My scrabbling fingers found the material covering the windows. Just flimsy cardboard.

The sharp edge of a dagger sliced through the material and pried the window open. The opening was small; the home must have been built pre-fire code. I *banished* the weapon and prepared to squirm through the gap. From the rest of the house came the sound of more curses, growls and vampires going all dust-in-the-wind. Red light pushed under the door and scattered in patterns across the threadbare carpet.

I pulled myself up and started to squirm through the window. The plan was to slip out, twist and land, catlike, on my feet. More human than cat, I landed hard on my butt. Above me came the bang of the bedroom door being kicked open. A few feet away, footsteps rattled the front porch.

Running at top speed, I darted out from between the trailers, found myself in open ground, and leaped behind a conveniently placed pickup truck. Even with vampire speed, I couldn't make it much further without being seen. And I can't move at preternatural speed very long without getting fall-over-pass-out tired, anyway.

Cringing behind the front tire, I *listened*, my heart thudding a loud tempo. *Stupid. Stupid. Stupid.*

Someone approached, half-running, half-walking for a dozen steps and then stopped. Not daring to peek around the tire, I reached out with my hearing and smell, recognizing him immediately. The spicy smell of soap and aftershave and a heartbeat that thumped at a unique timbre. Jason. The universe's way of confirming he was the enemy. I tucked my knees tightly to my chest, trying to be as small as possible.

A red light from a flashlight played around the truck. Standard issue Holder equipment. The red light minimized loss of night vision. He took a step forward and I squeezed my eyes shut like a kid hiding from the monster under the bed.

Kyle came clomping out of the house and walked over to Jason. Gauging from the sound, they were standing at the far edge of the trailer.

"Where did he go? Did you see him?" asked Kyle. I cranked my eyes open and the red light flickered over the truck again.

"No," Jason replied, puzzled.

"He can't be far." Kyle moved several steps closer to the truck, and I fought the urge to summon my short sword.

"I'm not getting anything, no reading, nothing," Jason said.

His partner stopped. "Yeah. Me neither." A tapping noise, like someone trying to start a frozen wristwatch echoed against the metal mobile homes. Holders carry vampire detectors, generally disguised as wristwatches. They work by detecting a consciousness that has been separated from its soul. My soul and I are on good terms. "I thought the new ones had a range of at least a mile?" Kyle asked.

"Yes, they do," Jason replied. Kyle moved back toward Jason and I risked a peek around the tire. The window I had just slipped through was illuminated by a flashlight's red glow. Jason asked, "Are you certain someone was in there?"

"Window was covered in cardboard and duct tape. And somebody tore it all to pieces, in a real rush to get out." Light from Kyle's flashlight joined Jason's. "Window is wide open. The door to the bedroom was locked." Kyle's arm swung and the light darted along the ground. "Something's not right."

Jason turned toward the trailer's front entrance, his flashlight following his gaze. "That yours?" He stared at the remains of the two vamps I dusted.

"No. All the ones I did were inside." The larger man used the bolt launcher to gesture back at the trailer.

"We should see to the body...or bodies," Jason said, turning and walking back in the direction of the first trailer in the row.

Kyle caught him in two quick steps. His hand landed on Jason's shoulder, stopping him and shining his flashlight in his partner's face. "What are you thinking, Lake?"

In the red light, Jason's pleasant features took on a ghastly appearance. He gave a nearly imperceptible shake of his head and continued back to the first trailer.

I shifted to the back tire and continued spying.

They moved ghostlike between the two trailers, their movements visible only via their flashlights and the red infrared glow that surrounded each of them. Pausing at the remains of the vampire, they continued on to the security guard. Just as I had a few minutes before, Jason crouched next to the body, his hand held palm down over the corpse's chest area.

"Is he turned?"

"No." Jason answered. "But he was *cleaned*. No trace of blood or injury."

Kyle turned his flashlight back to the nearby mound of vampire. "So who did *him?*"

"Or her," Jason pointed out. He stood up, his attention still on the guard. "Interesting. The magical residue is evenly layered and strong."

I got a tiny surge of pride. Coming from an obviously competent sorcerer, Jason's words were complimentary.

Kyle's flashlight illuminated Jason's angular features again. "Not the usual M.O. for immature or crazy vamps, huh? Whatcha thinking?"

Jason's only response was to gently pushed the light out of his face.

"So what have we got?" Kyle pointed the light back out toward the truck and I froze. "A Wolfe?" he asked with apparent distaste.

Jason's flashlight sent red light down Kyle's arm. "No response from the detectors, though." Kyle glanced at his wrist and grunted in assent. I took the opportunity to shrink back behind the tire and search for a means of escape. My butt hurt and I really needed ice cream.

The two men continued on between the trailers and around the back side. As soon as they disappeared around the corner, I darted in the opposite direction to hide in another grouping of trailers. They continued on, between the fence and the mobile homes, retracing my steps, until they reached the doublewide's porch.

In the thick gloom of substandard housing, I paused and watched the two men. Jason leveled his flashlight at the vampire remains and lifted his eyes straight in my direction.

I gulped, reassuring myself he couldn't see me, and slunk away.

Chapter Eight

Sometime around seven the next morning, I dragged myself out of bed, pulled on sweatpants, shoes and a jacket and stumbled out into the cold morning to feed Bill. I tossed his breakfast into the feeder and glanced towards the mountains. A classic New Mexico sunrise filled the eastern sky, spectacular and worthy of artwork that would sell for a fortune in trendy Santa Fe galleries.

I took one look at the beautiful morning, staggered back into my house and fell into bed. My preferred method of dealing with mornings is to sleep right through them. When you spend your nights killing vampires and evading your mortal enemy, sleep takes precedence over postcard sunrises.

I was several winks short of my required forty when the phone rang.

The answering machine clicked and a woman's voice barked, "Regan, it's Cypher. Get up! It's nearly ten thirty. I have some information for you, but I am not leaving it on this machine."

I staggered out of bed and into the living room. "All right, all right. I'm up." I refuse to have a phone by my bed.

Cypher is Commander of Brethren Intelligence, and therefore, my boss. Yet another relative in high places, Cypher was turned by my brother Argus.

Though her features would suggest Mongolia, Cypher isn't sure where she was born. Her earliest memories are of smoke, the stench of burning flesh and the screams of her mother. By the time Argus and

Breas met her, sometime around the year 1000, she was a teenager and the property of a Persian trader. Although Argus is the one who turned her, it was Breas who first recognized the uncanny intelligence in her eyes.

"Kyle Peterson," Cypher said, getting straight to the point.

"Yeah?" I wandered into the kitchen, pulled a bag of tortilla chips off the top of the fridge, put some water on for tea, and then hopped up on the counter top.

Paper rustling noises followed and Cypher began, "Attended high school in Chicago, Illinois. Joined the Navy, right after high school. Served for six years and returned home to Chicago. He was identified and recruited by the Holders about a year after that. No innate magic but he has the perfect worldview. As in black and white and entirely xenophobic."

"Sounds pretty typical." I added the sound of me crunching on chips to the paper sounds and stared out the kitchen window. Bill was stretched flat out on his side, like giant road kill, napping off his breakfast.

"Yes. Very typical." She turned another page and said, "Jason Lake." My stomach did an odd flippy thing. "He is what the Holders refer to, in their frat boy parlance, as a Legacy."

Yikes! I gulped down another chip.

"His mother, Sarah Astin, is an expert in Elvish dialects. Daniel Lake started out in field operations, like his son, but has since been promoted to a position in Tactical Command. His family, maternal and paternal lines, has sustained membership within the Holders for centuries."

I stared bleakly at the tortilla chip I held in my hand, feeling an uncharacteristic lack of appetite. As if in sympathy, the sky darkened. I leaned over the kitchen sink and peeped out the window. My redneck neighbor had set fire to a huge brush pile; black smoke billowed from the blaze. Unlike leaves, tumbleweeds have long opposed the idea of being raked and stuffed into black plastic bags. Fortunately, air quality laws are lax in the village.

Cypher continued, "Daniel Lake and Sara Astin were married after dating about six months. A standard Holder arranged marriage." My neighbor's bonfire flared up abruptly and Bill lifted his head and blinked sleepily in the direction of the blaze.

"A year later, their first child, Juliet, was born. Jason Astin-Lake came along three years later."

People poured out of pyro-neighbor's trailer house like clowns out of a tiny car and converged around the towering tumbleweed inferno. Apparently, they were convening a committee to determine whether the thing was truly out of control. Bill's ears swiveled forward, but he seemed otherwise unconcerned by the fire.

"The pattern breaks a bit after that." Cypher was all about patterns. "After twelve years of marriage, they were divorced, at which point Sarah took both children and left London. She accepted a teaching position with the University of Wales, Aberystwyth. Linguistics. Where, she remains to this day."

My teakettle whistled and I shuffled over to stove. "She *left* the Holders? I didn't think that was allowed."

"Not usually, no."

"Wow." I poured the hot water into a cup and added the necessary ingredients for tea.

"Quite. Juliet returned to London within the year, continuing her studies at a Holder-sanctioned school. Jason remained in Wales for three years before returning to London." She turned another page. "And when he returned, he did not attend a Holder school."

My neighbors were trying to put out the conflagration, which threatened one of their non-functioning cars, with a hose. I sipped my tea and contemplated using my cell phone to call the fire department. The rust and bondo-colored car was an eyesore, but burning wasn't gonna make it any prettier.

"He went on to Cambridge, where he got his M.Eng in Chemical Engineering," Cypher said.

"What?" I inhaled hot tea and coughed. "Jason's an engineer? Then why—?"

"Is he now a Holder?" Cypher finished. "Actually, the mere fact that he never attended a Holder school is much more intriguing."

"So what changed?" The wail of sirens announced the arrival of the fire department. Someone more concerned with neighborhood aesthetics must have already made the call. The rapid response time was due to the fact that the firehouse was just a couple blocks away. Happily oblivious to the chaos next-door, Bill folded up his legs and rolled, flipping from one side to another before slowly standing up. He shook and a cloud of dust billowed off his shaggy coat, PigPen style.

"A year after he graduated college, his sister Juliet died in a car crash. Juliet, by the way, was an up and coming star in the Holders. Within the year, Jason had joined the Holders of the True Light."

"So why, then? He's honoring the wish of a dying sister or—?"

"That would be a likely scenario. I found nothing in the Holder records to indicate exactly why he 'returned to the fold.'" Cypher's time spent in the Holders' records is best categorized as hacking. For a bunch of magicians, the Holders are fairly techno-savvy and have impressive security on their networks, but they are no match for Cypher. Besides, Cypher has other means of acquiring information, some of which make me squeamish.

"Hmmm. And the question of the hour?" I asked. The firemen were busy extinguishing the fire before it damaged anything important, like my house.

"Why are they, the Holders, there in Albuquerque?" Cypher sighed. "Nothing. I can't find anything. Yet." The "yet" had an ominous sound. "The very fact that I can't find anything is significant."

She changed the subject. "So, did you and Jason hit it off?" Her tone was even, flat, but I knew Cypher well enough to feel her smirk.

"*Et Tu*, Cyph?"

"I only ask," she explained, through an obvious smile, "because the very nature of your Thrall charm could get us the information we need."

A spark of discomfort bounced around in my head. "Yeah, but, then he'd be like...obsessed...and weird...and stuff."

"So?" Cypher asked. "He's a Holder, isn't he?" At my silence, she added, "I'm not asking you to sleep with him, Regan. Just a good kiss. Or a bad one. He is English and human and male." Cypher is quite certain that, with the possible exception of contributing to the continued existence of the human race, her favorite food, human males are worthless.

"True," I responded, feigning indifference. I tried to bring up Cara's face and felt instant guilt because I couldn't picture her face clearly anymore.

Jason was just another Holder, no different or better than any other, right?

"Just how far has Kadin spread the story?" I asked.

"Even Cullan knows."

"Dad knows?" I groaned.

The vampire chuckled softly at my groan. "Actually, I think Breas is the only one who doesn't know." I clenched my jaw and didn't respond. "He's disappeared again," she finished, sounding moderately concerned.

"Thanks, Cyph," I said, edging the conversation away from slippery footing. "Let me know if you find anything."

"Of course. I know I can count on you to do the same."

"Of course."

I hung up the phone and stared enviously at Bill who stood dozing in the sun. A thick cloud of charcoaled-tumbleweed haze hung in the air.

A second later my cell phone rang. I didn't recognize the number, but I had a hunch who was calling. And that hunch set my heart a-racing.

Chapter Nine

That afternoon, I knew exactly how teenage girls felt right before their first date, which in effect, this was for me. My sexual experience was limited to a couple of glorified one-night stands: the first, a deflowering at the hands of my favorite vampire pest; the second happened under the auspices of sealing a treaty between the Grey Brethren and the elves. In neither case did the guy buy me dinner or pin an ugly corsage on my chest.

I cruised around the mall parking lot, searching for parking, and blaming my chattering teeth on the weather. Cold, wet weather in Albuquerque is as rare as flat-chested unattractive women in superhero comics. Around noon, however, the wind started to blow and an hour later, a sky full of dark nasty clouds supplanted the usual blue sky. Rain in New Mexico was a good omen.

Not that I was sure what a good outcome for my date would be. After I found parking, at the edge of the lot, far from the theater, I fumbled the key out of the ignition and stared at the dashboard.

My case of nerves was irrational. In my lifetime, I have fought in a war on a demon plane, been a battlefield medic, changed my name more times than I can remember, and had a dozen regular careers, ranging from surgeon to carpenter. *It's just a matinee. Piece of cake, right?*

Before getting out of the car, I indulged in a little girlish vanity and peered in the rearview mirror. I'd gone all out, setting the blow dryer and a handful of mousse on my hair, and putting a few swipes of blush on my cheeks. The face in the mirror resembled me with pink cheeks and unhappily tamed hair. I locked my car and headed slowly toward the theater.

Jason waited outside, dressed in slacks, a dark green sweater, a black leather jacket and Doc Martins. I felt a guilty pang, realizing I was late, as usual. Then I reminded myself, he was the enemy and it's only proper to leave your foe in the cold, freezing his naughty bits.

"Hi. Sorry, I'm late." I noticed that his eyes picked up the green from his sweater.

He shrugged. "I haven't been here long." He reached into his coat pocket. "I went ahead and got the tickets."

Since no movie experience is complete without artery hardening artificial butter dripped over popcorn, I made a trip to the snack bar. Then we headed into the theater and sat down.

A middle-aged couple, several rows ahead of us, whispered and kissed. "They're havin' an affair," I offered through a mouthful of popcorn. "He's got a ring, she doesn't. They're entirely too lovey-dovey. The teenaged couple, a couple of seats behind them, aren't that affectionate." I gave Jason a wry smile. "Sorry, I'm a compulsive audience watcher."

He nodded, played along and scanned the theater. "What about them?" He pointed at a couple that sat with a pair of sullen teenagers. "Forced family outing?"

"Yep. Note all the teen angst. Second marriage, the kids must be hers. They keep giving step-dad the 'You're not my father glare.'" I pointed at a couple with an infant and a toddler. "Now for them, I got nothing. Happy families make for dull stories."

Jason sipped his drink through a straw, his eyes on the couple. I noticed he had nicely-shaped lips, wondered what it would be like to kiss a human. Heat rose to my face.

"How about this?" he offered. "Perhaps they are not truly human, but rather cleverly disguised demons. And demon children, of course, enjoy gory horror films."

My jaw dropped open and I shot a quick look at the family. Nope. They were human.

Seeing the stricken expression on my face, Jason winced. "Sorry. I was trying to be...creative."

I laughed, nervous laughter that gave way to real laughter. "No Teletubbies for demon children, eh?"

He flashed a relieved smile. "No, actually, I think the Teletubbies are demon approved." Our eyes locked and butterflies fluttered around in my stomach. Mercifully, the house lights faded and we both turned away.

Two hours later we stood outside, shivering. The wind had died down somewhat, but now the air had turned biting cold.

"Seems it might snow," Jason said, zipping up his jacket.

Squinting at the sky through my sunglasses, I shrugged. "Nah. It's just Nature's way of teasing a drought-stricken land."

"I—" Jason began, "I don't suppose you'd like to get some dinner."

I found an interesting spot of ancient gum stuck on the sidewalk and studied it. The more time I spent with him, the more chances I would get to trip over my own feet and *splat*, land in the truth.

My eyes moved cautiously back up to his face. So far, he was disappointingly nice and nowhere near the monster I wanted him to be.

"Japanese? Italian? Generic American?" I asked, inclining my head toward the line of restaurants that flanked the mall parking lot.

My hair, using the wind as an excuse, started to spring free of the mousse-imposed order. In any minute Jason was going to take a good look at me and decide he was on a date with a Japanese cartoon character. By my estimations, the restaurants were all within walking distance, but the icy wind shrank the definition of 'walking distance' considerably.

"We can take my car," Jason said, "I'm parked close by." A sort of instinctive hesitation kicked in and I just stood there, probably with a ten-inch-long-centipede-in-the-bathtub expression on my face. My eyes moved to his face where I saw nothing but open honesty.

"Okay," I agreed, my voice a few registers higher than usual.

I made note of the license plate on his dark gray SUV and then climbed into the vehicle and out of the wind. The engine started and the stereo blared out Counting Crows, singing about a holiday in Spain.

Hiding my sudden discomfort at being trapped in a car with a Holder, I stared out the window and used my sense of smell to investigate the vehicle.

Jason's car smelled mostly of Jason, fast food, and Kyle. No notable magical residue. But that wasn't too surprising. Magic spells are hard to cast and sustain when you are encased in iron and iron alloys. Iron and magic don't play well together.

We ended up at the Japanese restaurant, primarily because it had the shortest wait. Every day in Albuquerque, hundreds of houses were being built with fabulous kitchens, which apparently, nobody actually used.

As we walked into the restaurant, Jason's hand found mine. The combination of living warmth and magic lowered my IQ several points, and I didn't even try to get a table which offered an unrestricted view of the door.

We ordered and our meals arrived soon after.

"Where did you get your doctorate?" Jason asked.

I glanced at him, and gulped down some miso soup. "M.I.T. And you?" I steered the conversation back at him. "What kind of a background or degree do you need to work in security? Criminal justice?"

I heard his sharp intake of breath and he rearranged his hold on the chopsticks. "Chemical Engineering," he answered, a rueful smile crossing his mouth.

"Engineering? Really?" Since I was expecting a lie, surprise came easy. "Where from?"

Again, there was a perceptible pause. I so wished I could read humans the way I could vampires. "Cambridge."

Egad! The truth! "Cambridge? Wow!"

He scowled at the chopsticks and then his hazel eyes met mine. "*M.I.T?* Wow!" He smiled his crooked smile and something in my brain fizzled and sparked.

Ring! Jason's eyes climbed skyward accompanied by a sigh. The cell phone rang a second time. I picked up my chopsticks and started to eat my vegetable tempura, shoveling in rice along the way.

"Go ahead." I gestured with the chopsticks. "Really," I said, in response to the guilty expression on his face.

His longish fingers flipped open the phone. "This is Lake." I focused my hearing on the phone. Eavesdropping is a rude, but useful advantage of super hearing.

"Yeah, it's Peterson," answered the voice on the phone.

Howdy, asshole, I thought cheerfully.

Jason made "blah, blah, blah" hand gestures. "Yes?"

"Brethren assigned a Wolfe here at least six months ago." Kyle sounded smug.

Asshole, asshole, asshole, I sang in my head and dumped soy sauce on my rice.

Jason's dark eyebrows crept upward. "Really?"

"Yeah. That would explain the extra kills last night and what you said about the clean."

Keeping my face neutral, I carried on with the melodic Kyle bashing. *Sphincter-Man, Sphincter-Man, does whatever a sphincter can.*

Jason watched me, his expression as bland as mine. "I don't suppose we have a name?" he asked Kyle.

Kyle sneered. "Nah. Not yet. Say? Aren't you the researcher? I'm doing your job. Maybe I should get your pay, too?"

It's a bird, it's a plane, it's Sphincter-Man!

"They rarely keep detailed records. Particularly regarding field ops," Jason said. "I doubt that I could find out much else."

Jason and I made eye contact and he asked Kyle, "Eight o'clock?"

"You givin' me the brush off, magic boy?"

"Well...yes." A small smile crept onto his face.

Kyle grunted. "She'd better be damn good lookin'."

Jason eyes swept across my face. "Yes. Astonishingly." I chucked a chopstick off the table and dove after it to hide my face, which had flared hot beet red.

"Really! Who?" Kyle sounded genuinely surprised.

"Goodbye, Kyle." The connection clicked off. "Sorry," came Jason's voice from above me. Trying to buy time, I poked at the chopstick, pretending it was a scorpion.

"No problem." My voice squeaked and I picked up my chopstick. I sat up and stared at it glumly, keeping my senses well in check. I didn't need to know the composition of the suspicious dirt smudge on the wooden surface.

I got new chopsticks and we finished our meal. The sun hung low on the horizon when we left, but I slipped my sunglasses on anyway. I don't have to worry about turning into a torch in sunlight, but too much of the yellow stuff gives me pinkeye. We got in his SUV and drove back to the mall parking lot.

Jason pulled his car up next to mine and I felt a wave of mild panic. Cypher's suggestion (or was it an order?) rattled about in my head. The

Thrall charm she mentioned is a genetic gift from my Mom and is meant to turn a vampire from hungry predator to devoted friend—at least. In my Mom's case, it netted her a vampire husband. Triggered by certain types of physical contact—a kiss is quite effective—it produces frightening obsession in humans. The effect is limited to humans or vampires, so elves and demons are immune.

"Thank you," I groped for the words, "I had a very nice time." *I am so bad at this.* "You should leave Kyle at home more often."

My date smiled grimly. "Were it that easy." He looked away. After a second, he turned his head, our eyes locking.

Eye contact with Jason gave me an odd little stomach butterfly thing and that meant trouble. Those stupid butterflies have been responsible for very stupid behavior. Nature, in an attempt to be poetic, started dropping big fat raindrops on the car.

I got the impression he was debating something. *I wonder what the Holder policy is on dating? Especially for a blue-blood Legacy? No peeing in the gene pool.*

His eyes had a strange wistful expression. My hair, with perfect timing, flopped down in my face. He raised his hand and, with exaggerated slowness that reminded me of someone else, pushed my bangs off my face. My nice little shield removed, I stared at him, straight on.

"Regan? Is that your real name?" *Uh-oh.* "Or is it a nickname?" *Oh.*

"Morrigan." The name shot out of my mouth, proving that crucial connections had come unplugged in my brain.

"Morrigan? The Irish Goddess of War—"

"Goddess, War Witch, Raven. Yeah, I know." Raindrops beaded up and ran down the SUV's windshield. "The name, it was my mother's choice. My dad, he didn't much care for it, so he shortened it to Regan."

"Morrigan," Jason spoke carefully, sort of tasting the name. "Morrigan. Could I make you dinner sometime?"

"Dinner? Is that what they call it these days? Oh, and nobody ever calls me Morrigan. Makes me feel like an aging fortune teller at a low-end carny."

"If you got my assurances that my intentions are entirely honorable?" he said with a nice mix of seductive heat and sarcasm.

Gulp. "Um, then I'd assume you were the kind of kid who preferred

Barbie and her pink nightmare house over GI Joe and all his cool weapons of mass destruction." Pondering for a beat, I added, "Or...I'm five seconds away from a 'let's just be friends' speech."

The cute crooked smile reappeared. "Neither."

"Well, all right then." He was bound to have something snoopworthy in his home. "Vegetarian, remember?"

He unsnapped his seatbelt, reached into an inside coat pocket, producing a pen, and after some more digging, a business card. He scribbled something—left-handed—on the back of the card.

Our hands brushed as he gave me the card and loose connections in my brain hissed. "My address and home phone are on the back." I flipped the card, which claimed he worked for Renaissance Security Systems, over and studied the address. "Tomorrow too soon?" he asked.

"Actually, I have a performance tomorrow night. I usually work late Monday through Thursday—ten hour days." I unsnapped my own seatbelt and stuffed the card in my pocket. I really didn't need it anymore. I never forget a number. "Anytime after that will work."

"Next Friday, then?" he asked, and I nodded.

At a much quieter volume, Counting Crows were now singing about American girls. Jason and I gazed at each other, our sudden silence punctuated by the sound of rain. I studied his face, intrigued by the faint suggestion of stubble on his jaw. Because of their elven origins, vampires couldn't grow beards.

"I better get going." If I didn't get out of that vehicle, soon, he might try to kiss me. And he might be successful. I fumbled with the door handle before spilling out into the stinging rain. "See you Friday," I said, and bolted for my car.

Chapter Ten

A silver or gray car, it was too dark to tell which, sat (in my preferred space) in my driveway. I parked my car next to the interloper, got out and scowled at the showroom shiny Mercedes.

Bill, whose pointy-eared silhouette should have been near the gate, was nowhere in sight. A faint blue flicker of television light pulsed through the living room blinds. I wandered back to Bill's corral to confirm that he was eating dinner and went into my house.

First, I checked the fridge. A couple of six packs of overpriced microbrews had materialized on the middle shelf. *Marvelous*, I thought with plenty of sarcasm. Grabbing a beer, I clenched my jaw and walked into my living room.

Cypher's missing friend was in my living room, sprawled in the middle of the couch, drinking beer and watching a Spanish soap opera. Un-invited, as usual. On account of one kiss, Breas Montrose has secured an all-access pass to my life.

I twisted the top off the beer and took a long drink, debating where to sit. Knowing Breas, his position on the couch was meant as some sort of power play. I glanced at my comfortable recliner and sat next to the vampire.

"Why are you here?" I asked.

Not taking his eyes off the television, he responded, "Breas. How nice to see you. How are you? Oh, and thanks for feeding my horse." Not even a hint of expression touched his face or voice. Breas was as emotional as a rock. A tall, blond, gray-eyed, dangerously beautiful rock.

"Thanks for feeding my horse," I replied, trying to emulate his neutrality. "Cypher's looking for you. I think she's worried or something."

"She found me." His eyes, reflecting slivery-blue in the television's light, fixed on me. "How was your date?"

"Date?" I asked, innocent and wide-eyed.

"You're dating Holders now, aren't you?" He turned to the television where a busty blond had a shrieking fit and hurled insults and household furnishings at her cheating husband.

"The addition of the word 'blind' automatically negates the 'date' part," I explained. The blond woman threw a tacky gilded lamp at her husband and informed him that she carried another man's baby.

I speak damn good Spanish for an Irish girl. The Brethren Sword Master was a Spaniard and gave all instruction in Spanish. I had been given two choices: learn Spanish or bleed.

"The baby is his brother's," Breas said.

"I take it you've seen this before."

He nodded. "This was real popular in Brazil about a year ago." I frowned at the screen. Apparently it lost something in the Portuguese to Spanish dubbing, which was as bad as a Japanese Godzilla flick.

"And he's screwing the maid," the vampire pointed out, almost cheerfully. The maid appeared at that moment, took one look at the lamp carnage, and went screaming down the hall.

"Good lighting must be hard to find in Brazil," I said.

"Doesn't the addition of the word 'second' to 'date' negate the 'blind' part?" Breas asked, studying me with metal-cold eyes. Lying and omissions of truth are pointless with Breas. "I can smell him on you."

"Two Holders get assigned to New Mexico of all places. Something big is going down." I gulped down a mouthful of beer. "I'm just trying to find out what, exactly."

"How? By shagging the sorcerer?" He gave me a sly once over and added, "Poor S.O.B doesn't stand a chance."

"Shaddup." Breas and I communicate by sniping at each other. Once, long, long ago, on a continent, far, far away, we stopped sniping. I aim to never let that happen again, ever.

"I don't need to do *that*," I stated. "I have my ways. Vampire senses and whatnot."

"*That* is a lot more fun."

I ignored him and watched a car commercial in Spanish.

"Uh-huh. And you're jealous," I said after a minute, giving him a long stare.

Breas's mouth did something that resembled a rueful smile. "Nothing gets by you."

"Jealous." I laughed. "You're so jealous, you're greener than The Hulk."

The vampire set the beer bottle down on the coffee table and swung around to lean in on me. "Yeah. And you," his eyes dropped to my chest and back to my face, "are attracted to a Holder."

"Am not!"

He leaned in closer; his eyes had changed color, shifting to a dark blue-gray, a consequence of some elf in his pre-vampire lineage. "I could smell it when you walked in the room." His head cocked to the side. "You smell...charged, excited." Little waves of compelling Mesmer power emanated from him, pointless since I'm immune to its power.

"R-road rage. Traffic was b-b-bad." He hadn't been this flirtatious in years. "What are you doing?"

"Being jealous." He tilted his head and brushed his mouth against mine. Frazzled brain connections from my date with Jason spit out sparks like an arc welder. The contact turned into a genuine kiss.

"You, um, have beer breath." I squeezed the comment in between kisses. A high velocity collision between a beer bottle and his head might have been fun, but beer stains were a bitch to get out of a leather couch. Something subtler was in order.

Breas dropped his face to my neck, which made me nervous for reasons that had nothing to do with him being a vampire. He kissed my neck, using his tongue to draw figure eights on my skin.

Before he progressed any further in his repertoire of seductive skills, I said, "So when you were human ..."—my hand toyed with his short blond hair—"was your hair long?" He stopped kissing my neck and looked me straight in the eyes.

"Long braids, maybe?" I asked. "And a helmet with horns or wings? Like Asterix the Gaul?"

For a second, it seemed my ploy had failed and he was actually going to answer. Instead he pushed himself off me, reclaimed his beer from the coffee table and sat at the far end of the sofa.

Whew! I jumped up and relocated to the recliner.

Need to get Breas Montrose off your back—literally—in a hurry? Even the briefest mention of his past—the human years—is ten times more effective than the wickedest yew-wood stake.

If asked what I know about Breas, my answer would be, "Not a hell of a lot." That puts me miles ahead of most of the universe, for which the answer would be, "Nothing at all." His real name is neither Breas nor Montrose. All I know about his life, life before his unlife, is that he was a Gaul born sometime around a date followed by the letters "B.C." He refuses to talk about his past, which may have once been kind of fascinating, but now it's just a tired, tired shtick.

"Can I borrow your car?" I asked.

"Can you what?" An expression of authentic surprise broke through his stony exterior.

"Your car? Vroom, vroom, vroom." I pantomimed driving. "May I borrow it?"

He retreated behind his cold mask. "No."

"Please?"

"No," he said, finding something fascinating about a fabric softener advertisement.

I got up and sat next to him. "The Asterix the Gaul comment? I've got loads more where that came from."

He scowled at me, his eyes silver. "Books *without* pictures, Regan. Try one. Maybe you'll learn something." I ignored the gibe and smiled. "Why?" he growled.

"Anonymity."

"Oh. So I can take all the heat for your miscreant activities."

Huh. This from Breas, the perpetual grifter. "Come on. I'll be careful. I need a car that nobody's seen before."

"Nobody, meaning the Holder?" He gave me his world-weary expression.

I licked the tip of my finger and wiped at a tiny spot on his cheek. "Little bit of green still there—okay, got it." I tried the toothy grin and added the big innocent eyes. "Please?"

"No."

Not easily deterred, I got up and grabbed my coat. "Here." I held out my car keys. "A trade. My car for yours."

"Your Korean Piece of Shit? I don't think so."

I huffed and then detecting a change in his demeanor, asked, "What?"

Breas took my car keys, set them on the coffee table and stood up. "So? Where are we going?"

"We?"

"I come with the car, an added feature."

Soulless icon of death. What every woman looks for in a car. "Eh. I'd rather a GPS or an awesome stereo."

"It's got that, too."

"Holders, Breas. Do you purposely put yourself in situations where they can find you?" Brennus, his brother, is high on the Holders' list of vampires-that-need-a-killing-yesterday. Unable to actually locate Brennus, they settle for tailing Breas. Pointless, since Breas has no interest in a Hallmark card reunion with his sibling.

"So this does involve your boyfriend."

"He's not—" Biting back a retort, I folded my arms across my chest. "I need to speak with an informant." It was time I looked into the "scary" human Talis had mentioned.

He shrugged. "Okay. Let's go see your informant."

I mirrored his shrug, switched off the television, picked up my coat and followed him out the door. Breas Montrose has a well-cultivated reputation as the guy you *don't* count on in a fight. In my case, he can be surprisingly useful. Sometimes.

Chapter Eleven

Sleet, the sort of weather phenomenon that never happens in Albuquerque, pelted the car and roadway. "Maybe the Holders are here on account of the real winter weather," I muttered.

My chauffeur drove in icy silence. Breas refused to let me drive his precious car, complaining that I was too short and would mess up his perfectly adjusted seating. As we drove southward, farther into Albuquerque, the sleet turned into genuine snow and he grumbled about desert-dwelling humans who didn't know the first thing about driving in winter.

We were headed toward an old bank building in the downtown area. Once there, Breas circled the block a few times, before driving a few blocks back to a metered parking lot. I got out of the car and pulled my jacket's hood up over my head. Cold doesn't bother me as much as it would a regular human, but I'd rather not have a cold, wet head of hair. My vampire companion, unaffected by cold, wore a jacket for appearances. We started our walking tour through one of Albuquerque's less desirable neighborhoods.

It was the kind of neighborhood that was raucous on warmer nights: people sitting on couches on front porches, smoking tobacco and other combustible weeds, with a weird mixture of gangster rap and mariachi music blaring from parked cars. Thanks to the weather, the area was quiet. About a block from the building, a red car screeched around a corner and sped past us. Out of habit, and mostly for the mental exercise,

I memorized the license plate.

The bank building had been semi-abandoned for at least twenty years. For the first ten years, it had been inhabited by the usual motley crew of vagrants and drug abusers. Then Icarus claimed the place as his own, frightening away, and if that didn't work, killing the previous inhabitants. The surrounding neighborhood was made up of run-down office buildings and low-end rental housing. Despite, or maybe, because of, the presence of a demon, the old building was one of the safest places in the neighborhood.

Demon is a generic term used to describe any sentient creature from a plane other than Earth or Fey. Though coined by humans, it has gained broad acceptance, even among the demons themselves. Icarus is a demon from a plane whose name I can't even begin to pronounce.

Some people prefer the term alternate universe to plane, but that tends to evoke images of Earth as we know it but with a historical twist. Some Non-Earth planes are unimaginably different from Earth: fire, brimstone and toxic gases. As far as I know, none are populated by humans. Access between planes is easy if you can fold space-time like origami paper. In other words, if you've spent a century of your life in tempus mage training.

From his ugly brick bank building, Icarus runs a quiet little empire, where he traffics in pretty much everything. He owes the Brethren big time for past favors.

My *senses* turned up high; Breas and I slipped around back to a service door. Just outside the doorway, I paused, and stared at the ugly metal door.

"What?" Breas asked, emanating impatience.

"The spell. There is a guard spell on the door. Usually." I lifted my head and surveyed the side of the building. "It's gone. Mostly." The remains of the spell clung to the doorframe, floating in the breeze like gauzy party streamers.

He stepped up next to me and studied the door. "Wow," he said with unusual interest.

I noted the speculative expression on his face. "What? You know something?" He shrugged, shaking his head. I extended my sense of smell toward him and detected a lie. "Yeah. You do."

"You're not blocking me?" he asked, grinning down at me.

"No," I admitted. Vampires are easy for me to read since I can smell a vampire's emotions. Breas gives off emotions that make me nervous, so I usually keep my senses in check around him.

"Whoever did this is running some very dangerous magic," he said. He opened the door a few inches. We sniffed the air together. Nothing.

He pushed the door all the way open, and his lean form disappeared into the dark. Once I entered the building, Breas dropped back and let me lead. The door opened into a narrow hallway that ended in a stairwell. Contrary to what one might expect of a little blue demon, he didn't live in the basement, so I took the stairs leading upward. All the other times I've been there, the place was bustling, the air buzzing with faxes and phones and even some magic. Tonight, the only sounds were the faint whirring of electricity and the light tapping of snow on the windows. Icarus had a small staff of ten made up of a mixture of various demons and one fairy.

I paused at the doorway to the second floor.

"Smells like death," Breas said.

Breas Montrose, Captain of the Good Ship Obvious. Partially blocking my senses, I stepped into the hallway and crept across dusty industrial carpet.

"Ew!" I nearly tripped over a body.

Breas crouched at my side. "Fairy."

"Aw, hell, it's Marty." Marty was a flake, like all fairies, but he always made me laugh. Shutting down almost all my senses, I crouched next to the vampire. Marty had been dead for a while, his body too cold to give off any infrared glow. I pulled a little penlight out of my pocket and pointed it at his remains.

The fairy's little pointy face was frozen in shock. The cause, a significant scorch mark, bled out across his chest like a crazy inkblot. Nearly half his wings on one side had been burnt away.

"Yikes." I gasped and reached my hand, palm down, over his body and jerked it back. "It still burns. And the magic is all fuzzy and overlapping." Breas stood up and I pointed the flashlight at him. "What kind of creature does this?" I asked the vampire. "Makes this kind of magic?" Breas ignored me.

I studied Marty's usually cheerful face, now scrunched up in a terrible death mask, and remembered my purpose for coming here. *The scary human*. I contemplated the possibility that a human killed Icarus and Co., but dismissed the idea. I've never met a human powerful enough to channel this level of power. Not many Fey or demons could do it either.

Breas continued on down the hall, the light casting his shadow doppelganger on the grungy wall. I scrambled up, muttering a hasty goodbye to Marty, and hurried after him. More bodies, the remains of Icarus's staff, were scattered in the hallway, all powdered with the strange magic.

Icarus's office was accessible through a door at the end of the hallway, which opened into another hallway, and finally into an enormous windowless office. He had believed the setup was strategically advantageous. I always found it claustrophobic.

The demon, dressed in an improbably normal business suit, lay sprawled out, facedown, halfway across the floor. The same burn marked his back.

"In the back. A dishonorable way to kill somebody," I said.

The vampire chuckled. "You do it all the time."

"I'm a tiny, helpless, little half-vampire. Gotta take any advantage I can."

Breas threw me a baleful glance and wandered over to the Icarus's body. He shoved his foot under the demon and flipped him over. Icarus, purple eyes frozen in wild terror, clutched a small caliber handgun.

"I guess size does matter," Breas said.

"Always," I answered, giving him a sideways look before I began to explore the room. I heard the sound of the clip being removed and then popped back into the gun. "Clip is still full," he said.

I shrugged. Because some things that go bump in the night, go thump when hit with bullets, Wolfes are required to spend a certain amount of time on the firing range. But guns are too easy, cheating. I'm done with cheating.

An army of file cabinets, lined up in neat little rows, populated the room. I ran my hand in front of one, checking for traps, and then pulled it open. Icarus stored the majority of his merchandise off-Earth plane and used catalogued magical "tags" to retrieve the stuff. Since the indices and folders were all in some demon language, for all I knew the cabinet contained magic links to something as mundane as toilet seats. Business must have been good since this type of system required the services of a tempus mage and that didn't come cheap.

Breas sat down at the large oak desk that dominated the room. Setting the gun on the leather desktop, he proceeded to rifle through the drawers.

I walked over to the desk. "Find anything?"

"Besides porn?" He tossed a magazine up on the desk's surface as proof. "Not much. Pens, paperclips, staplers, the usual desk stuff."

Picking up the magazine by its spine, very gingerly, I gave it a shake. A little index card fell out. Breas and I glanced at the card and back at each other.

"Numbers, I think. Maybe," I said. "I don't read demon."

"You should. I think it's Sh'ree."

My daggers and short sword were forged by Sh'ree demons and a big chunk of the Wolfe induction ceremony is in the Sh'ree language. The Sh'ree, along with the elves, are the Brethren's closest allies. The only Sh'ree I know is "Dol tach no'e" which I think means, "You have lovely livestock."

I pretended to read the card while Breas pulled out more dirty magazines and shook them for evidence. The effort netted us four more cards and enough skin rags to make a teenage boy's head explode.

"The T and A file system. Dewey Decimal System for perverts." I studied the cards, hoping the language fairy would take a poop in my head.

"You have no idea what it says, do you?"

"Nope." I shook my head. "I'll get them to Cypher. For all we know they are in Sh'ree, in code." I placed the cards in my coat pocket. "Why are you here?"

"What?"

"Here? In Albuquerque?"

The tall vampire shoved the chair back and thumped his feet up on the desk. "Why am I ever here?"

"I dunno. I thought you and Asha—?" Something caught my attention. "I smell human."

Breas's eyes glassed over. "Increasingly," he said.

I frowned, wondering when he last ate.

"Guess who?"

"So much for the acuity of vampire senses," I grumbled.

Breas hopped up and we both surveyed the room. The file cabinets could provide plenty of hiding for someone who didn't set off vampire detectors. With an effective search radius of one mile, by now, the Holder's detectors must have been screaming like banshees.

We scurried away to hide behind the farthest row of cabinets. As we crouched behind the furniture, I gave him a grim smile. "You know, you're like a walking, talking Holder magnet."

"You know," he replied, "If you weren't here, I could lead them on a merry chase and get away."

"So what's stopping you? Go. Be my diversion. Shoo."

"Maybe I'll just use you as a shield, instead."

"My hero." I fanned myself in adoration.

Defying logic, Breas stood up and stepped out of the shadows as the two Holders entered the room. I watched him, pondering the possibility that he'd acquired a taste for a hallucinogen like Elf Dust, and made no move to join him.

The sound of a bolt launcher clicked and I cringed, despite knowing he could easily dodge the projectile. He didn't move more than a finger, a couple of fingers. His spell jammed the weapon and the bolt jerked out and onto the floor with a loud clatter.

Kyle cursed and I waited for Jason to take a shot. Silence.

"Old magic," said Kyle. "Check it out, Lake. We got one of the heroes of the War."

My mouth dropped open as I stared at Breas in amazement. Breas is capable of wielding earth-shaking magic, but it wasn't like him to reveal that he had any power unless absolutely necessary.

"No. Not a hero. More like a reluctant draftee," Breas answered.

"Why did you kill this creature?" Jason's familiar voice asked.

"I just got here. It's a little ripe for it to have been me, don't you think? Besides, I've got methods of killing that are much less dangerous to me than chaotic magic." He folded his arms across his chest and leaned back on the wall.

Huh? Chaotic magic! As far as I knew that stuff was just theoretical and only existed in books and moldy old grimoires. The kind of books I use as doorstops.

I listened to the sound of Jason's measured footsteps toward the remains of Icarus.

"He's right," Jason half whispered, clearly awed.

"He? It's a vampire—they don't do right," Kyle argued.

"I'm a vampire? Really?" Breas glanced at his watch. "Your nice Rolex tell you that? Funny. Mine actually tells time."

"Who killed him, Thing?" Kyle asked.

"Thing?" Breas stared at the Holder, his expression turning bored. "I don't know. You tell me. This," he gestured toward the scorched demon, "is why you lot are here, is it not?"

"And why is a member of the Grey Brethren here?" Jason asked.

"I assure you, I'm not Grey Brethren."

Jason took a step towards Breas. "What are you called?" he asked.

"What the hell difference does it make?" Kyle muttered under his breath.

"Dorian," Breas replied.

I heard the amusement in Jason's voice. "Dorian. As in Gray? Clever."

"I think so," Breas stood up. "Now what?"

"Kill him, Lake. Shit!" said Kyle. "What are you doing?"

Jason sighed. "I feel safer with a functioning weapon." I bit back a smile and drew squiggles on the dusty floor.

"Besides," Breas twitched his wrist and the gun fell out of his sleeve, into his hand, "I have one of these." Kyle cursed. "Much safer than chaotic magic," Breas added with a bitter smile.

I surveyed the vampire's calm face and pushed my senses at him. He emanated pretty much everything a vampire was supposed to be, violence and rage and death. And jealousy.

"I'm not interested in killing you, Dorian." Jason walked over to the desk. The sounds of the magazines being shifted followed. "Find anything useful?"

Breas kept his eyes on Kyle. "Icarus was a pervy little bastard."

"I'd say so." Jason pulled out the drawers, probably checking for secret compartments. "What happened here? A deal gone bad? Someone taking issue with Icarus's return policy?"

"Yeah. No receipt, no return. Or...someone was trying, successfully, to shut him up," Breas said. "Or maybe, it's just a diversion."

I wrote the name "Jason" in the dust and then obliterated it.

Diversion? Oh. Feeling especially dense, I started to creep away towards the far wall.

"Diversion?" Jason asked, as Kyle joined him at the desk.

I saw Breas's shoulders lift in a shrug. "Someone's cranking out Lesser Generation vampires. Maybe they'd prefer it if you two were otherwise occupied."

"Yeah? Maybe that someone is you," Kyle said.

Breas didn't bother to respond. I gave the vampire one last glance and then slipped away. Though turned by one of The First, Breas has never turned anyone. Well, as far as I know and that isn't much of a drive.

I skirted the far wall, pausing to check that Kyle and Jason were focused on their quarry, then tiptoed out the door and down the hall. Reaching the main hallway, I stopped, considering my options. My feet carried me to the doorway of the next to last office. The office's unfortunate inhabitant sat slumped over an ugly metal desk; his horned head resting on a computer keyboard.

Closing my hands around the collar of the ornate shirt he wore, Japanese food churning in my stomach, I hauled him away from the keyboard. The guy was a Sharet demon and, unlike Icarus, was tall and heavy. Freed from the support of the keyboard, he flopped sideways and hit the floor with a juicy thump. I cringed and threw my hearing back in the direction of Breas and friends. They were still engaged in mindless banter. The shrilling of the vampire detectors, working on a psychic level, had increased. I pushed my senses out farther, but picked up no other vampire. Odd.

The demon had been working on a letter, written in a language I didn't understand. My father's constant admonitions to study demonology echoed in my head. I saved the current document and shut down the computer.

Within a few seconds, I had the computer's case open and had extracted the hard drive. From what I understood of Icarus's organizational structure, this demon was the accountant.

After some rearranging, I found room for the hard drive in my jacket pockets. I left the building and made my way to the car.

Breas's lock spell was too strong, so I sat on the ground, my back to a tire, huddled out of the wind. Snow still fell and the world was very quiet. My eyelids grew heavy and I let them rest for a second.

"Is there anywhere you *can't* sleep?" The vampire's voice jarred me awake.

"In the arms of a bloodthirsty creature of the night" was not an answer to his question. I started to lose consciousness again as he lifted me into the car. In my line of work, sleep deprivation is a feature, not a bug. And when presented with the opportunity to sleep, I take it.

"Holders, demons, and chaos, oh-my," I muttered.

Breas chuckled. "You've been a busy, busy girl."

Chapter Twelve

Vampires are hell on houseplants.

Breas's continued presence in my house required a reorganization of my indoor vegetation, moving plants out of the spare bedroom and living room and into non-Breas designated areas. By now the plants were used to the routine, although I thought my efforts should be rewarded with something more than beer in the fridge. Something like a nice fat rent check.

Left with little room to work in my own bedroom, I built the computer in the spare bedroom. The hard drive I stole from Icarus's accountant needed the rest of a computer to be of much use.

Rather than spending Sunday afternoon asleep, the source of my indoor horticultural trouble was wide awake, stretched out on his stomach, on the bed. He was reading some deliriously dull book in ancient Greek and supplying useless advice from time to time.

After ringing three times, my answering machine clicked on and Cypher's voice barked, "Regan. It's me. Pick up."

Breas jumped up and answered. "Afternoon, Cyph. Yeah. No. Not yet. Not for lack of trying." Since their conversations just weren't ever interesting, I made a point not to eavesdrop.

After three tries and some sailor-worthy cussing, the computer booted up. Breas crouched at my side and handed me the phone.

"What have you got for me?" asked Cypher.

My speaking the words "Chaotic magic" was met with a long stream of curse words in several languages.

"Well, that explains the Holders," she continued in English. "So, who or what is responsible?"

"Dunno. Yet." I went on to tell her about the late and not-so-great Icarus. Allowing myself a little age-appropriate senility, I omitted any references to the Holders. Breas sat next to me and flashed a knowing smile.

"You searched the premises, thoroughly?"

"Er...em, no," I said. Breas stared at the computer screen and smirked.

"I'm getting a Holder vibe, love," said Cypher.

My elbow connected with the vampire's ribs, but he didn't lose the smirk. "They showed up while we were searching the place. But, um, I got the hard drive from the accountant's computer. Breas and I are going over it right now." I used my eyes to gesture at the computer. Breas reached for the mouse and pulled up the file manager.

Cypher sighed. "And by now the Holders have run a Clean-up team through the place. Can't afford to have humans learning they aren't alone in the world. By the way, why are the Holders, Jason Astin-Lake in particular, still a problem?"

"Jason *Astin*-Lake?" Breas snickered.

I fiddled with a section of my black hair and had a blond moment. "Huh? I'm not supposed to kill Holders, eh?" The screen flickered—I had dumped the hard drive in an old system—and an invoicing program popped up. Breas narrowed his gray eyes and studied the introductory form. I gestured at the "Search by date" option.

"You know what I mean, Morrigan."

"Wouldn't the Holders find it a bit odd if one of their operatives all sudden-like developed a pathological obsession with some woman? They might take an interest in the woman."

"Contrived as it is, you do have a good point. About it arousing the Holders interest, that is."

Whew!

Breas queried the invoicing system for purchases made in the last three months. The cheap monitor glimmered and a new window popped up.

I glanced at the results and reported to Cypher, "Nothing much in the invoices for the last three months. The only local purchase was some shaman in Taos." Taos is a mystical Mecca, attracting hordes of human psychics, gurus, and other metaphysical types. None has any real power (the Holders are quick to snap up humans with genuine ability), but all the ones I ever meet were harmless and gentle folk. "He or she—the name is J. Ward—purchased some Maram'ro wood and a cutting tool from the Sh'ree."

"It's a popular wood for constructing talismans," said Cypher.

"It also makes nice furniture," I said. My weapons were made of Maram'ro wood. The Sh'ree also use it to cover cooking pot handles, as it is very heat resistant.

"Um...anyway." We were getting off-track. "I have something I'd like to send you. Icarus had some index cards squirreled away in girly magazines. Could you look at them? They might be in code."

"All right. If they're in Sh'ree, I may have a long talk with your father," Cypher said.

I sighed. "Then you best be calling him now."

Fortunately, Cypher laughed.

"Oh, and the accountant, a Sharet demon, was working on a letter. It's probably just an angry letter to the government, but I'll send that along, too. Okay?"

"Okay. Call me if you get anything else."

"Of course. Thanks in advance, Cyph."

"And Regan?"

"Yeah?"

"Regan, this is important and, coming so close on the heels of the matter of the Sh'ree and Teile, crucial that it be handled appropriately." Cypher sighed, an odd sound for a vampire. "There are those who are suggesting the time has come to relieve you of your position."

I started to say that the vampires making that suggestion were those who had lost money betting on the demon war. But guilt jabbed me hard in the stomach, and I shut my mouth. Explaining my various misadventures was a full-time job, the duties shared by my father, Kadin, Argus and Cypher. Cypher's weary tone indicated she was the one in the hot seat this time around.

Instead, I asked, "Really? Why's it—chaotic magic—such a big deal?"

"History, Regan. Ancient history." With humor in her voice, she said, "I can recommend several texts if you are interested?"

"Only if they come in comic book format," Breas muttered.

"Er, thanks, Cypher," I replied with thin enthusiasm. Those dreary texts were the source of every prophecy or tale that began with the phrase, "It is written...."

I hung up. The thin hint of sunlight between the heavy blinds had faded. Almost dark. I yawned and wondered what it would be like to *only* have a day job. And then I realized I didn't want to know. I may not be a model employee, but I like being a Wolfe, if only because, as Talis had once said, it's prestigious.

With renewed determination, I started searching through Icarus's sales records.

Chapter Thirteen

Monday morning, at precisely nine o'clock, was the designated time for Koar Inc.'s technical staff meeting. Specifically, it was the opportunity for people with actual career aspirations to oil and wheedle their way into the upper management machinery.

I positioned myself as far back in the room, without actually becoming part of the wall, as possible. Sean Avila, one of my staff if I was inclined to admit to having staff, joined me and was followed by Joan Wallace.

Sean cleared his throat theatrically, and spoke in an announcer voice, "Today's staff meeting will be brought to us by the makers of Chapstick Brand lip balm."

"Ew. You mean Barry 'The Ass Kisser' Stanton is running this meeting?"

"Yep." My partner in office insurrection grinned; his bright blue eyes full of mischief. The rest of Sean is stereotypical Native American, pronounced cheekbones, shiny black hair and coppery-brown skin. The blue eyes are courtesy of some white man who had climbed an otherwise pristine family tree. The combination, blue eyes and all, had half the office's females setting up little Sean shrines in their cubicles. Beautiful men are the norm for vampires, so I liked him for his willingness to verbally eviscerate management.

"Frankly," I said, "I'm amazed Barry can stand upright. What with all the bending over and kissing Edward's ass."

Slipping back into announcer voice, Sean added, "And...joining us as a new sponsor—BenGay pain reliever."

"Where is Edward, anyway?" I asked.

"I don't know," Sean replied. "Maybe his garage door opener outsmarted him again." There was a slightly over-blown rumor that Edward had once been trapped in his garage by an opinionated garage door opener.

Joan made a sound that approximated a giggle. "Hey, Joan," Sean said.

Nudging Sean, I asked, "Have a good weekend?"

"Oh, yeah. 'Member that girl I told you about?"

I stuck both my hands out about a foot beyond my chest and made a PG-13 lifting gesture. Somewhere, a sexual harassment detector was probably going off.

"Yeah, her. We finally got together."

"Cool," I said, cutting him off before he supplied too much detail.

"How 'bout you?"

I paused a beat. "I went out, again, with that guy Eva set me up with. You know, the blind date? From Thursday?"

"All right. Regan-O finally got some action."

"Good morning. Good. Morning!" Barry's voice rumbled across the room, cutting off my retort.

Barry Stanton's presentations were punctuated with loads of techno-babble that even the technical types found incomprehensible and bright shiny ideas that usually pissed off at least half the staff. The other half rarely expressed much of an opinion, one way or the other, as they were attached lamprey-like to his ass.

Sliding on my attentive-eyes-brain-is-not-in-the-building mask, I pondered the contents of the hard drive I had pulled out of the demon's computer. Breas and I had spent a good part of Sunday night searching for anything notable on the disk. Still no answer to the question, "Who fried Icarus?"

"...this will ensure proper stewardship of the data," Barry droned loudly.

"'Stewardship'? That's new and it's actually a word. Must have gotten one of them Word-a-Day calendars," I whispered.

"Stewardship. Three. Whole. Syllables," Joan said.

"As I understand it, Regan O'Connell's new app can facilitate much of the process."

I choked my laughter into a cough when Barry stared at me. "I assume you mean the application my team developed for the school system?" I said, in my best imitation of a professional.

Barry was pathologically unable to read any human being. A balding football player gone-to-seed, he typically got his way by plowing verbally over friend and foe alike.

"Yes. Exactly. Your app should provide the best possible solution to our ongoing integration issues. From what I understand, it's solid. The clients love it."

Of course they do, you putz. And get your lips off my ass. "I have a great team," I said.

Any further pointless Barry drivel was cut off by Eva Osborne's dramatic and flustered entrance into the room. The Human Resources department didn't fall under the category "Technical Staff," so she got an automatic exemption from the Monday morning misery.

"I'm sorry," she gasped, her face so flushed I wondered if she was having a hot flash.

"It's Mr. Aguirre. He's missing."

"Did anyone check his garage?" Sean earned a withering glance from Eva. Joan made her odd giggle noise.

"This is serious," Eva said, filled with a sort of maternal indignation.

"Missing? How?" Barry asked.

"His ex came by his house, Friday, to drop off the kids. He wasn't home. Of course, she was pissed...um, I mean really mad." She took a deep breath. "She figured he forgot it was his weekend. She kept calling him. All weekend. Finally, she went back to his place, last night. He wasn't home, but there was blood on the kitchen floor. The police think it's suspicious." The room erupted in a flurry of concerned murmurs.

"Good riddance," said Joan. "He didn't know anything." Joan's eyes were hard behind her glasses.

I shrugged. Barry, with his extensive knowledge of techo-nothing, was a greater affront to nature than Edward Aguirre and his knowledge of absolutely nothing.

Assuming the meeting was over, I went back to my desk.

Barry, no doubt seeing the potential for upward mobility that had been presented to him, wasted no time sending out a flurry of emails. I scrolled glumly through the list. *And they say vampires are ruthless.* A great many of his correspondences involved my "app" and he saw fit to copy me on every scrap of mail he sent out. I highlighted the majority and hit delete. Because he needed the reassurance that his pearls of wisdom had been seen and treasured, the red light on my voice mail flashed like a nagging mother. *That sucking sound, Barry? That would be the vacuum in your head.* I wandered over to Joan's cubicle.

Joan sat hunched over her keyboard, absorbed in what I assumed was work—she could have been downloading porn for all I cared.

My knuckles rapped a tinny beat on the metal cubicle frame. "Hey, Joan."

Joan Wallace is a couple of inches taller than me and has a face that makes me think of a Kewpie doll; a tired, embittered Kewpie doll. Like myself, she has pale skin and black hair. Her hair, however, is a bit too black, suggesting the color came courtesy of Ms. Clairol rather than Mother Nature. I'd say she likes me better than most of her coworkers but that just means I would be one of the last shot if she went on a workplace-shooting spree.

"Regan," she said, regarding me with washed-out blue eyes.

"I just wanted to check on the upgrade to those forms. Barry has gone all 'I'm in charge here' and is hassling me about the delivery date."

Joan pulled off her glasses and rubbed her eyes. There were red marks where the glasses had perched on her nose, and I wondered why she didn't get contacts or that laser surgery.

"I'll have it done by this afternoon," she said, with less emotion than Breas at his expressionless best.

"Cool. Thanks." I started to leave, but paused when my eyes caught something new on her desk. "Who's that?" I pointed at the small, framed picture next to her computer.

"My boyfriend."

"He's cute," I lied. "What's his name?" Judging from the picture, he was Indian—as in India—and spent an inordinate amount of time in the gym.

"Roger," she answered.

"You been seeing each other long?"

"Yes."

I took another step and probably to Joan's irritation, stopped once more.

"Cool. Electra and...Wolverine!" A comic book sat on the desk's surface.

"You, *you* like Electra?" she asked, a hint of humanity in her voice.

"Honestly? More a fan of Wolverine, but—"

"There you are!" Eva came bustling around the corner. She had recovered from the morning trauma and dressed as she was—in a bright blue dress and matching eyeshadow—reminded me of a gigantic and possibly radioactive bluebird.

Eva's mouth opened and then she noticed Joan. "Oh, hi, Joan." Joan responded with a faint nod.

Slightly unsettled, it took Eva a few seconds to regain her composure. "Happy Hour," she announced. "The Owl and Thistle. Five-thirty. Morale booster. Just the girls."

Ew. "Just the girls" meant a group of drunken hens regaling one another with Letters-to-Penthouse detail of their mates' sexual shortcomings.

"I have a meeting," I said. Joan watched the drama in silence.

Eva's face lit up. "Really? Jason?"

"No. Not Jason. Work."

Forgetting her discomfort with Joan and grateful for an audience, Eva cooed, "I set them up. Regan and Jason." Joan blinked, a significant reaction. Encouraged, Eva added, "Jason is tall, has dark brown hair and beautiful hazel eyes."

"Uuuuh? Beautiful eyes? You looking to replace Kyle?" By my estimations, Kyle could be replaced by something with batteries.

"Of course not," she replied, as though I'd suggested she replace her coffee creamer with rat poison. "And he has an English accent."

"Not really a selling point," I said.

"Why not? Everybody loves an English accent."

"I'm Irish. As in Ulster?" Eva stared at me empty-eyed.

Evidently making an attempt at polite, Joan asked, "What's his last name?"

Eva answered before I could. "Lake."

I yawned. Joan's eyes dropped to her boyfriend's picture, her capacity for social interaction spent.

Eva patted my shoulder. "Just stop by for a few minutes, huh?" Her gaze swooped to Joan. "You should...come, too, yes?" She sounded as though she were trying to convince herself. Joan just watched her, unblinking and disinterested.

As soon as Eva had left, Joan said, "She only invited me because she had to. She's never invited me before." Despite her flat tone, she sounded like a dejected, unpopular teenage girl in a John Hughes film.

"You haven't missed anything." I peered around the corner. "Chicken and alcohol are a bad combination when the chicken is still alive and clucking." *And clucking, and clucking....*

Joan stared at me without comprehension, a suggestion of envy in her eyes.

"You should go. It would really rock Eva's world."

Underused muscles tightened into a smile. "You think?"

I returned her smile. "Yep. Have a beer for me." My steps actually took me out of her cubicle this time. "Live a little, raise some hell."

Chapter Fourteen

Regarding the rumor that Edward Aguirre was once trapped in his garage—it isn't true. Not entirely. One morning, the power went out, rendering the garage door opener inoperable. Edward couldn't figure out how to unhook the door from the opener, so his *car* was trapped. But like any water cooler fable, the story expanded to include a host of courageous emergency workers struggling to free hapless middle management from his two-car garage.

Edward, though well-meaning and amiable, was never destined for greatness.

So I found it hard to envision him at the center of a kidnapping plot or any other kind of scheme. What would be the point? A plot to breed an army of techno-illiterates?

After taking Bill for a slow ride along the irrigation ditch bank that ran by my house, I gave him supper and went inside to do some research. A quick background check turned up nothing unusual. Like many divorced middle-aged men, Edward Aguirre's finances were in shambles. The ex-wife and children gobbled up most of his money and the rest was lost to idiotic ego-boosting purchases. He needed a shoehorn to get his large butt into his latest purchase, a tiny red sports car. His only run-ins with the law were speeding tickets; a few earned recently and no doubt a function of the little red speedster. Though in danger of becoming a regular mass transit customer, Edward Aguirre was an otherwise tedious law-abiding citizen.

Bedsprings creaked as a rumpled Breas flopped down on my bed. The wide-open shutters, which filled the room with sunshine part of the day, didn't keep him out of my room at night.

"You just get up?"

"Creature of the night." He yawned and rolled over to stare at the ceiling.

"Edward Aguirre. My boss? He went missing this weekend."

The vampire closed his pewter-colored eyes. "Wasn't me."

"If it was you, you ate the wrong manager," I told him. A sliver of gray peeked under his eyelids. "Barry Stanton," I explained. "With Edward gone, he's the new emperor in town, or so he thinks. If you do get the munchies, knock yourself out."

"No, thanks. I have a bad track record with emperors." At my amazed expression—I think he'd made a reference to his human past—he asked quickly, "Why the interest in the missing boss? Sounds like cause for celebration."

"I like Edward. I don't like Barry Stanton." Elbows on the desk surface, I leaned my chin on my palms and stared at the screen. "About a month ago, there was a story in the paper. A woman reported her live-in-loser had gone missing. She reported that she found him lying on the sidewalk, just outside their seedy apartment, with a 'dark figure' crouched over him. She's an addict of some sort, so she didn't bother to check on him until the next morning."

"Dark figures are probably the norm when you're somewhere over the rainbow."

"Exactly. And when she went back out, he had vanished. But there were little spots of blood on the ground. Same as with Edward Aguirre."

"Except your boss is an ordinary middle-management nobody as opposed to a crack ho's boy toy."

"Well, yes," I said, with exaggerated patience. "But I just did a check and as far as I can tell, there's no reason why anyone would want to kidnap or kill Edward Aguirre."

"Probably a coincidence." He flipped onto his side and watched me with tarnished dull eyes. "Burglary."

"Nothing was taken. Not even his cheesy little mid-life-crisis mobile." I bit my lower lip and stared back at my un-invited houseguest. "There were no signs of a break-in so he must have let his attacker in."

"Invited, in other words." He smiled with his eyes. "So you figure both were attacked by a vampire?"

"Possibly. The question is, 'Is this my problem vampire? The mother of all Lesser vampires, so to speak?'"

"So we goin' to your boss's place?"

"You set off vampire detectors." I wanted the company, but was playing hard to get.

He sat up and rolled his shoulders, working out stiffness. "Well, somebody's gotta play chaperone in case the Holder arrives on scene."

Seeing his longing glance in the direction of the bathroom, I said, "You've got ten minutes." He hopped off the bed and went to shower. When he emerged twenty minutes (and an entire water heater's worth of water) later, I already wore my jacket and carried a set of car keys in my hands.

"You're not driving," he grumbled, digging through his coat pockets. "I value my un-life."

"Nah, really?" I whirled the key ring around one finger. His eyes lit on the keys—his keys—and yellowed.

"Consider it compensation for my propane bill." I hot-footed it out to his car before he could reply.

The key turned, the engine rumbled to life and Meatloaf's "Paradise by the Dashboard Light," blared out of the speakers. Breas switched the radio to a classical station, ignoring my smirk. Laughing, I scooted the seat forward, tilted the steering wheel and cranked up the seat warmers. I still don't see the point of paying that much for a car, but my toasty butt could make me rethink that position. I pulled out of the driveway and headed south down Corrales Road towards Westside Albuquerque.

The presumably late Edward Aguirre had lived in a mid-size pueblo-style home in a subdivision that jammed itself against the lands of the Petroglyph National Monument. The once majestic views, from high atop the volcanic mesas, were now obliterated by miles and miles of pink and gray roofs.

As usual, I drove around the block and surrounding blocks before I pulled into the small parking lot of the neighborhood park and playground. Breas dropped an arm over my shoulders as we walked through the park, past sun-bleached playground equipment and dingy yellow turf. It was contrived but I put my arm around his waist and played along.

There was a For Sale sign in front of the house next to Edward's. After a quick check with vampire senses to ensure that the home was vacant, we scurried into its shadows, made our way to the backyard and finally over the fence to Edward's place. Breas picked the sliding door lock, and I slipped into the house.

Four months before, Edward hosted an office party at his house. His harmless proclamation to his guests—"Make yourself at home"—gave me a kind of residency by proxy. I used it now to invite Breas into Edward's house.

Although crime tape still decorated the doors, the blood had been scrubbed away. I flicked my pen light on and did a quick once-over of the kitchen. Scene of the crime.

"Feel that?"

"Yeah," I answered, crouching next to Breas on the floor where the stains had been. For a vampire, even cleaned up bloodstains were shiny bright beacons.

The faintest hint, a residue of magic—ordinary, not chaotic—hung in the air.

"Fortunately, it is the rare burglar that uses magic," I said, directing the little light along the floor.

"Your Holder boyfriend taking up a life of crime?"

"Green's still not your color." I flashed the light on his face. "And I don't smell him."

"There have been so many people in here, it would be hard to pick anyone out."

I shrugged. "True." Our eyes met. "It doesn't feel like a clean-up spell, so either the vampire was a tidy eater and hauled the body away after—"

"Or Elvis was alive when he left the building."

Breas got up and ambled into the living room. He pulled out small red-light flashlight and its light darted around the room, pausing on the television.

"Gonna check for ESPN?" I asked.

"Couch doesn't look comfortable enough for my taste."

"Is that all I need? Breas deterrent? An uncomfortable couch?"

"Better than an un-invite spell," he responded, his voice ringed with humor. He moved to the entryway and motioned for me to join him.

The spell remnants made my skin tingle. "It's like Mesmer power, only in handy spell activated form. Only $19.95 through this special offer. Call now and receive the bonus Ginsu knives."

"Amateur." Breas sniffed imperiously. "A human could generate that sort of magic, as well."

"Back on that again, are you?" I dog-sniffed, two inhalations and a quick exhale. There were scent traces from at least a dozen humans, but the only vampire I detected stood next to me, providing irritating commentary. "What good would it do him, anyway? He's human. Can't very well turn humans to the undead state. Next, you'll be claiming he's our chaotic magic user."

"Why not? He's powerful, got strong innate magic. Almost as strong as you."

"I am not—" I closed my mouth, considering his words. "The whole bit with Lesser vampires started months before Jason even got to town. As for the chaotic magic...I dunno." I crossed my arms over my chest. "Besides, why Jason? Why not Kyle? He can probably do this level of magic with an energy conduit."

The vampire's eyes glittered in the pale light. "Yeah. And he's enough of an asshole to do it."

"Sphincter-Man," I sang.

We wandered around Edward's house. A few pictures of his kids stared at us from stiffly-posed school photos.

"Funny..." I said, the light illuminating a picture of his youngest son who smiled despite an idiotic sailor suit. *Could be worse, kid. In my day, they dressed little boys in little frilly dresses.* "With all the inbreeding and what not, the Holders still have very few really strong innate sorcerers."

"Elf blood only goes so far, spread thin," Breas spoke over my shoulder.

"Elf blood?"

Breas, who had been staring at the photo, shifted his focus to me. "You don't know?"

"Know what, exactly?"

His dangerous smile shimmered. "Go back far enough and you and

Lake might be cousins. Kissing cousins of the pointy-eared kind." His gaze returned to the photos on the wall. "The Holders' naughty little secret. Fight the enemy with their own weapon."

D'oh. Of course. Humans are a rather un-magical bunch, so any human with innate magic owes their talent to elf heritage.

"Holders," I said. "The xenophobic jerks have a corner on the hypocrite market."

My elf connection comes through both my mother and father. Rumor has it, Dad may have been as much as one half elf, although I've never gotten a straight answer on the matter. When it comes to his past, Dad is nearly as mysterious as Breas. At any rate, I'm a Heinz Fifty-seven mutt.

Breas's fingers touched my face. "Don't trust the Holder. Chances are he'll mistake you for a human with elf bloodlines, but...." He withdrew his hand and turned to investigate the next bedroom. "The Holders and the Brethren went to war over far less than you."

"Yeesh. You make me feel all Helen of Troy."

"A reference to classical literature, be still my heart." His blond head poked back out of the doorway. "If the Holders get wind of who and what you are, it'll make the last war look like a tea party." He disappeared back into the bedroom.

If he starts babbling about destiny and prophecy, he's leaving this place in a dustpan. I leaned back against the wall and frowned at the photos. "Assuming it's a vampire—"

"Why bother with this? All the turnings?" Breas emerged from the bedroom and finished my sentence.

"Takes a bit out of the vampire that does the turning, does it not?" I asked, my senses focusing on him.

Aware of the scrutiny, he studied me back. "Yeah. So I'm told."

Getting the usual stomach turning emotion off him, I moved my focus elsewhere. "It doesn't feel like anyone was turned here. You know? There's usually a little trace. Like energy or something. Especially with a Lesser Generation turning."

He curled his lip in disgust and nodded.

"So the vampire is taking his victims somewhere else? Why?"

"Or he has a human familiar doing the dirty work." He scanned the ceiling. "If your boss was turned, it was a long way from here."

"Yeah." Newly turned vampires often return to familiar territory, but there was no indication Edward Aguirre, dead or undead, had been here in days.

Car lights from a passing car—an SUV from the sound of the engine—flashed lightning bright in the living room.

"Speak of the devil—it's Paris, here to steal my Helen," Breas said, reading my reaction.

I laughed. "Let's go, Menelaus. They've probably already picked you up on their detectors."

"Regan O'Connell has gone and discovered books without pictures. I think I'm getting turned on."

Sparing him a withering glare, I led the way out of the house and back to the car.

Chapter Fifteen

The next morning couldn't have been more unproductive if I had spent the time playing Internet Poker.

Fresh from an overpriced managerial seminar—"Empowering your Staff through Communication"—Barry Stanton flitted from cubicle to cubicle.

Even without Barry's regular visits, I wasn't going to get anything done. Edward's absence had taken on the persona of a five hundred-pound gorilla. It sat behind me, scratching hairy armpits and clearing its throat. After playing a couple of hands of computer solitaire, I got up and wandered into Edward's office.

A round table surrounded by four chairs took up most of the right side of the room. Edward's desk, a modular desk/shelf combo, sat to the left. Because nothing said power like wood, all the furniture was finished in fake oak veneer.

Edward, where are ya? Give me a sign, huh?

Finding him with magic was out of the question, and not just because of my inabilities. It's possible to locate a lost person using a tracer spell, but because the spell forges a permanent bond between the souls of the searcher and searched—it's dangerous. The degree of bonding is a gamble, literally, with the odds skewed towards "tight." And like my Thrall charm, that much togetherness can result in pathological obsession for one or both parties. I liked Edward, but I didn't want to like him that much.

I snooped around his desk for the fifth time that day, finding that nothing had changed. A couple of books—a thesaurus and textbook from a seminar entitled "Managing Difficult People"—were the only things on the desk's surface.

I picked up the watering can that Edward kept in a far corner of the room, watered his plants, and left. My next stop was the break room where I collected my lunch—grilled cheese with tomato and green chile from a vintage refrigerator that wheezed and spluttered. Until Barry's interest in conversing with the peons waned, my cubicle was no longer a happy-happy place, so I headed for the lobby.

The lobby's furnishings were innocuous to the point of dull—white walls, a couple of goliath rubber plants, and a tan, vinyl living room set.

Not doing much to improve the décor, Joan Wallace sat on the loveseat and picked at a sandwich. Today she had traded in her bitter aura for a morose one. Despite an urge to go somewhere else, I sat down on the couch.

Spending time with Joan Wallace was a bit like being flung into a Salvador Dali painting. As in surreal to the nth degree. Today would be no exception.

I unwrapped my sandwich and did my usual "Hey." Her eyelids twitched, which I took to mean, "Hello, Regan. How are you doing?"

"Great," I replied. "I just love Barry Stanton. Don't you just love Barry Stanton?"

"I like New Mexico."

"Yeah?" I bit into my sandwich, the green chile and tomato bliss in my mouth. "What's there to like?" I asked, just to be belligerent.

"It's almost—" Joan paused, frowned at her sandwich. She peeled back the bread and yanked out a slice of cheese. "It's magical," she replied.

"'Land of Enchantment.' It's the state motto. You gonna eat that?" I asked, my eyes on the cheese. Joan handed the offending bit of dairy to me, and I set it on a napkin.

"You know what I mean?" she said. "There's a hum, energy, all around us." She was staring at me.

Well, yes, I did know. I felt it as a tiny tremor, like the tickle of a tiny insect on my skin. Power. Coming from my odd lunch companion! Joan must have had some innate magical power.

She didn't give off the Snap-Crackle-Pop-Kapow type of strength that Jason did. It probably wasn't enough to cast a simple spell, which would explain why she was working as a computer programmer and not chasing magical bugaboos for the Holders. The Holders are glad to get a hold of any human with even a hint of power, but someone like Joan isn't likely to get noticed.

Joan was loopy enough without knowing she had special powers, so I played dumb. "A hum? Like the Taos Hum?"

"No. I have to go finish. Bye." She scooped up the remains of her lunch and marched off towards the office.

My gaze slid over the room, stopping on a large wall clock, half expecting it to be melted and pouring down the wall, like the clocks in the painting, *The Persistence of Memory*.

Eating my sandwich slowly, I used the time to think.

The Holders wouldn't send their operatives to an out-of-the-way place like Albuquerque just to kill Lesser vampires. And yet, who shows up at Lucky's Repo Depot and does my job? Jason and Kyle.

I thought back to the night at Icarus's place and Breas's conversation with the Holders.

"He's right," Jason half-whispered, clearly awed.

Jason's reaction to the murder weapon, chaotic magic, had been surprise. Assuming that reaction was genuine, the Holders had been after something else. Regardless, the matter of the chaotic user must now be a prominent addition to Jason and Kyle's to-do list.

How was poor Edward's vanishing act connected to vampires, chaotic magic or "something else?" It would be foolish to rule out any possibility, but the chance of a Lesser vampire using chaotic magic was slim. Most Lesser vampires have a hard time tying their shoelaces. A likely candidate for that level of mischief would be a fairy or a demon, but that didn't explain the vampire connection.

Too many unknowns and not enough equations, I thought, as I finished Joan's discarded slice of cheese.

Back at my desk, two things awaited me. The first, a Wolverine and

Electra comic book, sat on my chair, a pink Post-it note stuck on its cover. Joan had written "I'm done" in tiny script on the note. *Cool.* I slipped it into my briefcase for reading later.

A bright red toy car was parked next to my mouse. I grinned and picked it up. *1967 Camaro, sweet.* No doubt part of the game Sean and I played. It started with him getting me a bag of green army men after I whined about my toy-free childhood. When he told me how he envied a childhood friend's toy dump truck, I got him a lemon yellow Tonka version. Last week, Sean and I had been talking muscle cars.

I made engine noises and pushed the car around my desk. Its tiny tires squeaked as it swerved around my teacup, triggering another memory of the night Icarus died.

A red car screeched around a corner and sped away.

Had that just been a car full of teenagers, or someone fleeing the scene of the crime? What if Icarus's murderer had driven right past me that night?

Because car licenses are made up of numbers and letters, they get stored in my head as two separate numbers. The first number is the license with all the letters swapped out for numbers—A = 1, B = 2, etc. The second number is a bunch of zeros and ones, where zeros mark the location of letters in the license. It sounds complicated, but numbers stay in my head, letters don't.

I dug the car's license out of my memory. It was a long shot, but I did some digging. Koar Inc.'s networks had the usual Internet safeguards to prevent the lecherous from downloading porn and the chronically bankrupt from shopping (not that I couldn't get around said safeguards, if I were so inclined), but nothing to keep me from committing invasions of privacy. I ran the license through Motor Vehicles and found that it belonged to a rental car company. A bored employee at the rental place told me everything I wanted to know over the phone.

A Susan Ward had rented the car, the day before I had seen it near Icarus's warehouse. The rental company reported the car stolen two days later, after receiving notice that the transaction was processed on a stolen credit card.

Ward? Where had I heard that name? The transaction from Icarus's sales log! *J. Ward purchased some Maram'ro wood and a cutting tool from the Sh'ree.* Coincidence?

Susan Ward's police report—her home had been burglarized—was her only interaction with law enforcement—ever. She was divorced, the mother of three grown children, and lived in Farmington, New Mexico.

I gave her a call.

"Hello?" said a voice that reeked of apple pie, cookies and wholesomeness.

"Hello," I said. "This is Tara Kane. I'm with Southwest Adjusters. I'm calling regarding the break-in."

"Well, now, you know I think I already spoke with someone from your company."

Not likely, since I made it up. "Yes. I apologize. We switched to a new tracking system and I think some records may have been lost in transition." She sounded so nice I hated to lie.

"Oh, that's all right, dear. What can I help you with?"

"You reported your wallet as being the only missing item. Is that correct?"

"Yes."

I detected a slight waver in her voice. "Is there something else?" I asked. "Something you noticed after the police report?"

"I'm not sure it's even related to the break-in. It may have been missing long before that, you know?" She paused. "It's a piece of jewelry. Honestly, I hated the darned thing. It was a gift from my mother-in-law."

"Well, it can't hurt to mention it in the report. In the event it *was* stolen and the police locate it. Could you describe the item, please?"

"It's a cross. Gold. And gaudy, so gaudy. It has all kinds of weird little stones inset in the center of it."

"Really," I said, letting my interest show a little too much.

"My mother-in-law is Russian Orthodox. I think she brought it over when she came to the U.S. It's old, an antique."

I chatted her up a bit more and learned that she had two grandchildren (from son, Jonah, the accountant) and that her other son William lived in California where he worked as an actor (this statement was accompanied by a wistful, why-can't-he-be-an-accountant-like-Jonah, sigh). Her daughter Jeanine had passed away; I didn't press for details.

After my conversation with Susan, I did a check on Jonah. He and the wife and kids lived in an exclusive subdivision in Denver. There were no indications that he slew demons in his free time or consorted with anything magical.

William's most notable acting credential was an advertisement for herpes medication. Perhaps because the universe despises too much of a good thing, the Ward's happy little family had shrunk by one when Jeanine killed herself about five years ago.

I started to rub the stiffness out of the back of my neck, stopping when my fingers contacted a slim chain. A small silver cross, Irish with a circle, hung on the chain. I fished it out of my shirt and closed my fingers around it so its surface, warm from contact with my skin, pressed against my palm.

My little cross was a vampire Bane, given to me by my friend Cara, although I doubt she had any idea of its power.

Could Susan Ward's cross have been a Bane?

I picked up the phone and dialed my home number.

"Good afternoon," I said when the answering machine picked up. "This is your roommate. Hello? Wake up! Get up—"

"You'd better be calling from your bedroom—naked," answered an irritated Breas.

"Tall, pale, and grumpy. I think I love you."

"No, you don't. If you did, you'd let me play with your soft pink parts." There was the hiss of a bottle opening and voices murmured from the television. "What do you want? There's a soccer game on."

"Soccer? How? I don't have ESPN."

I heard him swallow some beer. "You do now. Satellite. Hundreds of channels."

Rather than launching into the inevitable argument about the cost of his television access, I said, "Banes. The kind that work on vampires."

Breas was silent for a moment. "You should work on that temper," he replied in a sulky voice. "It's just television. And satellite was a better deal than cable."

"I'm not going to use one against you, you big mook!"

"Oh."

"The really powerful Banes, the kind that'll bring a guy like you to your knees, where were they usually crafted?"

The sound of the television increased, and I heard the *whumph* of a couch being sat on.

"Eastern Europe," he replied. "Crafted by Orthodox priests, usually." He took a swig of beer. "Why?"

I didn't answer right away.

Ordinary crosses and other religious symbols are no more effective against vampires than a Sixties era peace sign. But any object, provided it is made from a natural material—wood, stone, pure metal—can be imbued with vampire harassing magic. The most potent vampire Banes, the kind that take the bite out of the undead, hailed from the eighteenth century or earlier and were crafted by the clergy. Those holy men were innate magic users. Unaware of their power, they would inadvertently craft a Bane when they prayed over an object.

"Regan? What this all about? Your cross?" My cross was a weak Bane, capable of giving Breas nothing more than an itchy rash. Like all Banes, it had no effect on me.

"No," I answered. "Go back to watching the bouncing ball. I'll see you later."

Was someone using a Bane to control vampires? Setting them on the homeless? Was this someone behind the unfortunate change in management in Koar's Information Systems Division? If so, why?

"Regan. Hello." Barry Stanton's voice derailed my train of thought. He stood in my doorway, chest out, belly out farther—the king awaiting his general's report.

"Hey." I immediately launched into a stream of techno-speak that made Barry's heart pound, "Sean and I ran three tests. Everything was going great until the client's protocol…."

Barry left after about ten minutes, content that all was well in his newly usurped kingdom.

"I thought he'd never leave," muttered the five hundred-pound gorilla. "Ever stop to think he might have offed Edward?"

The imaginary simian had a point. I started Barry's background check.

"Forget vampire Banes. What I need is a Boss Bane."

Chapter Sixteen

"Where's Breas?" Lex asked. She was sitting cross-legged on the floor, a carton of ice-cream next to her, flipping through a fashion magazine. The harsh sound of ripping paper indicated she had found another perfume sample.

"I don't know," I answered, comparing my oak hat stand to one on *Antiques Roadshow*. According to the dapper appraiser, a grandmotherly woman's oak hat stand was worth well over ten thousand dollars. "Off doing something sneaky or illegal, probably."

I nibbled my lower lip, trying to suppress the growing unease that rumbled in my belly like food poisoning. My century long career as a Wolfe did bear a stronger resemblance to a blooper reel than a profession, but I'd never felt this degree of insecurity. But then, thanks to the intervention of my family, my job had never been on the line before.

Like a tongue worrying a sore tooth, my thoughts returned to Edward's disappearance.

Barry Stanton's background check had turned up nothing incriminating. Besides, he had an alibi. The weekend of Edward's disappearance, Barry and his buddies were in the mountains hunting Bambi and his woodland friends.

I set down the remote and headed for my room. Sitting on my ass watching the parade of high-end thrift store junk wouldn't keep me from getting fired.

"What are you doing?" Lex asked, as I dug around in my closet. She twirled in the doorway, cellophane-like wings fluttering, the velvety purple fabric of her dress following her motion.

"Locator map. It's dark. I thought I'd actually do my job. Killing crazy vampires?" I spread a map of Albuquerque on the bed. A locator spell, unlike the more complex *tracer*, is easy to cast, though not nearly as exacting. The Brethren taught a special variation on the spell, designed to identify any Lesser vampires. I hadn't gotten any blips on the map in a few days.

Bored, Lex fluttered back to her ice-cream and I breathed a sigh of relief. I don't like real magical folk around when I work spells.

I kill Lesser vampires to keep vampires safe from humans. Humans have an understandable unwillingness to be the *soup du jour*. And modern humans, particularly Americans, when confronted with anything "unsafe," have a tendency to overreact and call their Congressman. Lesser vampires, with their newsworthy Salem's Lot style antics, run the risk of adding "The War on Vampires," to the existing wars on terrorism and drugs.

Judging from the bright response I got in the downtown area, Tuesday was the night out for crazy vampires. The spell produces a circular response area between one to two miles in diameter, but that narrows things down a bit. Noting the approximate location, I folded and returned the map to the closet.

After changing into my gray hunting outfit, I returned to the living room. "I'm off to work, honey. Have dinner ready when I get home."

Lex hopped up, ice-cream carton still in hand. "I'm coming with," she said.

"Why?" The various perfume samples Lex had slathered on herself were battling for supremacy in my nose. I didn't want her in my car.

"Why not?" She beamed, showing spectacular white teeth. "Are you going to meet the human? Jason? Is he cute? Can I meet him?"

"No."

"He's ugly?"

"I'm not meeting Jason. And no, you can't meet him." I moved toward the door. "Come on, Lex."

"So he is cute, then?" Getting no response, except me opening the door, she asked, "Don't you want it?"

"Huh?"

"That wonderful feeling, in the morning, when you wake up together?"

"You mean that sinking feeling?"

"Regan, seriously? When you turned and saw Breas—?"

"Just like the Titanic. Glug, glug, glug." Straightening my fingers, I tipped my hand like an iceberg-afflicted boat. "Can we ever talk about something besides...sex?"

Lex shrugged, following me over to the car. "Like what?"

"Politics? World affairs? I have no idea."

We sat at a streetlight, just shy of a freeway overpass, under the mournful stare of a homeless man. He held one side of a brown cardboard box, on which he had scrawled: "Vietnam Vet. Please help." The Albuquerque Isotopes T-shirt he wore was too small to cover a stomach that suggested he was carrying twins.

Taking in his doughboy physique, Lex observed, "The poor in this country are oddly-shaped."

I scraped change out of the car's center console and handed it to Lex. "Yeah. Give this to him, will you?" Lex complied. A minute later, the light changed and I turned the car onto the frontage road and merged onto I-25 southbound.

My thoughts wandered from homeless veterans, to humans in general, and then to the Holders.

The fact that the Holders had sent a lone pair of operatives to New Mexico didn't negate the potential seriousness of the matter. The Holders' power among Non-Earth plane peoples was rather precarious. If they had to send an entire army out every time there was a problem, they'd look weak. A lot had changed since Mankind first discovered iron. Humans have advanced, but so have many of the other races.

Crackling plastic noises came from Lex as she grappled with the wrapper on a Twinkie.

"I'm surprised he's still alive," Lex said.

"Who?" I summoned a dagger and handed it to her.

Her dainty fingers wrapped around the leather bound hilt and she sliced through the plastic. "Jason. Breas has been remarkably tolerant," she replied, handing the dagger back to me.

The daggers and sword are like appendages to me; they can be retrieved or sent away instantly. They are stored on the Sh'ree plane when they are not being used to open sugary snacks or dispatch the undead. I thought the dagger away and hit the turn signal, preparing to exit the freeway.

"Jason's a fairly adept sorcerer. I really doubt Breas is spoiling for a fight." The second statement was equivalent to declaring the Pope Catholic.

"But Breas is in—"

"Lex," I warned. "Enough."

"You're so repressed," she said.

My target area, a neighborhood just south of downtown Albuquerque, suffered from an identity crisis. It alternated from block to block between yuppie gentrification and chronic neglect. I parked in a neighborhood where weed-free landscaping and fresh paint indicated regular tithing at the local home improvement store. Acting on instinct, I made my way to a small park that often hosted society's lost.

Lex and I sat on an uncomfortable metal bench, watched all the while by four men and a woman. The five sat in various poses on the playground equipment a few hundred feet away.

"Are they?" Lex asked, still nibbling on her snack. Here, in public, she kept her wings folded flat against her back.

"Yeah." It was nearly ten o'clock and there were only a few lights glowing from the surrounding houses and businesses. Sending my senses questing outward, I noted that one, a muscular dark-skinned man, seemed normal. Greater vampire? The others, all in varying states of unstable, appeared to have accepted the sane vampire as their leader; they whispered questions to him.

Even without a soul and most human emotions, a Greater vampire's retained memories and self-awareness render him (or her) a lot like the human he once was. There is a rumor that, over time, a vampire's continued sentience forges a weak facsimile of a soul. At any rate, this rarely applies to Lesser vampires. Lesser vampires return to "life" lacking most memories or a coherent sentience; the fragile magic that holds them together is often weak and unraveling. Once, I killed a Lesser by stabbing it in the toe.

Curious, I got up and walked over to the little group, Lex providing my shadow. The vampires watched me with thinly concealed zeal.

"You have strange taste in friends," I said to the sane vampire.

His facial features were a nice combination of Asian and African. "You too, cutie," he said.

One of his unstable companions licked its lips and leered at Lex. The fairy stuck out her tongue and the vampire lunged.

The vampire's fingers clamped around Lex's neck. Or they would have if I hadn't grabbed a handful of her dress and hurled her Twinkie-loving self out of the way. The vampire slid to a stop, whirled and dashed at me. A dagger sliced though his chest and disappeared before the vampire finished collapsing into small heap of dusty ash. His buddies hissed in astonishment. Then all except the Greater vampire glided in my direction.

Grandstanding is a poor choice in the middle of a city, in full view of humans, so I flicked the dagger in rapid succession, dispatching all three.

Lex returned to my side. "You suicidal?" I asked her.

She straightened her dress. "I knew you'd save me."

The remaining vampire stood up, his attention on me. "The infamous Regan O'Connell."

"This bunch yours?" I replied, waving at the four dust piles.

I got a whiff of emotions that added up to insulted. "No tact," he said. "Must be why you start wars—"

"Hey! The Sharet and Teile were already on the brink of war. I just gave them a teeny shove." I crossed my arms over my chest.

"Sweetheart, you planted your foot in their ass and kicked them over the cliff," he replied with a smile that was high voltage nice.

"Whatever. Who are you?"

He held out his hand. "Pete Tanaka. Confederacy."

I took his hand. Before I could actually shake his, he bent down and kissed the back of mine. "Er, Confederacy?" The Confederacy is the tongue-in-cheek name for one of the Brethren's southern business partners. "What are you doing here?" I asked, retrieving my hand.

He lifted his gaze extra slow, taking me in. "Watching out for business interests."

"What interests?" Lex asked. "The Brethren control this part of the country."

"Then why's this place got a Holder infestation?"

"Two. There are just two," I said. "And I've got it under control. You checking up on me?" The possibility that he was outsourced talent, hired by my family's enemies to catalogue my failings, occurred to me.

His smile glowed in his almond-shaped eyes. "This is about the Holders, sweetheart. If they fuck this one up, all the other races are going to take it as a sign of weakness."

"So what? You gonna hoist the Confederate flag, sing Dixie and ride to the Holder's rescue?"

"We don't take sides," he said. "But if some new trade routes happen to open up...."

Trade routes? What the hell?

Any moderately skilled magic user can move between planes using *existing* folds, but only a tempus mage can create new *permanent* folds. Besides taking a century to complete, tempus mage training is limited to those few, one out of ten thousand, who can pass the entrance exam. Tempus mages are a rare breed, bound by numerous rules of conduct. Creating items like Lex's pin or Icarus's filing system is perfectly allowable, but "folding" new trade routes or engaging in unsanctioned interPlanar commerce is a serious breach of conduct.

"Trade routes? There are no trade routes in New Mexico," Lex said.

"Yet," Pete replied.

"What do you mean?" Lex turned to me. "What does he mean?"

Ignorance is a weakness, but I asked anyway, "What do you mean?"

"Don't play games, O'Connell." He grinned. "You know exactly what I mean, don't you?"

He saved me from answering by saying, "Warm-blooded vampire. I could get used to that. You have any plans—?"

"She has a boyfriend," Lex said. "A two thousand-year-old, very jealous boyfriend. But I'm free. I'm Lex, by the way."

The vampire turned his attention to Lex. "A fairy." His hungry gaze swept her from head to toe.

Sliding up to within a foot of him, she ran a slim finger down his chest, stopping at his jeans. "Everything you've heard...it's true," she purred, curling her finger around his waistband.

My lip curled. "Ew. Get a room."

They both gave me a sideways glance and then locked eyes. I watched the couple for a minute, astonished by Pete's ability to ignore the toxic perfume cloud that surrounded Lex. Then, realizing I was staring, I turned my attention to the park.

Here in the already dusty Southwest, the remains of one vampire might go unnoticed, but several dust piles was a little suspicious. I did a quick disperse spell, sending the vampire particles swirling away, and then headed back to my car.

"Later, Lex," I said, ignored.

Lex is the universe's way of making up for all the sex I'm not having.

Chapter Seventeen

"We could download a virus onto his computer," said Sean. In just two days, Barry Stanton had managed to spread his acid-caustic influence to every corner of our Division. Sean, the ringleader in the disgruntled circus, had convened an impromptu rebellion in my cubicle. Everyone stared at me, faces shiny with anticipation.

With the exception of Eva, the rest of the world seemed to see me as their own personal Van Helsing, expected to slay life's everyday vampires. The expectation baffled me, since on a good day, with liberal application of makeup, I might look twenty.

Given my position, I should have behaved like a professional and told them to all get back to work, but I was bored and mildly amused by their antics. If I couldn't find Edward, the least I could do was torment his usurper.

Terry Moulder, recent survivor of a witless battle with Barry Stanton and new convert to our snarky group, laughed. "But we need to use his computer profile, right?" she asked.

Sean said, "Regan-O, she can take care of that. No problem." He smiled at Terry and she toyed with a section of her big fluffy hairdo.

"I, uh...." The natives were getting too restless. "Don't you have work—?"

My phone rang and I answered, glad for the interruption.

Eva, in a syrupy high tone, said, "Hi, Regan."

"Wow. You're cheerful. Are there doughnuts in the break room?"

Hearing the magic "D" word, Terry, Sean and the rest of the irate mob marched off in the direction of the break room.

"No. I'm transferring a call to you."

"Who—?"

"Bye now."

I listened for the click of the line transfer, my eyelid twitching.

"Hello. This is Regan." I spread a thick coat of professionalism over my irritation.

"Regan," said a male voice that shunted most of my blood in a southerly direction. "Hi."

"Jason. Um, hey."

"Sorry. I don't mean to bother you at work."

"You're not, um, bothering."

"Actually, Eva called *me*. Trying to find Kyle."

"Really? It's your day to watch him, then?"

His laugh made my toes curl and I grinned stupidly.

"He hasn't called her in two days. She's worried—"

"Smooth move, Eva." I squinted at my reflection in the computer's monitor. "I take it Kyle's moving on to greener, er, other pastures?" Apparently Eva's bid for more vertical, not-naked time with the Kyle wasn't going over well.

"Possibly. Honestly, Regan, I'd really rather not know."

"Yeah, well, me too. Eva operates under the belief that she should share the misery."

"Perhaps she and Kyle have more in common than they realize," he quipped glumly.

"So whatcha doin'? Security stuff?" I asked.

He yawned. "I was sleeping. Eva's voice on my answering machine—"

"Could wake the dead?"

"Precisely. And you?"

"Plotting insurrection, world domination, and suchlike."

"Ah," he said, sleep still in his voice, "workplace amusements."

"Yeah. Our new boss sucks like the great vacuum of outer space."

He laughed and the last blood cell waved goodbye to my brain and headed for a more pleasurable location. "I don't suppose I could take you away from it all? Lunch?" he asked.

"You know, if you keep feeding me, I may follow you home."

"I'm counting on it."

I could calculate square roots in my head by age seven, but reading didn't come so easy. In modern America, dyslexic kids can expect a little extra help and the reassurance that they are not stupid. Not so in nineteenth century Ireland. It took a while, but I eventually learned to read and write in English and I devised numeric tricks to get around problems like license plates.

According to Kadin, my father didn't believe I was his child until I was three. I don't hold it against Dad. It's not as though vampires were fertile bunnies. When Dad realized I had speed that made cheetahs green with envy, he was proud to take up the mantle of fatherhood. Proud and demanding.

My abilities with numbers have never made up for what he sees as a lamentable lack of interest in literature and language. I hate his disappointment, but the alternative, him learning about my defective brain, is far worse.

The answer to my question, "What is the connection between Pete Tanaka's 'trade routes' and chaotic magic?" was probably buried in a book, written in demon or formal Elvish, using magical alphabets that hopped around on the page all by themselves. A dyslexic's version of hell. My only option is to ask someone for help.

Because I never know what will get back to Dad, I have to be very careful who I ask what and how I phrase the question. My two best sources of information are Breas and Lex.

Lex is smart, but not in a nitty-gritty technical way. Breas is like a two thousand-year-old palimpsest, with text written over layers of poorly-erased text. In other words, you need a shovel to dig through all the crap.

Talis is brighter than the two of them put together, but the hallucinogens he's poured into his body have dulled his intellect. Nevertheless, I picked up the phone and called him. A generic male voice, the default message on the answering machine, asked me to leave my name and number. I hung up.

Breas is in town. I don't know why, but Talis sometimes vanishes when Breas comes to town. He always says "goodbye" before leaving, though.

I made a mental note to check on him later, scooped up my purse and headed out to lunch. Eleven-thirty had come very quickly.

Jason picked me up at work and we drove to a nearby Mexican restaurant. He steered the conversation toward me and we talked about my music. I started playing violin at about twelve as part of what my father deemed a proper classical education. I stuck with the violin, but everything else—literature, history, magic, arcane knowledge—sloughed off like a mudslide. Of course, I left all the bits about magic and the arcane out of the conversation.

While we talked, I watched Jason's hands, noting the halo of energy that surrounded them. Actually, it sort of issued from his entire body and that worried me. If I—with limited magical abilities—could sense his innate ability, he could certainly sense mine. I'm not magically observant; lower level innates like Joan probably fly under my radar on a regular basis. Was Jason's interest in me nothing more than a Holder recruiting tactic? The possibility made me sad.

"What's wrong?" he asked.

"Wrong?" I looked up and got trapped in his hazel eyes.

"You look pained."

"Pain? Oh, er, I think I'm getting carpal tunnel or something…." I rubbed my left wrist.

"Here," he reached for my hand, "Let me try." His fingers slid over mine and up past my hand, curving so that only their tips touched my wrist. The touch of magical energy almost too much, I gritted my teeth, holding my hand still. Breas crackles with magic, but I've never met a human with that much innate power. Plus it's really different when the person has a pulse.

He pressed his fingers against my skin and my eyes widened, recognizing what he was doing. Power, warm and medicinal like liniment, washed into my wrist.

Bold move, that. Doing magic. What now? A recruitment speech?

Our gazes locked. "Th-that feels marvelous. How'd you do that?"

"It's a trick my father taught me." He pulled his hand away, picked up a fork and moved the remains of Spanish rice around on his plate.

"Living up to your name." His left eyebrow crawled upward, questioning. "Jason," I explained, "means 'healer.'"

Little eddies of magical energy continued to swirl around my wrist, not fading until I got back into his car.

"We still on for Friday, then?" he asked. We were sitting in the Koar parking lot. I scanned the lot and then my eyes moved to the glass doors that opened to the lobby.

"Yeah. Six, right?" Someone, I think it was Joan, sat in the shadow of a large potted rubber plant. "I owe you lunch."

His smile drained the blood from my head. "Count on it."

I made my retreat before anything hazardous, like touching, could happen. Joan waited in the lobby, her eyes shining fiercely out at the parking lot.

"Hey, Joan."

"Regan," she said, my name dripping with glacial ice.

"You, um, going to lunch? Boyfriend, maybe?"

She lifted her eyes to catch mine. "He's dead." Her voice carried so much force; I felt the shadowy tendrils of guilt creeping up my spine. I brushed the sensation away. I've only killed one human in my life and his name wasn't Roger.

"Joan, I'm so sorry. Why are you here? I mean, shouldn't you be taking some time off, or something?"

"I'm fine," she said, her tone tepid, as the ice melted a little. Her cold blue eyes turned toward the parking lot. "Was that your boyfriend? Jason?"

Totally thrown on my mental ass by her abrupt change of conversation and the bombshell she dropped before that, I just stared at her. Finally, righting my brain, I responded, "No. I mean...I don't know what we, he...is. You know? We're at the stage where we're circling each other like a cobra and a mongoose." I shrugged. "I'm not good at relationships."

"Don't trust him, Regan."

"Huh? What do you mean?"

Her square face lifted to focus on mine, some sort of intense emotion—unrecognizable—burning from her eyes. The fire faded and she said, "I know his type. Too handsome, not trustworthy. Trust me."

With that she got up and walked out of the building, leaving me to stand alone, bewildered by the sheer peculiarity of the human mind.

Whistling a simple tune to dispel Joan's gloom, I wandered back to my cubicle.

Chapter Eighteen

A little row of beer bottles on the kitchen counter, lined up like soldiers awaiting inspection, was the only evidence of my vampire roommate. Well, there was all his crap in my spare bedroom, but the actual living dead guy wasn't home.

After collecting all the bottles and moving them to the recycle bin by the back door, I walked into my living room.

I pulled up the window blinds and looked at my front yard. A four-foot high adobe wall framed a small patio around the front door. Last year, soon after moving in, I'd planted a small fortune in lavender, thyme, mint and rosemary. The intent was to make the entrance inviting and fragrant. It was a pointless effort since I, along with all my guests, tended to come and go by the back door. There was the added problem that on a rare rainy day, the combination of herbal aromas tends to smell like cat pee.

At eight o'clock at night, midwinter no less, the patio was reduced to black clumps of dormant vegetation against the dark gray mass of the wall. Leaving the blinds open, I wandered over to my easy chair and fell forward into its soft arms. The chair reeked of Breas—a curious mix of shampoo, beer, and blood.

Breas is a jerk, but he's my jerk. I lay motionless, comforted by his smell, temporarily without anything to do. My locator spell hadn't turned up any Lesser vampires and I was taking the "if I don't force it, the answer will come to me on its own" approach with the chaotic magic problem.

I flipped over and stared across the room at the kiva fireplace. I think it was an original fixture in the house, although a couple of years ago, Argus had spent some money sprucing it up with new plaster and adding *nichos*, little inset shelves, to its curved exterior. The actual fireplace was about two feet off the ground and surrounded by a built-in tile-covered bench.

I sniffed the chair and studied Breas's scent. All vampires smell like blood to me, whether or not they've fed recently. But a hungry vampire smells of desperation, which is what I was picking up from the sofa.

For all his bloodthirsty posturing, I don't think Breas ever kills his meals. Most Greater vampires can use Mesmer spells to eat without resorting to murder, wiping all memory of the incident from their supper's memory. But for any vampire except Breas and his brother, Mesmer is an energy intensive spell and I suspect there are lazy Greaters who kill for dinner. Mesmer just bleeds out of Breas, no effort required, and I've never known him to carry the taint of murder—the smell of violent death permeates deep.

Murder and death. My stomach churned with guilt. At that moment, on the Teile-Sharet plane, a war was raging. All because of me.

I jumped up and headed into the kitchen where my cell phone sat on the kitchen counter. Grabbing the phone, I replaced it with my butt on the counter and punched in Talis's number.

"Hello," Talis answered, after two rings.

"Talis. You're still here."

"Uh, yeah. Why wouldn't I be?"

"Because...." Neither guy would admit it, but I suspected Breas had threatened to rearrange Talis's anatomy if he came within a mile of me.

"I was worried. You haven't answered your phone."

"Uh, sorry." He yawned. "How are you?"

"Okay. Well, no, not okay."

In the background, I heard Eithne meow and a plate rattled.

"You're not still worried about the demons, are you?" he asked me. To Eithne, he said, "Which do you want, girl? Chicken fingers or shrimp puffs?"

"Jeez, Tal, buy that poor animal some real food."

I could hear the insult in his voice. "She loves take-away."

I listened as he filled Eithne's dish with greasy fast food, and she made approving noises.

"So what are you going to do?" he asked.

"I dunno. I need leverage. What do Teile demons value most in the world? What do Sharet demons value?"

The question was rhetorical but Talis answered anyway. "The Teile are fond of human slaves. Female slaves. The Sharet are fond of blood sports, so cheap expendable sacrifices like...slaves are also desirable." The sound of fast food crunching between teeth came over the phone. "But," he added, "I know you don't want to go there."

"No." The needle in my moral compass had a hard time settling on one direction, but it had never pointed towards "Enslaving the Helpless and Innocent."

"What about the dragons? This is all on account of dragons. Stupid dragons."

"Yahtets are really quite intelligent."

"They let themselves be owned by Teile and Sharet demons. They can't be that smart."

"Well, no, but...." Talis sighed. "Maybe you're on to something, though."

"The last two wars were caused by excrement and intercourse—of the dragon persuasion." I banged my heels against the counter cabinet. "I need dragon diapers and condoms."

"Crates of them," said Talis.

"You don't suppose a couple of lifetime memberships to a warehouse-buy-in-bulk store could end all this?"

Talis laughed. "No, but with demons, who knows?"

"Think you have any time to talk about this, in person?"

"Tonight?" he asked.

"I was thinking tomorrow afternoon." I couldn't tell from his tone of voice if he expected company, but even now, with a drug habit, women still beat a well-trodden path to his bed. The last thing I wanted was another front row viewing of Talis the sex machine.

We made small talk for a couple more minutes and then said goodbye. I hopped off the counter and headed for my bedroom to get my violin.

I practiced in the living room, breezing through the second violin part in a Haydn string quartet. Play any instrument for more than a century and you get pretty good, regardless of talent. I was subbing this weekend for a violinist with a broken arm. The effort ate up about thirty minutes.

Violin tucked under my right arm and bow in hand, I walked over to the front window, lowered and shut the blinds. I sat down in the easy chair and took a deep breath.

And then I did that thing I do when no one else is around, my dirty little secret.

Magic.

Real magic, sorcery, not the pansy stuff like *unlocks* and obscures that even a non-innate can run with an energy conduit.

Wood is used as an inhibitor or regulator in magical reaction. Oak is particularly effective in controlling and directing magic spells. A few woods, like Maram'ro, don't react, but instead block or contain the effects of magic. For a vampire, strung together by magic, the effect of any pointy wood in the heart is a massive disruption of that magical energy, a horrific, extra combustible, short circuit. Extracts from some woods, like yew, are used to make potent vampire knockout drugs.

I don't know where ebony, spruce and maple fall in the range of magical reactivity, but the only time I've ever been able to do real magic is while playing a violin. Over the past six months, I'd been making real progress, managing, for the first time in more than a century to accomplish something more than making license plates fuzzy.

I started out as usual, with a Paganini caprice, which I then began to augment with my own variations, alternately letting the instrument sing, chirp, and scratch out melody.

A key to my recent success had been the discovery that by dragging the bow over the G-string with just right pressure and speed, I could get notes that were below the normal range of the violin. This night, as many times before, those deep scratchy notes were the trigger.

When cast, simple magic spells feel like a light electrical shock, a pleasant hum. Powerful magic, the kind of force I'm supposed to be able to use, is like standing in front of the speakers at rock concert. Deep sonic vibrations that carry to my bones and have substance and form. With the right music notes, I can form that substance into extensions of myself, extra hands almost.

My personal challenge was to lift any one of the iron fireplace tools from its stand. Harder than it sounds, because the tools are constructed of iron and resent being moved with magic. Talis and Lex, who are both competent sorcerers, can't use magic to move anything that contains iron. Breas can manipulate the metal, because vampires, like the humans they are derived from, have an immunity to iron.

At the first surge of energy, I switched to a tune of my own invention, in a gloomy minor key, and focused on the fireplace. My control was poor, so I groped clumsily at the little broom for a few minutes, my "fingers" closing on air. After I managed to move the little broom and shovel and drop—loudly—the other two tools, I lost interest and put my fiddle away.

Just in case Breas got home early and noticed the magical residue, I dug an incense stick out of a junk drawer in the kitchen. Bolstered by my success with the fireplace tools, I set the incense in a holder and spoke three spell words in Elvish. Nothing happened, so I tried again, really concentrating on the sound and timbre of the words. *Just like with music, only with words. No problemo, right?*

Wrong. The incense didn't so much as smolder.

Frustrated, I found some matches and lit the stick the mundane human way.

Chapter Nineteen

Sick leave, glorious sick leave. If it weren't for sick leave, I'd never get any time off. I stopped at a convenience store and bought a lottery ticket. Five days since Icarus had been murdered, and I was starting to think I had a better chance at winning Powerball than finding the chaotic magic user. Claiming a bad case of monkey pox (Barry bought that story), I took the afternoon off to visit Talis.

Home for Talis was a low-end apartment in a dangerous neighborhood. Relying on a weak glamour for disguise, Talis fit in easily with his human neighbors, most of whom just wanted to be left alone anyway.

I cruised by the apartment complex, circling the block twice. Talis's battered little car, cobbled together from the remains of several cars of different colors, sat in its customary parking place in front of his apartment. A handful of gangbangers loitered nearby. They returned my wave with nods as I pulled my car in next to Talis's.

Rather than my standard license *obscure*, I slapped a lock spell on my car instead. A really good conventional thief could get around a weak lock spell, but my car wasn't a likely target for talented criminals. One advantage of driving a nondescript, econo-box is the lack of giddy excitement it inspires in car thieves.

The doorbell elicited a faint cricket squeak, so I knocked hard on the door sending little flakes of paint, probably lead-based, eddying to the ground. Silence. I listened and knocked harder.

"Hey, Talis, open up." I summoned a dagger and hammered on the door's surface with the pommel. A weak groan came from the interior of the apartment and feet shuffled to the door. Talis must have been into the happy-powder.

Scratching noises followed and the door opened a crack. A fat black cat squeezed through the opening, meowed a greeting, and marched out into the sun, tail held high.

"Hi, Eithne. Bye, Eithne." Eithne disappeared into a yellowing evergreen shrub.

A dark face and pair of sky blue eyes peered through the crack.

"Big bad Wolfe."

"Talis, that joke is so old, it's smelly." His apartment was dark, but I could see that one of his eyes was dark with split blood vessels. "Let me in, huh?"

"Okay. You're alone, right?"

"Well, yes." I turned to scan the area just in case. So maybe he hadn't been into the feel-good stuff.

With an Eva-worthy sigh, he unlatched the security chain, opened the door and shuffle-limped away. "Lock it behind you."

"You all right?" The smell of blood, his, filled the tiny apartment.

"No." He collapsed on his car seat turned couch.

I locked the door and walked over to him. "Shit, Talis. What'd you do? Piss off a Baccalshi?"

"No demons. Worse. Fucking Holders."

I hurried to the apartment's one window, where I jammed a finger in between the cheap plastic blinds and studied the parking lot. "When?"

"'Bout...an hour? An hour ago."

An hour. I wondered how Talis defined an hour. "Hang on. I'll be right back."

A first aid kit is necessary equipment in my business, and I headed out to retrieve it from my trunk. I tested the air and examined each car in the vicinity. No sign of Jason's SUV, but I had no idea what Kyle drove. *Sloppy, O'Connell.*

Back inside, I picked up a lampshade-free lamp from the far corner of the room. Plunking the light on the milk carton and wood plank coffee table, I then sat down next to the Talis.

Talis's most spectacular injury was a cut that ran from the top middle of his forehead, skipping over his eye and dinging his cheek. The gash and likely concussion, probably accounted for his inability to run a *heal* on himself. If a magic user is like a computer, then the brain would be the processor. I bit back unease, thinking of my date with Jason the next night.

"What did they want?" I asked, cleaning and dressing his wounds.

"They were asking about—" His eyes met mine, pleading. "Ch-chaotic magic user."

"Yeah? And you told them?"

"Nothing. I don't know...nothing."

"This is your brain. This is your brain on Elf Dust. Sizzle."

He forced a smile, revealing pointy canines. "I don't do that crap anymore."

"Right. So what do you know? About the chaotic magic user?"

He flinched as though I had hit him. "Nothing."

My fingers moved along his arm, feeling solid bone despite the bruising. "Don't lie to me, Tal. Please."

"I'm not—"

"Talis. This is serious. You heard what happened to Icarus?" He nodded. "The Brethren expect me to sort this out. Me!"

"All I...all I know is all the Non-Earth plane folk are nervous. Complaining even. The last time somebody messed around with...that shit, well, it was ugly. Real ugly."

"Ugly, how?" I took one of Talis's hands. Hoping he wouldn't notice the actual manner of execution, I tried a heal spell, augmented with melody in my head, on the cracks in his ribs. My magic spluttered and hesitated and then hummed to life, hot power sluicing through my skin into Talis's.

You can't get something for nothing and heal spells hurt nearly as much as the original injury. The spell worked and Talis groaned and clenched his fist around my hand.

When the spell had run its course, he freed my hand and said, "Thanks and, uh, planes, splits, rips in planes or something like that."

My mind started filling with equations. "Rips and tears. Wouldn't that mean passages in time and—?"

"And instability." A little bit of the Talis I remembered glimmered in his eyes. "Planes could shift." He raised his hands and held them in front of him, fingers straight out, palms facing and several inches apart. "If they touch—*pow, blam.*" He clapped his hands together and winced in pain.

"Shit!" Fear crept into my belly. What was I supposed to do against magic of that magnitude? Pull out my fiddle and lull the perpetrator into complacency? Regan O'Connell, supernatural snake charmer.

Talis's breath whistled through congealed blood in his nose. I shoved aside my insecurities and stood up. "Got any Surreal?"

"For you?" he asked with obvious disappointment.

"For a friend."

He shrugged. "Oh. Sure. Red, wooden box in my bedroom."

I found the box and picked a single pill from his stash. Surreal comes from the Fey plane, and in addition to producing psychedelic hallucinations when ground and snorted, it is a potent painkiller. I crouched by his makeshift coffee table and used a dagger to split the tablet into quarters.

I handed him a wedge and said, "Here. This will kill the pain. Take one of the remaining bits every four hours. Try a heal spell before you take the second." He stared at the pill fragment without blinking. "Water?" I asked.

"Nah. I just never thought to actually—"

"Take it in its original, solid form? It was developed as a painkiller. Originally. Better than aspirin, it won't interfere with blood clotting."

"Regan O'Connell, M.D." He smiled and popped the drug in his mouth.

My eyes perused the room taking in nothing out of the ordinary. Talis's only constant possessions, his collection of first edition Edgar Rice Burroughs books—*Tarzan of the Apes, A Princess of Mars*, et al.— were shelved neatly in small bookcase.

"Did, did *both* the Holders do this to you?"

"The big one, Kurt? He sends the other one out to their car. For a map or some shit like that."

"So it was Kyle, not Jason?" Talis's dark eyebrows arched upward and I explained, "I sort of have a date with Jason, tomorrow. Reconnaissance, you know?"

Talis grinned. "He know you're a Wolfe?" At my headshake, he chuckled. "Jason, greenish eyes, strong innate, right?" I nodded. "When he came back, he stopped the other one. Kurt, Kyle, whatever, was seriously pissed. I thought they were gonna come to blows. Scared the shit out of poor Eithne."

Feeling relieved and more than a little confused by my relief, I started to collect my stuff.

"Hey," he said, taking a deep breath. "Breas is in town, right?" His chest rose with a deep breath. "I think I smell him on you," he added.

I scowled at his choice of words. "Yeah. He's in town."

My gaze took in Talis's battered face. I'm not sure whom I was angrier with. Talis or Kyle. Kyle was acting true to form, but Talis could have defended himself if he hadn't been hopped up on the drug of the month. Maybe. Talis's people lived by some kind of code of non-violence. I think clinging to that code made Talis feel like less of an exile.

Talis leaned back into his lime green and duct tape couch, and closed his eyes. "Tell Breas. Tell him I need to talk to him. I got a request from a customer. Right up his alley."

"I'll let him know." I didn't want any more details. "Oh, and Talis?" I poked his shoulder with my finger.

"Huh?" His eyes opened.

"Give me back my watch."

He flashed a sheepish grin, if that was possible with fangs, and handed me the watch. I slid it back on my wrist. The thing about kobolds is that they aren't really thieves. They'll return anything if you ask them, provided you notice it's gone.

Talis shut his eyes and I watched him, my mind on Kyle and Jason. Did Jason know what Kyle would do to Talis? Is that why he conveniently left? Good cop, bad cop? Anger started to warm the cold fear I had felt earlier.

"Revenge is bad for the soul," said Talis, pale eyes half open.

"You a mind reader now?" I reached over and pushed a section of his hair back, exposing a pointed ear.

With a groan he sat up, his pale eyes catching mine. "No. But I know you." He took my hand in his. "What happened with Cyrus Purcell, it hurt you more than him."

"I don't think so, Tal. I killed Cyrus."

"No, you didn't." He released my hand and slipped his arm around my shoulders, pulling me to him. "Sometimes living is a lot harder than dying."

I relaxed against his bony shoulder. "Sometimes, I wish I was fifteen and back in Ireland. Dirty hair, dirtier clothes, illiterate and irresponsible. As opposed to moderately literate and somewhat responsible."

Talis nuzzled his face in my hair. "Uh, for the record, I like the well-washed version of Regan O'Connell."

I allowed myself a minute more of hug therapy. Drug addicts shouldn't make you feel safe, but Talis did. Humans, unfortunately, came and went, but Talis was a constant. Somehow, over the course of many decades, he'd become my best friend.

"Well, I'm off." I disengaged reluctantly from the hug. "Got places to go, people to beat."

"Regan," he said, gently.

"Kidding." After another quick inventory check, I got up and headed for the door.

"Regan?"

"Yeah?" I stopped in the doorway.

"Be careful, huh?"

I turned the latch on the doorknob to the lock position and left Talis to his business.

Driving away, I contemplated his words. "All the Non-Earth plane folk are nervous."

A chaotic magic user who could rip holes in the fabric of the universe, and the Holders respond by sending just two measly operatives? Appearances notwithstanding, it still didn't add up.

Chapter Twenty

*C*ypher called to check in again that evening.

"I examined those index cards." She went on to tell me that the index cards from Icarus's office were the keys to a system of cataloguing his inventory. I guess he figured his secrets were safely buried in his nudie magazines. The Sharet demon's letter, taken from his computer hard drive, was a complaint to his landlord, protesting his impending eviction. Some Sharet demons are like crazy cat ladies. Believing the animals bring good luck, they often keep dozens as pets. Human landlords don't look too favorably on the ensuing onslaught of kitty poo and urine.

"For want of a kitty, an apartment was lost. That was a whole lot of worthless." *More clues bite the dust.*

"I'm emailing you all the information I found on Jason Astin-Lake. Encrypted as usual."

Breas, who'd been eavesdropping on our conversation, smirked. "Jason Astin-Lake. Didn't he play a doctor on 'Days of Our Lives?'"

"No. I think it was 'General Hospital,'" Cypher answered.

I crossed my eyes. "Pairs vampire comedy. The next great Olympic sport."

"Or reality TV program," Cypher said, and returned to the matter at hand. "The Holders don't entirely trust Jason either, which isn't surprising, given his past. His partner, Kyle, is under orders to report any peculiar behavior on Jason's part."

"Poor Jason," I said, instantly regretting it.

"Regan, you old softy," Cypher teased.

I flinched. "It's just that it sounds like he was manipulated into joining."

"Free will, Regan."

Before I could stop myself, I blurted, "I hate 'em all, stupid Holders."

"Apparently, you don't," Cypher replied. "At any rate, they have their place, in the scheme of things."

"Huh?"

"Were the Fey and demon races still prevalent on Earth plane, the humans might stop squabbling amongst themselves and actually unite against a perceived common enemy. So long as humans believe they are alone in the universe, they are far easier to manipulate.

"Most Non-Earth plane governments, recognizing the very nature of humans, tolerate the Holders as a necessary evil. Imagine if humans, manifest destiny and such, knew of the existence of other planes? In no short time, nearly all Earth-like planes would be filthy with iron-wielding humans.

"Besides, by strictly regulating the number of Non-Earth peoples who are allowed commerce on Earth, the Holders have handed us a virtual monopoly."

"Oh." I should have known that, but I've avoided even the topic of the Holders of the True Light for many years.

"Careful, Regan." She had a rare hint of concern in her voice.

"Always. Thanks, Cypher."

Twenty minutes later, Breas and I were driving south headed for dingy downtown neighborhood. This was the second night we had tried this, seeking out a Lesser vampire to interrogate, following my hunch that the purveyor of wacky magic was somehow connected to the plague of nutty nosferatu. Lesser vampires were poor conversationalists, but I didn't have anything else to do, besides fret about my date with Jason the next day.

"Keep this up and you're walking home." Breas's voice broke into my faraway thoughts.

"Huh? I'm just sitting here."

"It's raining angst."

"You can block me." As I could with him, Breas could shunt his senses away from me.

"You are entirely too dangerous."

"Cool," I said with little enthusiasm.

He parked the car and studied me. The engine was still running, Vivaldi chirping brightly out of the stereo.

I told him about my lunch with Jason. "What if he picks up on—? You know? That I'm not human? He must know I'm an innate, but what if he realizes there is more?"

Breas surveyed the surrounding block. "Now, I *am* jealous."

"Huh?"

"Haven't shared your concerns with Cypher, have you? You're protecting him." The stereo cut off as he twisted the key out of the ignition.

"I've never told anyone about us, either," I said, referring to the night Breas and I spent eliminating my bright future in unicorn capture. "Unless you told Cypher."

He retreated behind his cold façade. "No." The mere perception of hanky-panky with yours truly had put him on permanent hiatus with the Brethren. Breas relieved me of my virginity a few decades *after* the infamous kiss that got him kicked out of the Brethren. He was free of Brethren laws—those regarding me, anyway. But Breas had enemies, vampires who'd love any excuse to have him chopped into little bits.

"Will he turn you in as one of The Lost?" he asked. The Lost is the Holders' cute way of describing innately magical humans who have coasted under their radar, people like Joan.

"I don't know. Don't think so, but my people skills are nonexistent." I threw my companion a wistful glance.

Breas was so unreadable; I risked touching him with my senses. His indecision felt heavy and thick. "From what I read off him," he began, "his approach to work is more mechanical than fanatical." He fiddled with his car keys. "Chances are, his interest in you is—" Irritation mixed itself in liberally with indecision. "Solely romantic." He added the last bit with a sneer and practically jumped out of the car.

We spent more than an hour wandering around the neighborhood, hiding in urine smelling corners and building shadows whenever the numerous cop cars coasted past us. Breas and I were both too clean to be in the area at this time of night.

With the possible exception of Edward Aguirre, the homeless and otherwise unmissed were the usual source for the Lesser Generation vampires.

I was ten seconds away from going home, when I picked up a scent. She sat forlornly in a barren lot that even the weeds forgot. As we walked up to her, she continued chatting with the remains of her victim, a middle-age man. She was so incoherent it would be an exaggeration to describe the conversation as one-sided.

Finally noticing us, as we stood a few feet away, she pushed the dead man off her lap, muttering, "Don't need him." A couple inches shorter than me and probably Hispanic, she peered up through stringy hair at Breas and then sniffed in my direction.

Not even making the effort to switch to vampire face, she lunged at me. I sidestepped, stuck my foot out and sent her sprawling. She made a mewling sound when she hit the ground and then struggled to her feet. Her dark unfocussed eyes latched onto Breas. "You. I know you." He made a face like someone who'd stepped in fresh, squishy, dog shit.

The vampire tipped her head sideways and clarified, to herself, "No. Different, but the same."

"She doesn't even know what she is," I said. Not unusual for Lesser vampires. "Hey. What is your name?"

This time her brown face shifted, eyes yellowing and fangs spiking from her mouth. She had speed but little in the way of the facile danger typical of vampires. I stepped aside, like a matador, turning to watch her stagger to a halt. *Ole.*

She glowered, her eyes still yellow. "Why you so fast?"

"I always eat my vegetables." She watched me with all the comprehension of a teenager in a boring history class. "Never mind. What. Is. Your. Name?"

"Alice." She pronounced her name as though discovering it for the first time.

"Okay. Alice. How did you get this way? Like him?" I gestured with my eyes at Breas, who leaned against the side of a nearby building.

I felt his indignation. "Insulting your ride. Not wise," he asked. Alice followed my gaze and seemed surprised to see the blond vampire.

"Show her," I demanded, meaning that Breas should be more expressively vampire.

"No." He glanced at his wrist, a watch's light flashing briefly, and turned his face toward the street.

I rubbed my eyes and dodged another Alice attack. "What made you like this?" I offered up my feeble approximation of a vampire, yellow eyes and small fangs.

Alice's eyes changed back to brown and widened to show considerable amounts of white. "So dark and angry, stop staring at me," she whimpered, shuffling backwards.

I glanced at Breas, who shrugged and continued to watch the street. "Wow, cool, I never had that affect before," I said. Willing my face back to human, I rephrased the question, "Who bit you?"

Alice took a step toward me, studying my face. "Pretty man. Dark hair and eyes like grass."

"Really green, like mine?" I asked, my finger pointed at my eyes.

"Nah, like grass. Like grass."

O-kay?

"Light brown?" Breas's voice sent Alice twisting in surprise. "With a little green?"

She smiled, revealing beautiful teeth. A great smile. All that remained after the usual recipe: generous amounts of bad luck, spiced with even worse life choices. *Like Cara, I thought. Like Talis.*

"Yeah! Like grass, like grass." Alice's head bobbed in agreement.

"Oh. *New Mexico* grass." A certain dark-haired, hazel-eyed Holder immediately came to mind. "Did he have a name?"

"Hungry." She darted at me with even less skill than the previous attempts. I tripped her again and she crunched to the ground. She stood up, a used condom stuck in her hair. *That's just sad.*

"I doubt he formally introduced himself," Breas said, as I hurried over to where she fell.

"Shaddup." I met Alice's next charge head on; the smell of scorched latex signaled her passing.

I stared at the remains of Alice, anger roiling in my gut. "I have to stop this. No more Alices."

"She was dead before she was a vampire."

I stared at Breas's impassive face. "No. She was alive. As long as she was alive, she had hope. She could've turned her life around."

Oddly, it was Breas who looked away, his dark scanning our surroundings. "The reluctant Holder goes bad."

It took me a second to realize what he meant. "No. Jason has no—"

"You said so yourself. You're a poor judge of character, O'Connell."

The emotion in the vampire's eyes—concern—caught me off guard and the silence stretched before my reply.

"No," I said, with as much conviction as possible. "He isn't another Cyrus Purcell."

♫

PARIS, FRANCE 1928

Cyrus Purcell shivered. Winter's cold squirmed through even the smallest opening, chilly fingers challenging the building's virtue; but that was not why Cyrus shivered. He trembled in giddy anticipation. Tonight. Tonight, the vampire girl would come to him. She simply had to. His work on the prostitute would insure it, right?

He had first seen the vampire girl several months before on a warm summer night. The occasion, a party thrown by an elf lord masquerading as an English lord. None other than Kadin Farahani, commander of the Grey Brethren's security force, had escorted her.

She was new to the city. Later he would learn she was Irish, originating from somewhere in the north of Ireland. Belfast, wasn't it?

He had introduced himself and employed all the charm afforded by his looks—chestnut brown hair, sea green eyes and finely chiseled features. Initially wary, as the evening progressed her reticence gave way to flirtatious humor.

She was coquettish, but hardly wanton and he considered the kiss a victory. Her lips were warm as though she had fed recently.

He hadn't had any direct contact with her since that night, though not for lack of effort on his part.

He had followed her whenever he could, whenever he could find her. Like all her kind, she was elusive. Some nights she didn't appear at all. Her haunt during the day was an upscale apartment on La Rue de Rivoli.

After the passing of weeks, her elusiveness lost its charm, his simple desire turning to obsession. Summer's green faded, giving way to bloodshot autumn, and then winter washed away all, leaving gray. All save his unyielding desire, which burned red-hot, kindled by denial.

Cyrus brought his hands to his lips, their heat reminiscent of the touch of her mouth. She'd been toying with him. He, no fool, knew that. But with that kiss, something had passed between them, a persistent need that needled him night and day.

Getting her attention would require a forceful act, dramatic savagery to impress one whose existence was steeped in death.

In truth, what transpired this night with the whore was no different from any other night in his laboratory. With instruments and even his raw senses, he recorded the last moments of her life, measuring the fragile energies that broke free from the woman's dying flesh. The sweet exhilaration of the whore's death still lingered in the laboratory.

The Holders of the True Light knew little of the exact nature of his experiments. They thought he sought a cure for vampirism, or perhaps the ultimate weapon against the children of the night. Placated with the occasional report, they funded his efforts. They knew or at least suspected that his subjects were often human, the castoffs, the detritus of mankind. But what did they care?

They were, of course, fools, caught up in their own self-righteous notions of good and evil, the rightful heirs of the Earth versus Non-Earth interlopers. Small-minded dolts who could not comprehend the power vampirism had to offer the human race.

He was so wrapped up in his reverie, he didn't immediately realize that she stood in the doorway. His left fist clenched in an attempt to control the shudder of anticipation that rolled through his body.

Her eyes, green as ivy, were fixed on the corpse in the corner. No emotion played across her face, but that was not unusual for her kind.

"Do come in," he said.

At the sound of his voice, she lifted her eyes, brilliant green orbs, and studied him.

"That was an invitation. You are invited in." He smiled.

The vampire stepped into the room, her gait smooth and catlike. Dressed in trousers and riding boots, every bit of her clothing was matte black. Black, like her hair, which she had bound back in a loose braid. The quintessential hunter. She appeared to be in her early teens, but he suspected she'd been "alive" at least twice as long. Which, of course, made her young for a vampire.

A few quick feline steps placed her in the corner where the whore's corpse lay. She glanced at him as he closed the distance between them. In his pocket he clutched a fragile vial of yew extract, concentrated, enough to drop even a large vampire.

Her face remained passive. "Why'd you kill her?" she asked. For the passage of a second, he thought he saw a flicker of sadness cross her perfectly symmetrical face. But that could not be possible. He knew that for certain. Those eyes were not always green.

He studied her. She appeared frail, standing there a few feet away, a thin waif. She tilted her head to look at the corpse and his eyes were drawn to her throat, her slim neck. Were she an ordinary human girl, he could snap that neck in a second. But he would not do that. Not until he had....

"You killed her to lure me here," she stated, answering her own question.

He smiled, confident of his charms. "Yes." Her hands clenched and unclenched gracefully. Those hands, the hands of a musician. What he would give to know their touch.

Then she crouched by the corpse. One moment she stood, then the next she was down by the dead girl's body. Vampire speed never ceased to amaze him. His hand closed on the vial of yew extract for reassurance.

"She's still warm," the vampire girl said.

"Yes. I'm sure her blood, what's left of it, is still quite edible."

The vampire had no response. Instead she brushed two slim fingers across the whore's face.

And then she flowed to her feet.

She took a step toward him. "She was my friend."

"Come on. Now let's not get maudlin. She was your pet, your familiar."

Another quick vampire step shortened the distance between them.

"She was my friend," she repeated, and this time he saw genuine emotion. "Her name was Cara. Cara Ryan."

He stared at the slim figure—her angelic face etched with definite sorrow—and felt the first flicker of uncertainly. Had he made a mistake? It made no matter, he had enough extract to disable her. Then she would be his.

Her head tilted, like a dog listening for a kind word. The sadness had fled her face and was replaced with calm. "You killed her. She will have justice."

The vial, specially designed to burst and spread its power, hit her in the chest just before she reached him.

She yelped in a manner reminiscent of a startled dog, took two quick steps back, her arm lifted, using a sleeve to attempt to wipe the chemical off her face.

Cyrus pounced, employing the second weapon in his arsenal, an aged wooden cross on a leather cord, a Bane imbued with the power to steal a vampire's strength. The instant her arm came away from her face, he shoved the cord over her neck. Confident of the Bane's power, he grabbed her wrists.

Blinded, she struggled in his grasp, but the Bane did its job. Cyrus swung his left leg out, sweeping her feet out from under her. Her head clunked against the hard floor as he shoved her down.

He sat on her thighs and pinned her wrists to the floor. Reacting to the caustic yew extract, her eyelids fluttered and the muscles around her eyes twitched. Oddly, the extract had no effect on her skin.

Stirred by the sudden awareness of her under him, the rhythm of his heart increased. He licked his lips, held in thrall by a sudden need for haste and a tightening in his groin. He arranged his hands so that one held her wrists, freeing the other to remove her shirt.

Her eyes opened enough to show slivers of ivy green.

"Get off me," she said, and one of her wrists twisted in his grip.

Working the buttons on her shirt, he ignored her. The Bane would leave her with less strength than an ordinary human girl. Black fabric parted revealing the pale perfection of a breast. He delighted in the strange warmth of her flesh and her reaction to his touch, a startled flinch.

As he toyed with a pale rose nipple, he realized her chest rose and fell as though breathing. A vampiric affectation, clinging to a parody of the life she lost?

The nipple hardened, he gave it a tug and moved his hand toward her waist. Distracted by her odd clothing—he wasn't used to removing trousers from women—he didn't instantly heed the pricking sensation on his arm. The pain intensified and he glanced up, his eyes widening at the source.

A dagger's tip had scratched a short red line down his arm, pausing at his wrist. A Wolfe's dagger! The dark ebony-like wood intertwined and melded into a silvery metal edge. The weapon of the elusive spy-assassins of the Grey Brethren.

As he watched, she twitched her wrist and jabbed the weapon into his left wrist, driving it precisely through nerves and tendons, taking the strength from his hand. In a second she pulled free of his grasp and slashed a second dagger at his chest, driving him off her.

And she was on him, in one instant, their positions were reversed. The fine edge of a dagger stung his throat.

"You. Are. Not. Yourself," she told him. "The kiss," she continued, "it had to be the kiss, the Thrall Charm, that has driven you to such perversions."

"The kiss? You flatter yourself." he replied, though he knew there was some truth to what she said. "A Mesmer spell. You used Mesmer on me." Despite his predicament, he smiled. "I'm flattered."

She shook her head. "No. It's much more than that." With careless ease, she grasped the Bane, snapping its cord and tossing it aside.

"You touched...the Bane...but how?"

She sighed. "I was born a vampire. Cullan O'Connell is my father." At his expression she explained, "Of course it's possible. If it were truly impossible, I would not be here. A more appropriate word would be...improbable."

She moved the dagger away from his throat and rocked back onto her heals. "I'm calling the *gendarmes*."

"Wait." He had the means to deal with the police, but he'd rather not overplay his hand with the local authorities over one prostitute.

Remembering that slow movements placated vampires, he reached with languid ease and closed his right hand around her wrist. Sitting up, he moved his face within inches of hers.

"I did you favor, really." With a lift of his eyebrows, he indicated the dead whore. "Among your people you are nothing short of nobility. Surely, she is not an appropriate companion—"

"She was worth a hundred of you," she snapped, trying to free herself from his grasp.

Cyrus clenched his fist, realizing that her lack of strength was independent of the Bane. The bones beneath his fingers were thin. "She was...trash."

Her eyes widened. "I'm *calling* the gendarmes."

"No, you're not." Cyrus yanked her arm with a calculated snap. She yelped and thrown off balance, fell on him.

The pain was so intense that for a few scant seconds it registered as something other than pain, an amorphous deadly shock to his system.

The dagger, clutched in her hand, had been driven into his chest by the force of her fall. Though she instantly pushed herself off him and jumped to her feet, the weapon remained, half its length buried in his chest.

His compulsion for her greater than his agony, he struggled to his feet, weapon jutting from his chest. Horror plain on her face, she took a step away from him. "Bloody hell," she said.

But mortality was too great for even the Thrall Charm; he fell to his knees, the impact sending painful vibrations through the Wolfe's dagger.

Wolfe. A Wolfe's training includes magic.

"H-heal me," he said through clenched teeth, imploring her with his eyes. But she stared beyond him—her expression desolate—to where the whore's corpse lay. His muscles began to weaken and he fell forward, stopping his fall with an outstretched arm. "H-heal me!" he pleaded in a harsh whisper.

His fading vision caught the motion of her kneeling before him. Managing to lift his head, he met her eyes. Bolstered by the indecision he saw, he demanded, "You have the ability. Do it."

"No. I don't. I can't." She moved back, her expression hardening. "I won't."

His arm buckled and he fell. The dagger was thrust, twisting in his chest. For a fleeting moment, all pain evaporated. *She did it. I am saved.*

And then there was nothing.

The city had never seemed so huge, dirty and sprawling; the cloying stench of humanity confused his keen senses. Though normally diminished by cold temperatures, the smell of the sewers, fecal and rotted, was strong this night.

Talis found Regan just where the vision had predicted—sitting, huddled, knees pressed to her chest, in a dark alley.

He had been sitting on the bed in his tiny Paris apartment, lost in the heroic exploits of John Carter in Edgar Rice Burroughs's *A Princess of Mars*, when the vision struck. The page faded away as though his eyes had succumbed to a rapid case of macular degeneration. A breath later, his vision expanded to the dim scene.

"Regan," he said, moving before the vision faded, the book falling on the bed, his hands outstretched. Half-blind, he tumbled off the bed. The pain of his knee hitting the wooden floor drove away the vision.

He cursed his impulsiveness. The one instance when he wanted to see all a vision revealed, he'd interrupted it with clumsy bumbling. Pulling on shoes and a coat, he had charged into the night.

Precognitive power had always been a curse. Up until the day he had been born, the power had only manifested in elves. A treasured gift in elves, precog power was an abomination in kobolds.

It had been six years since he told his father about his ability—six years of living as an outcast, a member of a despised race, struggling with a power that belonged to his people's greatest enemy.

Chilly tendrils of fear grew in his belly. The visions rarely provided him more than the foreknowledge of death.

With a lineage tracing to the most aristocratic elves and vampires, by all rights she should have spurned his friendship. Untroubled by status or disfavor, Regan O'Connell treated him as an equal, unknowingly earning an ironic loyalty. There wasn't much he wouldn't do for her.

It had taken nearly an hour to find her. The bitter ferrous smell of human blood was so overwhelming he thought her dead. "Regan." He crouched and laid a hand on her shoulder, relieved by her sobs.

He pressed his face against the back of her head. "It's all right. It's me. Talis." She trembled and he slipped his arms around her, pulling her to him. For a time, all he could do was cling to her, afraid some cruel fate might yet still her heart. "You're hurt. Let me—"

"No," she moaned.

"You've lost too much blood."

"N-not mine. Cara's...Cyrus's. Killed."

"Killed? By who?"

"Me," she replied, and told him what had transpired.

"You can't blame yourself." Talis loosened his hold enough to run fingers down her arms. A bone shifted and she gasped in pain.

Clearly sensing him beginning a healing spell, she said, "No. Don't."

"But—"

"I didn't heal him, Talis. Why should—?"

"There was nothing you could do. Shhhh." He wrapped his fingers around the broken arm, and spoke the words of the spell. Magic knitted bone to bone and Regan moaned at the agony of healing.

"C-Cara, her blood, my hands. I may as well have killed her myself."

Talis fiddled with a section of her hair, his narrow fingers working the strands free of dried blood. "I don't understand."

"Stupid, curious, stupid. Didn't think. I kissed him. I had no idea what it would do. She's dead because of me."

"No—"

"It *is* my fault." Regan shook free of his grasp and crawled a few steps away. Back pressed to the wall, she stared at him. "I kissed Cyrus and the Thrall Charm took his mind." The absence of light stole the color from her eyes, leaving black orbs in a spectral face.

Talis closed the distance to kneel before her. "No." He took her chin in his hands and leaned his face toward hers. "He was evil long before you met. Many have died in his laboratory—humans, demons, Fey—any he could lure. He was searching for something. I don't know what, but it was something only found in the death of others."

She took a deep hiccupping breath and averted her gaze. "I watched him die, Talis. I think I might have enjoyed it."

"No, you didn't."

"I'm a vampire—"

"You are that and more." He moved so he could wrap his arms around her. "Shhhh," he whispered, but silence was beyond her.

"His heartbeat. I cuh-can hear it, thumping, slowing, slowing...." With two rasping sobs, Regan begin to cry.

Wordless, he lifted his right hand, and set his slim fingers to dancing in the air. The sleep spell dropped like a blanket and she slumped unconscious in his arms.

He couldn't bear the sound of her crying.

Chapter Twenty-One

*A*nother spectacular New Mexico sunset, brilliant purple and pink, at my back, I drove toward Jason's apartment, keeping the car just under the speed limit; my usual desire to break traffic laws absent. Little feathers of doubt tickled my nerves. What if Breas was right? What if Jason had gone rogue and was monkeying around with world-shaking power? Was I going into the lion's den?

Jason Lake's apartment was located in the Northeast heights, across the street from a high-end gated community filled with super-sized houses plunked on anemic lots. I pulled into his apartment complex and navigated to Building D. Though not luxurious, the complex was far from inexpensive. The landscaping consisted of chemical green grass and ruler straight hedges. The buildings themselves were probably no more than a decade old. Holders must pay a pretty good per diem.

I slid into a guest slot across from his building. A tall, dark-haired guy was coming towards me, moving with an unassuming and smoldering sexuality. *Wow*, I thought, realizing the guy was Jason.

"Hey, Jason."

"Hey," he parroted, stopping a few feet away. His chest rose and fell in a mildly exaggerated fashion, a faint sheen of sweat clung to his skin. He glanced at his watch.

"I'm not late," I said with mock defensiveness.

"No. You're not, though I was sort of counting on your being late."

"Oh, really? Did your previous, um, date run over the allotted time? That explains the pantin', sweatin' and suchlike." I gave him a quick once over. The T-shirt, sweatpants, and running shoes made his actual activity pretty obvious.

He had the annoyingly attractive grace to blush. "I thought I could get in a quick run before you arrived."

We exchanged smiles and walked the short distance to the stairs. A couple of teenage girls stood at the base of the stairs, smoking and trying to look adult. Seeing the object of their apparent stakeout, they chimed in unison, "Hi, Jason."

"Hi." He nodded in their direction. As we started up the stairs, one broke her adoring gaze to glower and blow a lethal cloud in my direction.

"Must be the accent. Chicks love an English accent," I observed, tilting my head in the girls' direction, after we had cleared the stairs.

He unlocked and opened his door, gesturing inside. "Really? Is that why they stand there, day after day? I thought they were just trying to give me lung cancer."

I stepped into the living room, going through my usual discreet reconnaissance routine. "Single grown-up guy with English accent. *Mucho* swoon-worthy for American teenage girls."

His keys rang on the coffee table where he tossed them. I turned, catching him watching me with his peculiar wistful expression. With a small smile, he turned away.

"Would you mind if I grabbed a quick shower?" he asked.

I scrunched my face up in mock distaste. "Actually, I'd prefer it if you did."

He laughed. "Can I get you anything to drink? Beer? Wine?"

"Wine would be nice." We wandered into his kitchen where he poured a red wine, checked on dinner, cheese lasagna, and then headed off to the shower. "Make yourself at home. *Mi casa, su casa*," he said, before disappearing into the bathroom.

Sloppy, Jason, sloppy. Jason's seemingly harmless words made me a resident of his apartment by proxy, able to invite anyone or anything in. A guy in his line of work should know better.

I sat on the sofa and surveyed the room. The furniture was nice enough in a rental-furniture-angular-masculine-Mission style sort of way. A newspaper lay on the coffee table next to his keys. I started to flip through the paper and then picked up his keys instead. They tingled with a faint magical residue, but were otherwise quite ordinary. Car keys. Apartment keys. Key to the mailbox. *Hmmm. The mail.*

My hearing was tuned pretty high in Jason's direction. So high, in fact, I could hear him undressing, the soft rustle of cloth sliding over skin. Embarrassed, I tuned down my sensitivity.

As soon as the shower came on, I scurried into the kitchen where I'd spied a pile of mail on the counter. After a paranoid glance around the kitchen—with my luck he had a Nanny Cam buried in a cookie jar—I flipped through his correspondences. Much of his mail was addressed to "Jason Astin." Besides that, nothing unusual. I scanned his phone bill, but there wasn't anything informative. *He must make all his long distance calls via cell.*

Bored, I opened drawers and cabinets, but found nothing more interesting than an "It Steams; It Sautés; It Raises Your Children" infomercial cooking appliance. Mr. Astin-Lake was a sucker for a good sales pitch.

The bedroom and bathroom were down a short hallway, immediately off the kitchen. I stood in the kitchen, getting chewed out by the voice in my head, "Have you no shame? Taking advantage of his trust." In the end, I used Lex to justify my snooping. Lex would want to know what Jason's bedroom looked like.

His bedroom was fully furnished—king-sized bed, two side tables and a large dresser. I studied the room debating where to start. On a hunch, I walked over to the bed, sat and pulled open the top drawer of the bedside table. A large manila folder, addressed to "Mr. Jason Astin-Lake" lay on rows of neatly folded socks.

I noted its exact position in the drawer and slid it out gently. Prying apart the fastening tabs, I latched my fingers around the contents and pulled the papers out. Someone had scribbled a note on a sheet of white paper.

Jason,

Here are the documents you requested. Let me know if you need anything else.

Alex

I peeled back the top sheet and my vision blurred. Somewhere inside me, something dark and bloody screamed and twisted, and I almost dropped the pile of papers.

Written on a coversheet were the words, "Document number: bdr789587-1928, *The Nature of Lesser Generation Vampiric Turning, Energy Transformations*, Cyrus B. Purcell, March 1927."

It shouldn't hurt. Not after all this time.

The shower still ran even though part of me willed it to shut off. My shaking fingers fumbled with the cover page, and I stared at the handwritten report of the man who killed my best friend. *Oh, shit, breathe O'Connell, breathe* The writing, feathery and spider-like, covered page after page with obscure paranormal discussion.

Focus.

The report, as best I could tell, detailed the physiological and psychic processes involved in turning a human into a vampire. I skimmed through the pages, horrified and fascinated. This was the result of his experiments. *Do you have any idea how he got this data, Jason? Do you care?*

Though it was obvious that most Lesser vampires were unstable, I really never knew why.

As is well known, at the point of death, the soul and the sentient consciousness, bundled together in an ephemeral energy cluster, leave the corporeal body. Vampire blood commits the grievous sin of splitting the two asunder, leaving the sentient consciousness in the body while casting aside the soul. In laymen's terms, the differences between Greater and Lesser Generation turnings can be described thusly: The affect of Greater Generation Blood, one of The First, for illustration, is much like a surgeon's scalpel, cleaving cleanly between the soul and the sentient consciousness, leaving both whole and unharmed. By the Fifth Generation, the blood dilution is far too great to cleave so smoothly; the weakened blood acting more like a dull blade, sawing and ultimately tearing the soul and sentient consciousness apart. The damage to both, and most notably the sentient consciousness, is tremendous and leaves us with a creature despised even by its own kind.

The vast majority of the data consisted of mathematical equations, which made a lot more sense than his verbiage.

Reaching the end of the Purcell's report, I found another by an Alec Gagnon, titled *"Ephemeral Power Transformations - 1939."* Like the previous report, it contained several pages of written explanation (in

French) followed by even more pages of equations. Mr. Gagnon frequently cited Cyrus Purcell's research. Judging by the equations, the report was divided into two sections; the first dealt with statistics and the other with vibrations and harmonics.

The shower switched off. *Damn.* I went over the equations, trying to commit something, anything to memory. I put everything back together, closed the drawer and slunk back to the living room.

The wine sloshed like a stormy red ocean as I picked up my glass. I set it down. Trying to appear as casual as possible, I opened the paper, and attempted to read. Something stopped my feet with a thud as I stretched out my legs. Bending down, I saw a laptop computer-sized briefcase. More water noises came from the bathroom as Jason switched on the sink faucet. *Not enough time.*

I sighed, sat on my shaking hands and pretended to be absorbed in the news, where I remained until he emerged. Smelling damp and soapy, dressed in black jeans and a black sweater, Jason walked into the room, a quizzical expression on his face.

"You all right?"

His concern triggered guilt, and the scent of freshly washed man triggered a reaction much lower in my body. "Er, yeah, why?"

"You don't look well."

I forced a smile. "I'm okay. It's just been a long day. I skipped lunch."

"Dinner is nearly ready," he said, still sounding a bit too concerned.

I followed him into the kitchen where I propped myself up on the counter, arms crossed to hide my shaky hands. Obviously much more self-sufficient in the kitchen than me, he proceeded to cook string beans in a way that made them smell appetizing. Taking advantage of his distraction, I ogled the cook. The man wore black well, the color accentuating long legs and a nice butt.

We talked, him dodging anything about his work, me avoiding much about my personal life. As we ate dinner, I pondered his interest in Cyrus's research.

Breas had a point. I was a terrible judge of human character. But I was certain of one thing: despite being affiliated with the same organization, the man who sat before me was the antithesis of Cyrus Purcell.

Chapter Twenty-Two

*A*fter dinner, we ended up in the kitchen, leaning on opposite counters, facing each other like backwards bookends. As far as I could tell, Jason wore a real watch, as opposed to a vampire detector. *Reasonable enough since vampires can't drop by without an invite.* I smiled at the irony. My human bloodlines exempt me from the invite clause.

"What?" he asked, referring to the smile.

"Nothing." I set my empty wine glass down and fiddled with the long sleeves on my top.

With great effort, I met his eyes. His were mostly green, with just enough golden brown to keep them in the hazel range. He took a step in my direction, reached past me to set his empty beer bottle next to the wine glass.

"You have beautiful eyes," he said, and I realized how close he stood. At this distance, his innate magic hummed, sending little vibrations that generated sympathetic oscillations in my own magic.

"Th-thanks."

Jason put an end to further conversation by covering my mouth with his. Guilty fear erupted in my stomach; a war broke out between my conscience and key parts of my body. *This is wrong*, my brain warned. *A quick kiss won't trigger the Thrall charm*, argued parts of me that hadn't been used in decades.

He tasted like beer, which reminded me of Breas, and he also kissed a lot like Breas. *It's like kissing a living breathing Breas.* His hand felt warm where it encircled my upper arm, and my knees started feeling less than solid.

I have to stop this, I thought. Except, I couldn't. His heat surrounded me, while the sound of his heart drummed just off beat from my own, the pace of both our heartbeats quickening.

Jason worked a hand under my shirt and rubbed my back. I shivered, aware of the strong possibility that I might have sex with this human. The notion of naked skin on skin time with Jason was delightful. Except, Jason struck me as a "sex with the lights on" kind of guy. One look at the tattoo on my left hip, the mark of my Wolfe rank, and my cover would be blown.

Innate magic passed from his hand and into the sensitive skin on the small of my back. I let out a little whimper and arched my back, pressing against him. Everywhere our bare skin touched, heat and wonderful electric magic sank into my skin. I lifted one leg and started to slip my thigh up his leg.

On cue, the phone rang. Jason leaned in, intensified the kiss and did something with his tongue that made most of my muscles and a few bones turn to jelly. *Shit.* After the second ring, he paused, his mouth still touching mine, and after the third, he pulled back and sighed. The answering machine clicked on and following Jason's perfunctory message, Kyle voice barked, "Lake. You there? You better be. This is important. Answer the damn phone."

"You really should…." I was horrified by my weakness. *What have I done?*

Leaning in and brushing his lips over mine, he squeezed my arm and then stepped back to pick up the phone. My hearing focused on the phone; my legs wobbled.

"I'm here. What?"

"You're breakin' my heart, Lake. You never called." When Jason didn't respond, Kyle asked, "Did you go through the stuff Alex sent you, yet?"

Jason paused, his eyes, irritated but otherwise sane, fixed on a spot on the floor. "Yes," he replied.

"And?"

A muscle twitched in Jason's jaw and I got the hint. "I should probably be going." I started toward the kitchen door.

He held his hand up to indicate, "Wait, a second," accompanied by a pleading expression, so I said, "Okay. I'll go read the...paper." The laptop sprung to mind. Even as I walked into the living room, I kept my hearing focused on Jason and the phone.

"You got company?" came Kyle's voice as Jason headed into his bedroom.

"Yes."

"Eva's jailbait friend? Did I catch you mid-fuck?" Jason didn't bother to respond.

Asshole I thought, picturing Talis's bleeding face.

The sound of bedsprings creaking indicated Jason now sat where I'd been just an hour ago. He opened the drawer and pulled out the paperwork.

"According to Cyrus Purcell," Jason began quietly, "when a human is turned into a vampire, his soul is split from his sentient consciousness. The effect is much like splitting the atom. Tremendous energy—magical energy—is released." Jason shuffled the papers. "When the sire is a Greater Generation vampire, the process is quick and does little damage. The released energy is powerful but very short in duration. Lesser Generation blood, on the other hand, tears the soul and consciousness apart, creating long duration chaotic ethereal energy."

Jason stopped speaking and Kyle took a second to digest the information. "Chaotic? Like the magic that killed that demon—Icarus?"

"Chaotic magic is largely theoretical. Few people, human or otherwise, have ever bothered to study, much less use it."

"But it's powerful, isn't it? Barbequed that demon and his staff."

"Chaotic magic and its precursor, chaotic ethereal energy, are powerful and unstable. The instability gives it higher potential energy, but it also makes it extremely difficult to control," Jason replied.

I pondered Jason's words and tried to picture Mr. Gagnon's equations.

"According to Alec Gagnon, the only way to utilize chaotic magic would be to store chaotic ethereal energy and then release its potential energy as chaotic magic." I heard Jason's sigh when Kyle didn't get it. "I believe someone is storing the potential energy from Lesser Generation vampire conversions."

"Yeah? Who?" Kyle paused, thoughts rumbling around his tiny brain. "That vampire? Dorian?"

"Doubtful." Jason sounded bored. "I believe he was just as surprised as I was to find the remnants of chaotic magic."

"So maybe he's the one doin' the turnings."

"Possible. Though his use of Brethren magic would probably negate that. The Brethren aren't likely to welcome a Lesser Generation vampire into their ranks, even a stable one."

"So he is Brethren," said Kyle.

"As you would say, 'He's a vampire, they lie.'" Jason continued, "Chances are, he was there for the same reason we were. To get information."

Kyle cursed. "He's the Wolfe." I almost laughed out loud.

"Yes."

I jammed my fist in my mouth, holding back laughter. *Breas the Wolfe. Funny.*

"We still don't know for certain if this is connected to the primary problem," Jason said.

Huh? There's a primary *problem?*

"It's possible, though." With unsettling insight, Kyle added, "I don't think we are getting the full story from Headquarters, Lake."

"No. I don't think we are…." Jason paged through the documents. "I need to think about this some more."

"'Think,' huh?" Kyle snorted. "Tell me that isn't what you plan on doing with Jailbait. What you need is a game of naughty professor and cute co-ed. You need to get laid."

"Kyle." Jason's voice was calm. "Regan and my relationship with her is not a topic of discussion. Ever."

Matching Jason's tone, Kyle responded, "I wouldn't get too sentimental, sorcerer. Remember who and what you are."

Jason muttered, "Goodbye," and hung up. He remained in his bedroom for a couple of minutes, and I felt uneasy for more reasons than I could count. In a pitiful attempt at relaxed, I leaned back into the couch and stuck my feet on the coffee table. *Manners? Who needs 'em?*

After hanging the phone in its charger, he sat next to me on the couch. I felt his indecision—unusual, because I can't read humans unless they are practically bleeding emotions—as he reached out and took one of my hands in his. He fanned my fingers out, and I remembered Breas's comment about elf blood in the Holders' sorcerer bloodline. Like mine, Jason's fingers were slim, the bones of his fingertips elongated. Jason's elven heritage must have conferred immunity to the Thrall Charm. Relief ran through me like adrenaline.

The primary problem. What or who was the primary problem? The Holders were hiding stuff from their own operatives. *Why?*

Jason let go of my hand, dropping his arm over my shoulders. I shifted position on the couch, snuggling against his chest, my mind whirling like helicopter blades. Cyrus Purcell's research. Who would have access to that research? A million "what ifs" coalesced into one single possibility with a few variations. I glanced at the laptop, but it didn't seem quite so interesting.

Jason's arm was warm. Every place his body touched mine radiated heat. I tilted my head so my cheek pressed over his heart and his blood flow roared in my ears. I turned down my hearing and closed my eyes, listening to the sound of his heartbeat.

And I woke up when Jason tried to move his arm. "Sorry. My arm fell asleep," he said.

Like any good soldier, when presented with the opportunity, I sleep. Blowing my bangs out of my face, I yawned. "Me, too. Sorry." I sat up and stretched. "I better get home."

On wobbly legs, another yawn peeling out of my mouth, I moved over to the door. Jason scooped up his keys and followed me. My Korean P.O.S. glowed dully under the streetlights and Jason scrawled "Wash Me" just above the fender.

"Cute. You've damaged its protective armor, broken all the spells and suchlike."

He studied the dirt on his fingers. "Really, and this would be fairy dust?" He smiled his crooked smile.

Irony, much? "Yeah. Now it can't fly." I examined his fingers. "Do you have any idea how much fairy dust costs? You've got a fortune all over your hand."

Humor twinkled in his eyes and he stroked his fingers across my cheek. "Back to its rightful owner then."

"Oh, goody." I smiled wryly. "I can fly." Jason leaned down, tilting my face to his and we kissed. The rubbery knee thing happened, and I shifted back against my car for support and he leaned with me. His magic pushed through my skin and tangled with mine. When we came up for air several minutes later, I had a fistful of his sweater and was wrapped up in his arms. *If I don't get out of here, we'll end up doing it in the car.*

"Speaking of magic…." I tried to smooth the crumpled sweater and got sidetracked by the underlying muscle. *Yum.* "Black magic. If your teenage fan club saw that, they'll be crafting a Regan voodoo doll and sticking it full of pins." I winced. "See, there they go."

"And here I've gone and destroyed your magical protection," he said, eyeing his handiwork on my car's fender. I pulled out my keys, and he took the hint and moved a step backwards.

"Ah well. Car is made mostly of iron. Should be safe from all kinds of magic." I watched his handsome face, which had an interesting expression. Realizing I was pushing the magic discussion too far, I added, "You know? Like in fairy tales? Iron repels magic?" He gave a tiny nod.

"I better get home and check on Bill."

"Bill? Your flatmate?" Jason asked, with a distinct hint of jealously.

I grinned. "Bill, my horse. You know? Goes 'neigh,' eats hay, converts it to fertilizer?" *I don't have a flatmate. I do, however, have a soulless squatter.* I paused, about to get in my car, and then leaned on the open door. "Thanks, again." What I could only assume was indecision crossed his face and I remembered Kyle's earlier comment.

"The Irish band I play with is performing Sunday afternoon at the Owl and Thistle. Two o'clock. Drop by, if you'd like." I kept my tone neutral.

Indecision temporarily gone, he stepped forward and kissed me over the car door. "Bye, Regan."

Breas wasn't in when I got home. Good thing, too. The vampire might have tried to take advantage of my runaway libido. Given my current state, I might have let him.

Chapter Twenty-Three

My hand swatted at nothing, and the buzzing sound continued. *It's the middle of winter, how can there be a mosquito in the house?*

I flailed again, waking myself up.

Lex's leaf pin, sitting too close on my dresser, hissed like an exotic cockroach. Without moving any more muscles than necessary, I reached out, and closed my hand over the cloisonné green surface.

"Sh'Tah," I mumbled, my hand released the pin and slumped off the side of the bed.

The bed shook. "Hey," Lex said.

"Hey?" I said into the pillow. "It's the ass crack of dawn. What are you doing here?"

"Humph. Well, you didn't have to answer," she responded, still cheerful.

"Right." I closed my eyes, extending my senses toward the guest bedroom. "Breas is home. Go say 'Hi.'"

"Really?" The bed shuddered and she bounced out of my room.

The sounds of exasperated vampire improved my mood. Pulling on clothes I found on the floor, I headed outside to feed Bill.

I returned to find Lex perched on a stool at the kitchen counter, alternately spooning cookie dough onto a baking sheet and into her mouth. *Pete Tanaka*, I thought, noting her high-collared shirt.

"Breakfast. Yummy." I pulled up a chair and dug a blob out of the pre-made tube of dough. "You're up early."

"It is nearly mid-afternoon back home."

I shrugged. Keeping track of time differences on Earth plane is hard enough.

"How was your date?" she asked.

I picked a chocolate chip out of the dough. "All right, I guess." I really didn't have much basis for comparison. "Nice?"

Lex's amber eyes glowed mischievously. "Nice, meaning mind-altering sex or nice...polite, boring, handshake at the door?"

"Somewhere in between."

"Really? Kissing? Heavy groping?"

"Yeah. Pretty much."

"You should just sleep with him," she suggested. "Break all the tension. Lose the mystique."

"It didn't work with Breas. Why would it work—?" I stuffed more dough in my mouth.

"Wait a minute. You kissed. So why isn't he," she pointed toward the door, cheeks puffed up like a cookie dough loving squirrel, "at your doorstep, hopelessly obsessed?"

Caught by a sudden memory of Cyrus, I winced. "Breas says Holder sorcerers have a tad bit of elf in their bloodline. He's probably immune."

"Maybe he was already hopelessly in love with you."

"Not likely. He's emotionally unavailable or something. A girl waiting at home, maybe."

The swooshing of the shower made me frown. "You woke the beast."

"You told me to," Lex replied. "He was quite unpleasant, by the way."

"So, Lex," I said, changing the subject, "Tell me about chaotic magic."

Her canted eyes widened and she raised her hands, thumbs hooked together, palms outward, doing the fairy equivalent of warding off the evil eye. "I'll tell you nothing. It's nothing you should be—"

"Lex. It's me. Un-magical me. I just want to know more about it."

A long string of exquisite sounding Fairy words dripped from her mouth.

"Yeesh! You kiss your mother with that mouth?" The first things—sometimes the only things—anyone learns in any language are curse words. I picked up the remaining dough in the plastic tube. "Talk to me, fairy, or the cookie dough gets it."

"Now you are just being cruel."

"It's genetic." I shifted my eyes a little in the yellow direction.

"Okay, okay. Just don't hurt the cookie dough."

The sun through the window started to sting where it hit my back so I thought my eyes back to green and handed her the dough. She spooned another heap of dough onto the baking sheet, considering her words.

"All magical creatures...." She gestured to herself and me.

"Not me."

"I cannot explain this to someone who is so magically constipated."

I crossed my eyes. "Ew! And sorry, no more commentary."

After a scolding frown, the effect negated by the cookie dough stuck to her mouth, she continued, "All magical creatures carry the stuff"—she held up the cookie dough—"the raw ingredients of magic in their blood."

I wrestled down a quip and nodded.

"To cast a spell, we"—she arched her eyebrows, challenging me to disagree—"take that stuff...energy, and convert it to true magic. So in essence the strength of a spell is defined by the innate magical strength of the caster. Right?"

"Yeah?" I agreed to be agreeable. Magic class was where I perfected sleeping with my eyes open.

"Chaotic magic"—she made the warding sign again—"doesn't rely on a user's innate magical ability or strength. The 'raw stuff' is chaotic energy."

I took a minute to combine Lex's explanation with what I had learned at Jason's apartment.

Spell casting consists of two phases: preparation and release. The "stuff" that innate magic users possess bears a closer resemblance to a stiff spring, than cookie dough. Through words or physical motions, sorcerers compress or stretch the magical energy in their blood. This creates a type of potential energy, which is then released in the form of a spell. Chaotic magical energy, however, starts off brimming with springy potential energy, no preprocessing required.

"So someone with little or no innate magic could cast some mighty gnarly spells," I thought aloud. "Because of the built-in potential energy, it is naturally more powerful."

The fairy's hands traced out the warding sign. "But it is dangerous.

And unpredictable."

"It's about outcomes, right?" I asked, thinking about Alec Gagnon's equations. Seeing the blank expression on her face and remembering that English wasn't her first language, I elaborated. "If regular magic were a wagon, sitting at the top edge of an incline, it would only have two possible actions. Stay in one place or with a little push, roll down the hill at a predictable speed. But with chaotic magic, the wagon suddenly has an unlimited amount of possible actions. Some possibilities don't even require a push, right? It could roll down the hill, fly, explode, anything, right?"

Lex's jaw dropped. "How do you know all that?"

"Cyrus Purcell," I answered, the name bitter on my tongue, "and a colleague of his. Reports. Jason has their reports in his possession."

"Really? Then the Holders *have* been studying chaotic magic," she said, speculation glowing in her amber eyes.

"Probably. Since few humans, even the innate sorcerers, are very powerful, it would be an advantage."

"But at what cost?" Lex leaned toward me. "Regan. Why are you asking about—?"

"Chaotic magic," I finished for her and told her all I knew so far.

She lifted her pretty little face, her expression absolutely grave. "Regan. Whoever, whatever is using this magic must be stopped."

I blinked, taken aback by her humorless demeanor.

"Seriously, Morrigan." *Uh-oh.* "That word, 'outcomes.' Yes. There is rarely *just* one outcome when a chaotic spell is cast." She paused, scrambling. "Cast a spell to unlock a door and the door unlocks and a dam bursts fifty miles away. Understand?"

"Whoa," I said in my best Keanu Reeves voice, "Pete Tanaka's interPlanar trade routes. A possible bonus outcome of a powerful chaotic spell, right?" *Or worse still, a major reorganization of Earth's geography.* She nodded and then we took the next few minutes to eat the rest of the cookie dough, including the future cookies on the sheet.

Breas ambled into the living room, fresh from the shower.

"I smell wet vampire," I said. Not unpleasant, except it made me think of a certain damp human. *Sigh.*

Thinking for a beat, I turned to study my houseguest, who was channel surfing in my comfortable recliner. I walked over and sat on the chair's arm. "So does it hurt?" I asked. He ignored me. "Having your soul cut away? Does it hurt?"

"At what point have I ever indicated that this was an acceptable topic?"

"Never. So?"

"I don't remember. Go pester Cypher or Argus—"

"I'd rather annoy you. You heard what I told Lex, no? About Purcell's report?"

"Yeah. I'm real proud of you, reading something without pictures."

"Not even any illustrations or charts. Bleh." I swiped the remote from him. "A Lesser vampire turning generates chaotic energy. Did you know this?"

"No." He smirked and pushed a mind warping mix of affection and loathing at me, trying to muddle my senses.

"Liar. So, why does vampire blood only *turn* somebody who's on the verge of death?" Unless a person has gone through Familiar Rites, vampire blood can make a healthy someone sick enough to wish they were dead.

"Purcell must've addressed that issue in his research."

"Probably. I didn't get very far in the report."

"Little something called the 'spark of life.' Binds everything together in the physical body. Unless it's really weak, the spark binds everything together like super glue."

"Everything meaning soul and sentient consciousness?" I asked and he nodded. "So, where were you last night?"

"Hmmm? Night? Vampire? Eating people?" he replied.

I marched into the spare bedroom. After digging around in his luggage, I walked over to the closet. I opened the door and cursed.

"Dammit, Breas." I stomped back into the living room. "You can't be selling forged artwork out of my house."

"Who says it's forged?"

"I learned from the master." Before venturing into the land of honest-day's work, I had tried my hand at Breas's less-than-legal means of generating income.

"You're so dull since you went legit," he said.

"Uh-huh. Whatever. Talis, everybody's favorite purveyor of IQ-dropping fun, would like a word with you. You dealin' drugs, now?"

"I deal in difficult to procure items. Drugs are anything but," he replied, insulted.

"Whatever. Get out of my chair." He ignored me. "Move!" I took a deep lung filling breath. "Please." I shoved the word out.

He grinned and moved to the couch, full of passive-aggressive smugness.

"You two are so in love," Lex said.

"Shaddup," Breas and I chimed in unison.

♪

ALBUQUERQUE, SATURDAY NIGHT

"Doesn't seem you've made much progress, Jason."

Jason Lake piloted his SUV south along University Avenue, just one of a multitude of drivers driven to distraction by a cell phone. None, except Jason, however, had the misfortune to be speaking with Daniel Lake.

"Perhaps," Jason said, "if I had more information—"

"You've been given all you need," replied his father.

"Yes, but—"

"How difficult can it be to find someone in a city the size of Albuquerque? It isn't London, after all."

Jason clenched his jaw and throttled the steering wheel. "The Albuquerque metropolitan area has a population approaching eight hundred thousand."

Daniel Lake ignored the information. "What is your next plan of attack?"

I'm going to spend today's per diem at a nudie bar, he thought, as his SUV swept past a local strip club. "I'm going to speak with the kobold, BelTalis'aresh, again."

"And what do you hope to accomplish? According to Kyle—"

"Yes, I know." *You're spying on me, Dad. Except you don't even have the decency to be sneaky about it.* "Perhaps Kyle's previous persuasion will make the kobold more cooperative this time around."

Brake lights flashed red in front of his vehicle, mirroring the stoplight, and he stopped at the intersection of University and Central.

The sky was rapidly turning blue-black as the sun dropped below the western horizon.

"Uncivilized creature," Daniel said. "I suspect it only understands violence. Do whatever is most expedient." He laughed, a dry arrogant sound. "Give the Clean-up crews something to do."

"You're not suggesting I kill—"

"Of course not," replied Daniel, with mirthful sarcasm. "How's your little American friend?"

"Who?"

"Regan. Irish derivation, isn't she?" Daniel's voice carried just a little less disdain than it had when discussing the kobold. "Kyle seems to think she's an innate."

Jason shivered. The car behind Jason's honked, he waved an apology and pressed the gas pedal. Once he had finished his turn onto westbound Central, he replied, "Apparently the kobold *did* score a few blows to Kyle's head."

"So it isn't true, then? She's not an innate?"

"Of course not." Jason was surprised at the comfort of the lie. Even if Regan were successfully recruited, the Holders wouldn't sanction his relationship with her. The Holders would want to spread their magical bloodlines as far as they could and Regan would be paired with someone of limited or no innate power. Affairs went hand-in-hand with arranged marriages in the Holders, but Jason had no intention of sharing her with anyone.

"A pity. If the likes of Kyle could sense her power, she'd be powerful, indeed."

"Yes. A pity," replied Jason.

Just before he hung up, Daniel said, "Make me proud. Make Juliet proud."

The end of Jason's conversation with his father didn't dispel the chill. Right hand still gripping the cell phone, he fumbled with the dial on the fan control until heat rushed from the vents in a wild exhalation.

He thumbed the phone's rubbery buttons until Regan's phone number appeared on the display, and he debated the merits of calling her.

Kyle knew she was an innate. How long would his lie hold? How long before Daniel sent agents to confirm Kyle's assertion?

Even if he were not driven by a strange possessive need for her, he knew recruitment would not be easy for Regan. Were she to resist—and Jason had no doubt she would—the Holders would respond with a harsh determination, if necessary using a *memory trim* to clear away inconvenient parts of her personality.

Regan was better off without the magic and machinations of the Holders. How could he protect her, ensure that the Holders didn't disrupt her life?

He had a life once. Then Juliet went and got herself killed.

Juliet. What exactly would make her proud? They had been close as children but in the last years before her death—

The back of a red minivan with a bumper sticker that proclaimed, "My child is a superstar at Oso Azul Elementary," was hurtling at him. His tires shrieked and the anti-lock braking shivered through the brake pedal.

His SUV stopped inches from the van's bumper. A little boy's face, presumably the superstar, looked out the back window and stuck out a tongue.

Jason frowned at the phone and tossed it on the passenger seat.

Jason's earlier encounter with BelTalis'aresh had been his first with any of the Fey. The elves loathed the Holders and preferred to let the Grey Brethren run interference and broker any deals between the humans. Fairies, who generally followed the elves' lead on political matters, did likewise. All Jason knew about kobolds was that they were a dark-skinned variety of elf, much despised by the fairer elves. There was an insinuation that kobolds were criminal by nature, which seemed to be borne out by BelTalis'aresh's neighborhood and current vocation.

Drug dealer. Con-artist. Thief. The kobold's profession had no bearing on what Jason had to do this evening.

Jason pulled into the apartment complex's parking lot, very much aware of the predatory stares of a group of young men who clustered around a car, one building over from the kobold's. Seeing sufficient evidence that the creature was home—blue television light leaked from crooked window blinds—Jason got out of the vehicle. He augmented the car alarm with a repulse spell. More than passing contact with the vehicle would produce nauseating vertigo.

Assuming the doorbell was still broken, he knocked. After a minute, he knocked again, this time on the window, knuckles rapping against glass.

A few seconds later, a lock clicked and the kobold peered through a small crack between the door and its frame.

"Oh. It's you," BelTalis'aresh said.

"Could I speak with you?" Jason asked, glancing at the group of dangerous looking youth. "Inside?"

"I'm kind of busy. Busy healing from the last time you spoke with me."

Jason grimaced, embarrassed. "Yes. I know." He held his hands up. "I just want to talk. Like civilized...people."

The door opened enough to show the kobold's leery expression. "Civilized people. That would rule me out, right?"

Realizing the kobold had taken some sort of insult from his words, Jason clarified, "No. Actually, it would rule Kyle out—"

"Come in," the kobold interrupted. He sighed and stepped aside.

Jason entered the apartment and squinted in the dim light. Behind him, BelTalis'aresh closed the door.

"You're not doing much talking." The kobold moved toward the couch. He paused in front of the television, pale eyes watching Jason with suspicion.

The apartment was as Jason remembered it, shabby but somehow tidy. The only real furniture was a small mahogany bookshelf in the far corner.

There was nothing outwardly criminal about BelTalis'aresh. If anything, he seemed harmless, wrung-out and tired. Jason had the impression of an old soul trapped in a young and misused body.

This poor creature's blood? Would that make you proud, Juliet? It would be easy enough. What Kyle could do with fists, Jason could with magic.

"Where's your cat? Eithne, wasn't it?" Jason asked, for lack of anything else to say.

"She's out hunting."

Jason cleared his throat. "Eithne. It means 'little fire,' does it not?"

The kobold nodded and dropped his gaze from Jason. "You want something to drink. Pop? Water?" he asked.

Faded blue jeans and an orange sweatshirt with the words "University of Texas at El Paso" hung loose on the kobold's thin frame. Jason was relieved to note the gash on his face had nearly healed, and he showed no signs of pain from what had likely been broken ribs.

"No," Jason said. "Nothing, thanks."

"I need…" the kobold darted a look at Jason and said, "some water." He turned and walked into the small kitchen, pulled a plastic glass from the cabinet and filled it with tap water.

When BelTalis'aresh returned, Jason asked, "How did you come to have a cat?" The kobold gave him an amused look. "You don't strike me as a cat person," Jason explained.

The kobold's smile revealed canines reminiscent of a vampire's. "I'm not," he answered. "You come here to talk about my cat? You quit the Holders? Picked up employment with the Humane Society?"

Jason returned the smile. "No." His smile faded. "I came to apologize. For Kyle."

After a loud slurp of water, the kobold asked, "In exchange for what?"

"I'm sorry, what?" Jason asked, perplexed.

"You apologize in exchange for...information?"

Oh. The Fey believed no good deed went unpunished, nothing was free.

"Nothing. Really. I know Kyle behaved...look, he's an ass. A bully." The kobold watched intently. Jason met his cold-eyed stare. "I know you didn't provoke him, as he claimed. I'm sorry, BelTalis'aresh. Really."

The only response the kobold gave was a slow blink and another sip of water. Jason kept his gaze level, eyes on the kobold, although he felt altogether uncomfortable. When it became too difficult to maintain eye contact, he dropped his stare to the cup in the kobold's hand. Brown fingers with a distinctive elongation of the distal phalanges— fingertips—partially obscured a convenience store logo printed on the cup's white surface.

Jason glanced at his own hands. Though not as pronounced, his fingertips showed the same elongation, the mark of elven blood. If all races of Fey could be traced to a common ancestor, would that make BelTalis'aresh a distant cousin, several million years removed?

At long last, the kobold spoke. "Talis."

"Excuse me?"

"Only my parents call me BelTalis'aresh. Usually, I'm just Talis."

Jason nodded. Talis said nothing, still watching Jason with mild suspicion. Casting about for anything to say, Jason again noticed the bookshelf.

"Are these"—Jason crouched before the shelves and pulled a volume from the shelf—"Edgar Rice Burroughs?"

Looking up he caught the bright gleam of pride in Talis's eyes. "First editions," Talis said, showing his odd dentistry again.

"Brilliant." Jason laughed. "T*he Warlord of Mars*. I was about twelve when I read the Mars series." He tapped the book. "This was my favorite."

Talis nodded.

As Jason flipped open the front cover, a sheet of paper fell out.

"Uh, don't lose that, please," said Talis.

"Of course not." Jason picked up the paper and replaced it in the book. Someone, perhaps to avoid damaging the volume, had written an inscription on the paper.

Hey, Tal!

Look what my Dad found in a Boise used bookstore. Boise! My Dad! Go figure.

Love Always, R.

Though nearly illegible, the script was ordinary human; little circles dotting the "i's" suggested a female writer. Interesting but not illogical. A thousand years ago, the Fey Dominion had declared sexual congress with humans unlawful. The prohibition probably did little more than make such couplings spicier. Talis had Fey good looks and no doubt human as well as Fey admirers. Jason replaced the book and scanned the rest of the titles.

"I have a friend," Talis said. Hearing the cautious tone in the kobold's voice, Jason looked up at him. Talis cleared his throat and continued, "My friend is expected to deal with the business with the..." his thin face tightened in pain, and he spat out, "chaotic magic user."

Jason kept his face neutral, feeling like a naturalist who had just happened upon a rare and extremely shy animal. He gave Talis an encouraging nod.

"My friend is over her, I mean, *his* head. And if I knew something,

something that would help you, I would tell you. If only to protect my friend." The kobold looked genuinely stricken. "But, I don't. I think you know more about it than anybody else. Right?"

"Yes," replied Jason. "And that doesn't amount to much." Thinking he had seen a flicker of hope in Talis's bloodshot eyes, he asked, "Your friend is a Fey, then?"

Talis ignored the question, instead asking, "You know it was the Sh'ree who cleaned up the mess on the Sharet plane, don't you?"

"I know of a rumor that the Sh'ree had the means to control a chaotic spell," Jason answered. The mess Talis referred to was the near destruction of the Sharet plane by chaotic magic.

"No rumor. Truth." Talis climbed over the back of his couch, sat, and set the cup on the coffee table.

"How?" asked Jason.

Talis rubbed slim fingers over his eyes. "Harmonic magic." He leaned his elbows on bony knees and stared at the television.

"Bloody marvelous. Power that only manifests in Sh'ree demons. And the Sh'ree aren't exactly rushing to our aide." Jason shook his head. "Not that the stiff-necked Holder leadership would accept their assistance, anyway."

Talis stared at his hands, which had developed a pronounced shake, and said nothing.

"I wonder," Jason mused aloud, "if a tempus mage would be of any help?" Talis cocked an eyebrow high and looked at Jason. Jason kept talking, grateful for someone with half a brain to discuss the matter with—even a drug-addicted kobold trumped Kyle's mental prowess. "The magic wielded by tempus mages, cosmos magic, involves manipulation of probability curves, does it not? You wouldn't happen to know an inexpensive tempus mage, would you?"

Talis flashed his fangs. "Inexpensive tempus mage. That's an, uh, oxymoron." He pushed hair off his face in a manner that reminded Jason disturbingly of Regan. "Yeah. I know a mage. He's a...jerk. Besides, a chaotic spell alters probability curves in an infinity of unpredictable ways. The addition of a cosmos spell further alters probability curves, making things more unstable."

Talis blinked blue eyes. "Did I say that?"

Jason could only nod.

"Sometimes...I remember things."

Hardly an uncivilized creature, Jason thought. "You attended the Sh'ree College of the Arcane?"

"Graduated." Talis gave Jason a look of abject misery. "And you'd better go. I need a hit. Watching me shoot up. It's a dreary spectator sport."

All the human addicts Jason had ever known were self-absorbed and impossible to pity. In Talis's case, he wondered what drove an apparently intelligent creature to such self-destructive behavior.

Jason pulled a business card out of his pocket, walked over to Talis and set the card on the coffee table. "Is this why you didn't squash Kyle like a cockroach? This habit?"

Talis shivered. "No." His fingers, graceful even with drug-craving induced tremors, scooped up the card and vanished it. "Violence," he said, meeting Jason's eyes, "is not the way of my people."

Jason's eyebrows lifted. "Really? But the elves say—?"

"Thirty thousand years ago, the elves attacked the prosperous fishing village of Cartref y Môr, starting a fifty year campaign to rid the Fey plane of all my people. Except those who didn't resist. Passivity saved us."

Jason was astonished. Of all the adjectives ever applied to kobolds, "peaceful" was one he had never heard.

"You didn't know?" Talis asked.

"I didn't attend Holder schools. The gaps in my knowledge of non-Earth plane history rival the Grand Canyon," Jason admitted.

Talis shrugged. "Funny, that. Kyle knew. Rubbed my face in it, literally."

"Kyle's an asshole," Jason muttered. He turned for the door. "Thanks...Talis."

His thoughts dense from Talis's revelations, Jason forgot the repulse spell until his fingers brushed the vehicle's door handle. *Stupid.* He removed the spell from the SUV and cast a counter spell over himself. Unfortunately, the queasy magic already in his system would have to run its course.

Though nauseous, Jason managed an ironic smile. He had learned more in ten minutes with Talis, than in a lifetime with Daniel Lake.

At this rate, he thought bitterly, *I'd probably get more information from the vampire, Dorian, than my own people.*

Chapter Twenty-Four

My harmonic magic chose Sunday afternoon to make an unscheduled visit. It wasn't the first time it happened, but as usual, it was a pain in the ass.

I started playing with the Kaylee Dragons soon after moving to Albuquerque, a replacement for a fiddler who had moved to Boston. It worked out so well, they kept me on. The majority of our gigs were at the Owl and Thistle bar, although we did play the occasional folk festival.

The Owl and Thistle was a few blocks from the University on a trendy stretch of Central Avenue. The Sunday afternoon crowd consisted of a mixture of alcoholics getting an early start on drunk and shoppers pausing to let their overheated credit cards cool.

We were running through a group of reels when I got sloppy and let my mind wander, fingers marching mechanically over the fingerboard. The waitress swept by, balancing a round tray full of foamy beer.

Beer. Breas. Breas and I had spent another evening trying to locate the pointy-toothed byproducts of chaotic energy generation. Specifically, any that might be coherent enough to explain who turned them and where. No luck.

Unconsciously, I poured my frustration into improvisation after improvisation, teasing the melody into more exotic modes. The fiddle, warmed up and responsive, vibrated as though it were enjoying itself.

Power rushed through my blood and just before I came to my senses, I decided magic was better than sex. Not that I had much basis for comparison.

The waitress shrieked, dragging me from musical ecstasy. I saw a disaster of monstrous proportions by Breas's estimations: three of the six glasses on the serving tray were cloven vertically down the middle, and beer ran in a sudsy stream onto the floor. The bar filled with collected *Ooh's* and *Ah's*.

Whoops.

Charley, the Kaylee Dragon's guitar player and de facto leader grinned and held his hand up. "The power of great music, eh?" he said, unaware of the truth in his statement.

The best I could manage was a feeble high-five and a sick smile.

Nifty power. Should serve me well if I run into any dangerous dishes.

I spared the poor waitress any more cuts to her paycheck for broken glassware by playing the safest versions of every song thereafter. Our set finally done, I packed up, and beat a hasty retreat via the back door. Too cheap to pay for parking in the vicinity of the bar, I hiked several blocks to the free lot where my car waited.

Along with Jason.

He leaned on my car, arms crossed over his chest, by the fender where he had scrawled "Wash Me." His neck inclined forward in a weary bend, he stared at the black asphalt. I stretched my hearing toward him, taking in the slow rhythm of his heartbeat.

I was about ten feet away before he noticed me. A slow smile spread across his face as he watched me over his sunglasses. He stood as I reached the car.

"Hi," I said, glad my eyes were hidden behind sunglasses. I unlocked the car and put my fiddle in the back seat.

"Hi. Sorry I missed the performance."

I shrugged and got in a surreptitious ogle. He wore blue jeans, hiking boots, and a royal blue sweatshirt that followed the contours of his shoulders and chest.

"Work?" I asked.

He nodded and tilted his head in a doglike fashion. "You've got that odd expression on your face."

"What expression, exactly?"

"Wary, suspicious, as if I'm—"

A damn Holder? The guy whose buddy beat up my best friend?

"Sorry. I guess I got a vibe, Friday night." I rolled my stiff shoulders. "Never mind."

"Vibe?"

Determined to avert any relationship talk, I slumped against my car and asked, "You okay? You seem distracted?"

"Clients. Seems I'm expected to solve their problems without actually being told what the problems are—"

"Sounds like all the clients in my business." I grimaced. "Of course, often, my clients genuinely don't know what the problem is."

"Well, that is a possibility. Although in this case, I think the deceit is intentional."

"Really? Why?"

Familiar indecision swept across his face. "They don't trust me." He reached to my face, pushing back bangs.

"But how can you do your job? Isn't it more dangerous, then?" I bit my lower lip. "Flying blind and suchlike?" I took his hand, lacing my fingers in his. "Why work for someone who doesn't trust you, anyway?"

"Paycheck?" He freed his fingers to press his palm flat to mine and then slid his fingers back between mine. The movement of magical energy, his and my own, was overpowering.

Fighting back the urge to—I don't know—I said, "Chemical engineers are generally the most employable of all engineers."

Continuing to alternately weave and free my fingers, he spoke after a second's hesitation. "My sister Juliet was killed in a car accident six years ago. She was employed in the same—this—line of work." My fingers followed his as he stretched them apart from each other. "I guess you could say, I'm picking up where she left off." His fingertips touched mine and then slid to my wrist, his thumb drawing idle circles on my pulse.

"I'm r-really sorry." I gulped, my brain thrown offline by the information he had just volunteered and the magical touching thing. His other hand pushed my sunglasses up, exposing my eyes and I squinted in the sun. "Bright light, ouch."

That damned wistful expression made an appearance. "You're beautiful, Regan O'Connell." He replaced my sunglasses.

"Shucks. I bet you say that to all the girls." *Wife? Fiancée?*

"Stunning, then?"

"Me?" I blushed like an idiot.

"Humility only makes you more so."

"Really? In that case...no, not me. I'm a troll."

Kissing Jason was like staring into the sun, blinding and almost painful. Breas, like Jason, was an innate magic user—even before being turned—but as with everything else Breas, his arcane energy was contained in steely control. Jason pretty much wore his ability on his sleeve and the effect was staggering.

He slipped an arm around my waist and pulled me away from the car. Away from the car's magical interference, our energies sizzled against each other. He pushed my sunglasses up on my head and did the same with his. Our lips touched and he ran his tongue along my lower lip.

The warm touch of his hand on my back made me jump and press closer to him, my stomach pressed to his groin. *Oh, my.* He was undeniably attracted to me. I slipped my arms around his neck and let myself enjoy the kiss.

Ring! Kyle, with a phenomenal sense of timing, called Jason before weak, weak me did anything too stupid. With a mutual groan, we broke the kiss. I staggered backwards, collapsed against the car and flipped my sunglasses back down.

"Yeah?" Jason joined me in supporting the car, his arm around my shoulders. The grounding affect of both of us touching the car, and all its iron components, helped settle the static in my brain.

"Did you say you'd be ready to run the tracer spell by tomorrow night?" asked Kyle.

"Yes. I only require one more element."

Tracer spell? My eyes swept Jason's face. *You really don't want to do that.*

"You know, I was doing some research and apparently this kind of spell can be dangerous to the caster. Real dangerous," said Kyle.

Jason's arm tightened around my shoulders. "I'm aware of that, yes." *Research, shit. He's lying, Jason. He's been talking to somebody. He's spying on you.* I scratched my arm. *Like me*, I thought with a guilty twinge.

"I don't see that we've been given much of a choice," Jason argued.

"Well, I guess if anybody is gonna find Ward, it'll be you."

I felt Jason's sigh. *Ward?* The sticky gears in my sexually addled brain began to turn.

When he hung up, I said, "You should know, I'm a hacker with all the requisite ethical flexibility. You know? If you need information?"

He pulled me close and pressed his face into my hair. "Thanks, Regan."

On the way home, I got hit by a heavy dose of guilt. What the hell was I doing making out with a Holder, a member of an organization that condoned the beating of a hapless, drug-addled kobold? An organization that killed my best friend.

And worst yet, I was swapping spit with a guy who was probably engaged, or worse, married. The Holders wouldn't let a guy like Jason stay single for long. I ground my teeth together, contemplating the ugly reality that I was becoming "the other woman."

"Woman on the side. It sounds like a way to order a salad. Dressing on the side, please."

Lex batted her eyes. "So?"

"So? So I—" My eyelid started to twitch. "That's it! No more relationship talk." I jerked my chin in the direction of the spare bedroom. "Go wake up Breas."

The fairy glowered. "No. You can't order me around, by the way. I'm the second cousin twice removed of King Oberon."

Loitering and cookie dough eating, royal pain in the—

"Please, Lex, I've got new information."

Lex lifted her chin. "No."

"Come on, Lex, it's Breas," I said. "Remember, 'Mmmm Breas'?"

"He wakes up nasty." Lex's pixie lips pursed. "I thought vampires were supposed to be aware, even when they sleep."

Running my tongue over my blunt teeth, I stared at the bedroom door. "Not Breas. He sleeps like a log and wakes up like a pissy cobra."

"No." The fairy rebuffed any further pleas by marching off to raid my refrigerator.

I walked to the spare bedroom, pausing to admire the nice wooden door I had installed last month. The door swung open without a squeak and I cursed my good carpentry skills. Breas didn't move.

Without any of my customary stealth—I'm naturally sneaky, it's hard to be otherwise—I stomped into the room and stood by the bed. Dressed in a T-shirt and sweatpants, he slept tangled loosely in the sheet and comforter, looking disturbingly human. Except for the not-breathing part.

I plunked my butt on the edge of the bed. Extending my senses gingerly, I felt nothing. *Still asleep.*

I shook his shoulder. His eyes sprang open, venom yellow, and his hand snatched at empty air where my hand had been.

"Hey. I need your help," I said. Instinctively, a dagger visited my left hand.

Closing his eyes, he reached out with exaggerated slowness that circumvented my instincts, slipped his arm around my waist, his grip tightening like a boa. He pulled me down, my back pressed to his chest. "I was having...the best dream." His fangs grazed my neck.

"Really? Me too." I winced at the teeth on my skin. "There was this vampire. And he came to stay at my place, and he paid rent, and didn't leave embarrassing bite marks on my neck." I nudged him with an elbow.

"Hmmm. What a peculiar vampire."

"Indeed." The elbow bumped his ribs a little harder. "Seriously. I need your help."

He loosened his snake hold, his fingers tracing sinuous trails down my arm. "Really? As opposed to trying to kill me?" His hand closed over mine on the dagger's hilt.

"Reflex." I banished the weapon.

His cold hand slipped under my shirt, touching bare belly, and I flinched. I felt his low laugh and he pressed his face against the back of my head. "You smell good."

"Soap. It does a body good." His hand sent a shimmer of warm energy through my skin and I struggled to speak. "W-we really need to talk. I have new information."

"Mmmm...information," he said into my hair, spreading his hand to lie flat on my stomach, a couple of his fingers slipping under my jeans.

This is precisely why I wanted Lex to wake Sleeping Beauty. My eyes came to rest on the thick adobe windowsill; the hint of sunlight thrusting impatient against the heavy shutters.

"Breas, I can't do this."

"S.O.S." He moved his hand away from my skin and rolled over to stare at the ceiling.

"Yeah, same old shit." I mimicked his pose, crossing my arms over my chest. We both studied the ceiling with the intensity of a comic book freak poring over a new Electra episode.

"So, what's this new information?"

Flipping off the bed, I gestured to the living room. When he didn't move, I grabbed his wrist and tugged hard. I pulled him into the living room.

Breas collapsed on the couch and Lex sat next to him, beaming adoration. I set my laptop on the coffee table and told them about the name Ward, which I assumed was the J. Ward from Icarus's records, and Jason's upcoming attempt at a tracer spell.

Slumped into the corner of the couch, Breas yawned and said, "Tracer spell. Dangerous stuff for puny human sorcerers."

"Yeah. I know. So I have to find J. Ward before that happens."

Using a stolen password and ID, I logged onto the Holders' systems. According to Cypher, the Holders had recently stripped a great deal of information completely off their systems, but I queried for J. Ward anyway. The search turned up a big goose egg. I tried the surname Ward, no first name, and got a listing of five people. All were deceased except one—Michael Ward. His current duty station was Oslo, Norway where he worked as a laboratory researcher.

I scanned the listing of dearly departed. *Whoa!* One name caught my eyes. "Jeanine Ward." Recently deceased. There was no photograph available and only a sketchy physical description—blond hair, blue eyes.

Giving Breas a final worshipful look—he was pretending to be asleep—Lex floated to my side. "So when do I get to meet Jason?"

"Not talking about anything relationshippy."

"Is he hideous? Is that why you are being so evasive?"

I jumped up, stomped into my room and re-emerged with an envelope that I handed to Lex. The Holders had assigned Juliet Lake to none other than Kadin Farahani. Brethren surveillance photos include a few of Juliet's meetings with her brother, Jason.

"Jeanine Ward. Supposedly died five years ago. No other details." I swirled the mouse cursor around on the computer screen. "Susan Ward's daughter. She has to be, right?" I turned to Breas who was watching me through slitted eyelids. "By died, I guess they mean was *turned* into a vampire?"

"Or one of the Holders' flock grew a coat of black wool." His yawn revealed harmless human teeth. "I still believe there is a human involved."

"Humans. The root of all evil."

"'Xactly," Breas said, stretching out on the couch.

I smiled at the vampire. "I hate to say this, but I think you're right. Jeanine is still alive. That is, assuming Susan Ward's stolen cross is a Bane. Jeanine Ward is using it to control vampires. Or at least, one vampire. She must have captured a Lesser and is using it to make other Lessers."

"Wow," exclaimed Lex, finding the photos, "Jason is cute." Breas spared the fairy a baleful stare and closed his eyes.

I don't like using my home computer for much hacking so I logged off and powered down.

"Even when we figure out where she is, we still have the problem of dealing with a chaotic magic user," I said. Lex's hands flew as she made the warding sign. "I need another go at the reports—Alec Gagnon's, in particular."

"The ones Jason has?" Lex asked, her tone a tad too bright.

"Yeah."

"After you have sex, and he's sleeping soundly, you can steal the papers," the fairy suggested. Breas's eyelids twitched.

"Lexxxx!"

"You are soooo repressed." She scooped up a photo—Jason sitting in a café with his sister—and shoved it in my face. "You really don't want to?"

"That's not the point."

"Do you want *me* to?"

"No," I replied, and saw the corner of Breas's mouth lift. "I mean...no." I considered my options. "We could break into Jason's apartment," I suggested, my focus on Breas. "Tonight, maybe?"

He didn't respond and a quick check revealed he was falling asleep.

I got up to stand next to him. "Hey! You can't sleep now."

"How'd you ever get a doctorate? Cliff Notes? Vampire. Daylight." He threw his arm over his face.

I pulled his arm aside and glared down at him. "My plants need light. I'm opening all the damn shades."

"Yeah. Sure," he said, consciousness already fading. I scowled at him until the nice angry feelings degraded into infuriating fondness.

Lex laughed. "You've got it so hard, Regan. Two gorgeous men—"

"Shaddup, Lex."

Chapter Twenty-Five

Scientific studies have proven that the delicious pain induced by eating green or red chile releases endorphins, not unlike the reaction derived from many narcotics.

Monday morning was as good an excuse as any for using my favorite legal drug.

A hot cloud of spicy steam gushed out as I peeled open the take-away dish. I was two bites into taste bud heaven when Terry Moulder poked her head into my cubicle.

"Morning!" she said. I shrank my senses away from her; her mixture of hairspray and perfume was forming compounds that should have been banned by the EPA. "Have you seen Sean?"

"Not yet, why?"

She shrugged. "Just wondering. I stopped by his cubicle, but he's not in yet, so—"

"Sean called in sick," Joan's familiar monotone cut in as she materialized in my doorway.

"Really?" According to Barry's latest imperial edict, when calling in sick, we were required to make voice contact with a supervisor, climbing up the chain of command, if necessary. The links, in this case, would be Barry or me.

"He said you were on the phone," Joan explained, answering my unspoken question.

"Okay, thanks. I'll let Eva know." I'm the weakest link in the chain of command.

Sparing a glance at Joan, who hovered in my doorway like a brooding gargoyle, Terry asked, "How about happy hour? Tomorrow evening? Sean, too, if he's feeling better."

"Thanks, but I've got a client meeting," I lied.

"I'm meeting old friends," Joan added with surprising quickness.

"Maybe later in the week," I said, hoping to diffuse any hurt feelings. "Or maybe, you could go with just Sean?"

At my leer, Terry sighed. "I'm married, Regan."

Right, I thought, shrugging an apology. Terry spent so much time studying Sean's ass, she could write a doctoral dissertation on the subject. At that moment Barry Stanton shuffled by, sparing us all a cursory look, lost in managerial obsessions.

Terry rolled her eyes and headed back to her cubicle. Joan remained.

"The latest upgrade is on Bester," she said, referring to the company share drive.

Enveloped in a nice, warm, green chile buzz, I nodded. "Thanks."

Probably spraining a host of facial muscles, Joan's face morphed to amiable. "Are you still dating Jason?"

I leaned back in my chair. All this interest in my love life. *I should start a newsletter.* "Yeah. I guess. Does making out in a parking lot count?"

Instead of answering, Joan said, "Kyle's using Eva for sex."

"Yeah," I agreed, wondering how Eva couldn't see the truth. It was obvious even to Joan. "Well, he's an asshole. Just ask Jason."

"So you trust him?" asked Joan.

I blinked, my mental equilibrium tilting like an adolescent girl in her first high heels. "Who? Jason?" Joan nodded.

While mulling the question over, I studied the interior of my cubicle. The origami cranes sat in a row on the top edge of the computer monitor, apparently having flown to higher ground. The green army men, still sitting on the desk, beamed smug triumph.

I met her eyes. "Yeah. I trust Jason. Fortunately, he doesn't take after his partner."

She nodded, the forced pleasant expression returning to her face. "Good luck," she muttered and wandered away.

"Thanks," I said after her, returning to my breakfast.

The last steaming forkful was about to reach my mouth when the idea popped in my head.

What was it Angry had said to Talis? *"Listen to me, boyo. I'm telling you, we could make a fortune. The addictive power of this stuff far exceeds Elf Dust. Demons, Fey, we could get them all addicted and charge a king's ransom...."*

Chile. I could end the demon war with chile.

Chapter Twenty-Six

*B*reas was a bored, bored creature of the night. Otherwise, he never would have agreed to accompany me that evening as I ran errands. Unfortunately, trips to the grocery store and the hardware store weren't a cure for vampire ennui.

I pointed my car towards my favorite comic book store, my mind back on the research papers in Jason's apartment. "There's only one way I can get another look at Purcell's research papers. I need someone with superb larceny skills," I said, offering up a chance at burglary, hoping to minimize the snarly vibes Breas threw off like spears.

"Hmmm," the vampire grunted. I frowned in his direction and considered suggesting he try running amuck and devouring villagers. Except, I lived in the nearest available village. I abandoned any attempts at conversation and pulled into a strip mall.

Having nearly ended the demon war—the combination peace treaty/trade agreement would be signed tomorrow at precisely 9:30 p.m.—I had no choice but to face the chaotic magic user, provided I could find her. As I negotiated the speed bump heavy parking lot, I mulled over everything I knew so far.

Breas broke the silence by asking, "Why do you put up with him?"

"Him, who?"

"Talis."

"I don't know. Why do I put up with *you?*"

Breas smirked and stroked the nape of my neck with his fingers.

"Because I make your pulse race. Awaken carnal desires."

Ugh. I shove his hand away and then stopped the car in front of a small shop. "You need to lay off the soap operas, Breas."

"You and I, we *are* a soap. Uptight virgin gives it up to the handsome bad boy." Before I could reply that our story arc was past tense, he said, "You haven't answered my question."

"Talis is my friend."

"He's a junkie."

"So? He has a kind heart. He's sweet—"

"Sweet?" Breas's teeth shone in the streetlights. "He's 'sweet' on you."

"No, Breas. He's not. He doesn't much fancy humans or vampires." I returned Breas's smile. "That's why I like Talis. No phallicly-motivated bullshit."

Breas laughed.

"Besides," I said, "I feel sorry for him. He didn't use to be—"

"Regan O'Connell. Always bringing home the strays." The vampire leaned towards me, his cool fingers brushing my skin as he fished the little Celtic cross out from under my shirt. "Thinking about Cara?" he asked.

"No. I'm thinking about Cyrus Purcell. Choices. Mine."

"You feeling guilty?" Dim disgust showed on Breas's face.

"Well, not so much guilty. I'm just wondering if letting him die was—"

"The best punishment? As opposed to a urine-soaked jail cell and all the man-love he could get from his smelly cellmate Pierre?" His eyes narrowed at the letters on the storefront sign: Lightman's Comics. "Yeah. That would have been a fitting punishment. But, I'd wager Purcell was well connected and covered his tracks meticulously. Not an easy guy to bring to justice."

"No, but—"

Breas sat up straight and unsnapped his seatbelt. He fiddled with the button on the seatbelt latch, snapping it open and closed.

"I got a great deal on my trade-in," he said. "One moral compass for a couple of yellow eyes, a set of pointy teeth and immortality, but—" *Snap, snap, snap.* "You did nothing wrong. It's not like you went on a rampage, killing every Holder on Earth."

"I thought about it," I replied, wrapping my hand around his in an attempt to stop the annoying noise.

"But you didn't. Revenge, on a grand scale, is the province of the human species. The old 'Your grandfather killed my grandfather, so I'm killing you and every member of your family, ethnicity, religion,' kind of bullshit."

"Yeah," I muttered. "I don't kill 'em, I date 'em."

"A far crueler fate."

"Shaddup."

Breas followed me into the store, grumbling about "books with pictures." After I made my purchase, I stopped to peruse the shelves long enough to get him good and antsy before finally leaving the store.

"Regan." The female voice cut frosty through the night air. Breas and I had just exited the store, almost colliding with the owner of the greeting.

"Joan. Hey."

Joan, emanating her special brand of gloom, frowned at me, her eyes settling hard on Breas. "What are you doing here?" she asked.

"Latest X-Men comic," I tried to say brightly, but her darkness smothered my artificial cheer.

Pale eyes unreadable, she stared at Breas. *Like he isn't already full of himself. Don't encourage him, Joan.* The vampire, for once, had nothing to say. "Oh, yes. Wolverine, right?" she said, only briefly hauling her gaze from Breas.

"Actually, this one's Wolverine and Gambit centered." I forced a smile. Joan nodded, her eyes glued to my companion. *Oh, good grief.* "Joan, this is my, um, friend, Bre-Dorian. Dorian, this is Joan." I wondered if she had even heard me, since she just kept watching the vampire. Breas didn't bother with a handshake, which was strange because normally he would do it just to fluster the person even more.

"Well, then, it was nice seeing you." I pushed Breas toward the parking lot. "See you at work."

Still off kilter from the Joan encounter, I walked in silence toward my car.

"Well, she's nearly completely insane, isn't she?" Breas said.

I screeched to a cartoon stop. "Huh? Really?"

Breas continued over to the passenger side of my car. "Isn't it obvious?" he asked, leaning over the top of the car.

My brain told my feet what to do and I moved over to the car. "I can't read humans the way you can, but she's always seems a little strange."

"Strange? Morrigan Siobhan O'Connell, Princess of the Happy Land of Understatement."

"Heh." I unlocked the car and slid into its comfortable confines. Breas did the same.

"She is the sort that hurts and cuts herself. Can't you smell her blood?"

Lost in thought, I started the car and headed home. "No. I wasn't really using *senses*."

"Sloppy Regan, real sloppy," he scolded, instantly irritating me. Parental tones from Breas are just too incestuous.

"So what about Jason?" I goaded.

"What?"

"Jason? Sane or completely Clockwork Oranged?"

"Déjà vu. Had this conversation, not going back."

"It bears knowin', Breas, since Jason may be the only one who can stand up to the chaotic magic user. What if he's as unstable? What if all the inbreeding has made them all unstable?"

Breas turned away, apparently watching the silhouettes of ancient cottonwoods zip by along Corrales Road. "Mildly depressed, but not dangerously," he said after a moment.

"Really?"

"Dead sister, possible father issues, crappy job. The stuff that human pathos is made of." Breas shrugged.

"That all?" I asked, scanning him.

Breas flipped open the glove box and rummaged around idly. "Nothing significant. Sort of preoccupied, nothing significant."

Whatever that means. My mind took an unexpected leap back to Joan.

Joan Wallace. Joan had innate magic power.

"Bloody hell." My car's tires issued a high-pitched complaint as I slammed on the brakes and jerked the vehicle over to the side of the road. The outlines of startled horses, in a roadside pasture, flashed in my headlights.

Breas, both hands pressed on the dashboard, scowled at me. "No turn signal, no warning. You've gone native, O'Connell."

"You'd have to be crazy to use chaotic magic, right?"

Passing car lights intermittently flashed Breas's eyes to silver. Several seconds passed and then he said, "Joan Wallace a.k.a. Jeanine Ward?"

"Yeah. Crazy hunch or—?"

"Well, it would explain how she knows I'm a vampire."

"Joan knows you're a vampire? Checking memory. Nope. Didn't mention that!" My fist connected with his upper arm.

"Ow," he complained, rubbing his arm. "Some humans can recognize us. Actually most can, but"—he shrugged—"most seem to *choose* not to."

"If she had been a Holder, she would've had training." All this time and the chaotic magic user might have been right under my nose! Helen Keller probably had greater powers of observation than me. I thunked my head on the steering wheel and accidentally hit the car horn, sending the horses skittering away.

"Why would I suspect her?" I asked, the question largely rhetorical. "I doubt she has enough innate magic to even see through a weak magical glamour, much less wield chaotic magic." Except if she was storing potential chaotic energy, she didn't need to generate her own magic.

"She probably thinks you're my familiar." Breas stifled a laugh. "This could be fun. I've never had a familiar."

"And you still don't." I hit the turn signal and waited for a chance to merge into traffic. For a village of only a few thousand people, the main drag was filthy with cars.

Lex was happily ensconced on the couch, watching a reality TV show about weight loss. She leapt up and flung herself at Breas who easily dodged her advance and headed for the kitchen; destination, the fridge, no doubt.

Ignoring them both, I scrolled through my cell phone's list, found the number and hit call.

"Hello," Joan answered.

"Hi, Joan!"

"Regan." The voice grew icicles on my phone.

Breas emerged from the kitchen, beer in hand.

"Yeah, hey, I had a question—"

"You like to play with fire, don't you?" she asked.

Seeing the look on my face, Breas handed me the beer.

"J-Joan? Did I just hit a speed bump in time? Bounced right over the spot where you made sense?"

"I think you know what I mean," Joan or perhaps Jeanine said.

After a gulp of alcohol, I answered. "I just wanted to check on your progress on the, uh, Carlson project."

An ice hard moment of silence followed. "I'm talking about your pet vampire." Another beer in hand, Breas moved to stand in front of me.

Wild animals make very poor pets. "Vampire? Stick to Electra comics, Joan, because the Anne Rice stuff is making you, um, delusional."

I could hear Joan breathing on the line as crazy little thoughts ran Keystone Kop-style through her head. "I knew there was something about you. All that innate power. Icarus knew you, but he wouldn't tell me anything—"

"Icarus?" *Oh, heck. She's the "scary human."* "You mean the guy who made wax wings and flew too close to the sun—"

"Icarus, the demon." Joan's sigh hissed over the phone line.

"Still hitting speed bumps, still airborne. In other words, huh?"

"Does your boyfriend, Jason Lake, know about Dorian?"

"J-Jason is not my boyfriend. And there's nothing to know. Dorian's just a friend."

"Your friend, the vampire?" Joan asked, sounding amused.

"He's not a vam—" Okay. Now that lie was too ridiculous to articulate. I rubbed my suddenly sore head and stared at the Brazilian soccer team logo on Breas's shirt.

"Who are you, really?" she asked, almost lucid.

"You're giving me an aneurysm. You know who I am. Regan O'Connell. Mild-mannered project manager."

"I know," she said. "That name pops up in a report."

My eyes locked with Breas's. "Report?" A block of ice started congealing in my stomach.

She answered with the name, "Kadin Farahani."

"Huh? Sounds like a 911 terrorist." *Sorry, Kadin.*

She breathed heavily into the phone. "Either you're lying or you really are—" She rang off abruptly.

"Shit! Shit! Shit!"

Breas's mouth did something between a smirk and a grimace. "You have a Holder problem. A bat-shit, crazy, Holder problem."

"What?" Lex asked. "What Holder? Who was that? Why don't you people ever tell me anything?"

Lex, along with Breas, was at least a little fond of withholding vital information, so I blinked at her, emulating Breas's unreadable exterior for several seconds. Once she was good and annoyed, I told her about Joan Wallace, now Jeanine Ward, rogue Holder, and possible destroyer of the world.

"So, what are you going to do?" the fairy asked, picking up a commanding tone.

"Me? Against a chaotic magic user? She'll kick my ass. She could probably kick all our asses." If everyone felt the need to take on parental tones, they should handle the problem. Except if I didn't handle the problem, Joan was going to keep killing people, somehow turning them into Lesser vampires.

"The Holders, they've linked me to Kadin. How?" I asked.

Breas shrugged. "Maybe they saw you together somewhere. That's bound to happen. They tail him everywhere."

"So? She just thinks you are a girl who spends a lot of quality time with vampires," Lex said.

"Not a whole bloody lot of those around, least not with heartbeats. And she called him a pet. Meaning she doesn't think I'm a familiar. Throws a whole new spin on things."

"Pet. Now, see that's why I don't pay rent," Breas said.

"Not funny." My phone rang. "What?" I growled into the phone.

"Oh," the voice said, dismayed. "I'm sorry, Regan. I didn't know who else to call."

"Eva? What's up?"

"The kids are at Carl's and I can't find Kyle. I don't know who to call. Regan, I—"

"Eva, you're rambling. What's going on?"

"It's Edward. Edward Aguirre. Regan, please help."

Why me? Eva has an army of relatives. *Do I give off a vibe?* "Where are you?"

"At home. Please hurry."

"I'll be there in a few minutes."

"Lex. Hold down the fort." Lex's delicate features scrunched up. To stave off any arguments, I said, "See if you can put something more effective, spell-wise, on Bill's paddock." I never listed this address anywhere, but I didn't want anybody taking out her crazy frustrations on poor little Bill.

Chapter Twenty-Seven

$\mathcal{A}$lbuquerque's North Valley is an eclectic mix of heavy industrial, nearly slums, and million dollar estate properties. Eva's neighborhood struggles to keep its head just a little above run-down. The lots are large and like my neighborhood, many of the residents are fond of sprinkling dead cars around their property like wheeled garden gnomes.

We walked up Eva's front path, dodging overgrown vegetation—mostly dead now—and a cat—very much alive—that attached itself to Breas. Totally decimating his reputation as evil dead thing, animals love Breas Montrose.

I rang Eva's doorbell, while the cat rubbed against the vampire's legs and he did his best to ignore it. Scrabbling sounds followed as Eva worked an armory of locks.

"Regan. Oh, thank God." Her brown eyes took in Breas.

"Hey, Eva. This is my friend, Dorian."

Eva did a finger handshake with Breas. She rubbed his hand before letting go. "Your hands are cold." Stepping back, she gestured, "Come in, please."

We followed an uncharacteristically quiet Eva through her living room and kitchen and on to a door I assumed led to the garage. She paused, her hands shaking, before finally opening the door.

I tensed, smelling vampire instantly, and grabbed Eva's shoulder. "Hang on." Hearing no movement, I said, "Okay, turn on the light." Eva's brow furrowed with confusion, but the light, dull flickering fluorescent, hummed and lit the garage.

The three of us passed through the doorway and stared at the cluttered garage. In addition to a sleeping vampire, the place was littered with the detritus of years of habitation. There was so much crap—toys, boxes, broken appliances—you couldn't fit a clown car in her garage.

"Goodwill charities, Eva. You do know they do pick-up?"

Thrown by my levity, she took a second to collect herself. "Regan. I found him like this." She rolled her eyes in the direction of the undead Edward Aguirre. "When I checked—I'm sure he wasn't breathing."

You checked? Hiding my horror at the image of Eva checking a vampire for a pulse, I walked over to Edward, bent and mimed, checking for a pulse. Even if he woke up and made a grab for me, I could easily evade him. "No pulse." Returning to Eva and Breas's position by the door, I said, "You've got a dead guy in your garage. Yep." I glanced sideways at Breas. *Two, actually.*

"You sure?" She peered at me, before moving her eyes to Breas. "I know this sounds crazy. But I swear…." She clamped her hand over her mouth. "I swear he moved."

"Moved?" I reached for a shocked expression and missed. "And you called me because of my Fox Mulder style wit?" I smiled at Breas. "Scully, this looks like an X-File."

"Regan." Eva's big brown eyes filled with hurt.

"Okay. Well, why didn't you call the cops?" I asked, for lack of anything worth saying.

Breas draped an arm around my shoulder. "And tell them what? She has a frisky dead guy in her garage?"

Eva noted the touching, and I hoped she really wasn't seeing Kyle anymore. "He's not that, um, frisky." I glanced at the more mobile vampire at my side.

"When did you find him, exactly?" Breas asked.

"Just now…well, about a half hour ago?"

"And when's the last time you were here, in the garage?" he continued, trying to work out the Joan/Jeanine related chronology.

"Uh. Not for a couple of days. I don't come in here much."

Nah? Really? I scanned the clutter. Fuzzy-hot bits of what I now recognized as chaotic energy clung to Edward, indicating he had been turned within the last day or so. I couldn't figure out why he was so groggy. Could it be the residual effects of the Bane?

As if he realized night had fallen and he should be acting more bloodthirsty, Edward, currently lying on his back, lifted his balding head.

Eva gasped and I ground my teeth together. When he pushed his thick frame to a sitting position, she started shrieking like a car alarm.

Fangs brushing my ear for emphasis, Breas said, "If you don't shut her up, I will." The new vampire cocked his head sideways and stared away from us, at the large metal door.

"Eva. Hey. You're only going to, um, get his attention. Shhhh." After a few seconds she ran out of air and quieted down. I guided her gently toward the kitchen door. "Wait here." In place of screaming, she launched into a host of Hail Marys, crossing herself in a way that reminded me of Lex's response to chaotic magic. It was about as effective, since Breas watched her with open amusement.

"You have to get her out of here and *make* her forget," I whispered, indicating that he should use Mesmer power on her.

"I'm not a Holder or a bloody Man in Black. I don't do memory trims or 'flashy-thing' people."

My eyebrows crawled upward. "You realize *you* just made a movie reference. I *am* rubbing off on you."

"Yeah. Like ringworm."

"Please, Breas. I'll deal with him, but she can't remember this. Please."

His arm shifted around my shoulders, his smile missing his eyes. "What's in it for me?"

Offering my best world-weary expression, I said, "My undying gratitude."

"Not nearly enough and nowhere near enough fun."

"You're kidding."

"No. As you'd say, 'not so much.'"

"Fine! Whatever. Get her out of here." I shrugged off his arm.

Eva let Breas lead her out of the garage, not expressing any concern over me being left alone with the undead management. Amazing the power a handsome man can have over a woman.

Edward shifted position and blinked in my direction. "Connell. O'Connell?"

"Edward." *What are the odds, the maniacal world-destroying wacko turns out to be my co-worker? Next, she'll be leaving vampires in the company break room.*

My senses picked up the usual dark miasma of confusion, anger, hunger and hate and nothing much else. I asked him, "Where did Joan take you?" I had a gut feeling she didn't store her pet vampire in her primary residence.

"Joan?" He climbed to his feet with surprising grace, and I shifted my weight to fighting stance.

"Yeah. Joan Wallace. Strange?"

"Joan," he said, and I sensed no comprehension.

He stretched, newly strengthened muscles tightening and loosening, and sniffed the air.

"I feel young," he said. I grimaced. Still balding and a bit paunchy, the addition of yellowy eyes and fangs to Edward's placid visage felt more B-movie than threatening.

He put his hand to his mouth and touched his new dental work. "Wow."

"So pointy, so sharp." I said. "Do you remember anything? Where Joan took you? Anything?"

"Blood?"

"Er, yeah, tasty. Joan—Wallace. Where did she take you?" He sized me up the way I take in the apple *empanadas* at the local bakery. I sighed. "If I tell you I taste like vampire, will you answer the damn question?"

"Vampire?" The expression on his fanged face was priceless.

"That would be you."

"Joan Wallace," he replied in a manager voice, "has an attitude problem."

"Really? Did you two have a run-in? Write her up?"

"Blood." His yellow eyes focused on my neck. He rushed at me with uncanny speed but not much grace. His feet got tangled in a tricycle and sent him flailing onto his face where he snarled and kicked. The tricycle came free of his foot and whooshed at me. One of the petals skimmed along my head, the rear tire made solid contact with my forehead and a starburst erupted in my vision. I wasn't trained to deal with flying yard sale junk.

I heard the *scrape-scrape* of his loafers on the dusty garage floor, but my eyes were still out of contact with my brain. The smell of stale cologne, blood and desperation enveloped me. A pair of hands grabbed my sweatshirt and yanked me forward. I stopped my motion with outstretched hands.

My vision started to clear in time to see Edward's hungry face. My hands were braced on his chest. He gave another pull and my weak arms gave way. As I stumbled into his grasp, I made a fist over his heart and summoned a dagger. There wasn't enough time to summon a dagger and *then* drive it into his chest. Cold breath rushed over my neck and then he shoved me aside. I tripped backwards over the tricycle and for the second time in a few days, fell hard on my ass.

Slow Kill is a cruel way to execute a vampire. Materializing a dagger directly into the heart doesn't kill instantaneously. The vampire suffers, in excruciating pain, for a minute or two.

I'd never done Slow Kill before and Edward's reaction assured that I wouldn't want to do it again. The sound he made would have put a banshee's teeth on edge—long and undulating, cat sex meets a car crash. By the time he finally dissolved into a pile of hot ash, I was cowering on the floor, hands over my ears, humming an out-of-tune version of "Camptown Races."

After my ears stopped ringing, I stood and listened for the sounds of concerned neighbors, hoping the garage walls and insulating layer of junk provided enough of a sound barrier. All I heard was Breas telling Eva, "You didn't hear anything," and Eva agreeing in a monotone voice.

Suddenly, I felt really tired and...sad. Since a dustpan or broom wasn't visible in Eva's clutter, I trudged back into the house.

Several minutes later, Breas and I stood at the edge of Eva's property. "What do you think? What was that all about?"

"Sending a signal to you? Or more likely, the Holders." He frowned down at the orange cat, which had resumed its devotions to his legs.

"Damn. Her bit about not trusting Jason. She knows him and Kyle." I tried not to yawn. "Joan's little gift, the vampire, was pointless though, because Kyle's dumped Eva."

Breas stared at my head and then pushed a few fingers through my hair. His fingers came away with blood. "Hmmm. That makes you a target. Jason—"

"Yeah. Except she knows my life comes equipped with a vampire." I reached up and pressed my palm against the small cut.

He licked his fingers. "She doesn't know where you live, right? No trails."

"No, Breas," I said, irritated by his tone. "The house is technically Argus's. I pay him rent and he pays the bills. Lights, phone, propane." I glared at him. "Your ole buddy Argus? You owe him rent."

Breas grinned and picked up the cat. "Not me. Pets don't pay rent, do they, Morris?" The cat mewed in agreement.

"Only if cat burglars are considered pets." I tried not to smile. The cat in his arms made the vampire oddly endearing.

My smile turned upside down. Breas was a tough S.O.B., but the rest of my friends weren't quite so indestructible. If Eva, through some weird intuition, hadn't had the good sense to call me tonight, she might have been out of the matchmaking business for good. What was Joan up to? Who might she target next?

An answer to either question was worthless because, at the moment, I could fit what I knew about chaotic magic in a thimble. I needed to get my hands on Cyrus Purcell and Alec Gagnon's reports. Tonight.

Chapter Twenty-Eight

I kept having a recurring fantasy about Jason.

In my fantasy, we were sitting on his couch, gazing into each other's eyes, and...having an honest discussion about the chaotic magic user. Fantasy Jason knew I was a Wolfe; he knew I knew he was a Holder. Sometimes all that honesty culminated in fantasy sex.

Reality was a good deal less pleasurable and a lot more illegal.

After checking my barn—I don't have a garage—for the presence of fresh off the assembly line vampires, Breas, Lex and I set out to spy on not-fantasy-Jason. We sat in Breas's car, watching Jason's apartment. I had tried the break-in the night before, only to be foiled by Jason, who chose to stay home all night. This night we were in luck. Around ten o'clock, Jason trooped out of his apartment.

When I saw him lift his arm to study the detector on his wrist, it looked like I had made a mistake in bringing Breas. Jason tapped the device, gave the parking lot a cursory examination, shrugged and then got into his SUV.

After Jason had driven away, I let out a huge sigh and turned to Breas. The vampire was staring at me, familiar smirk in place.

"Well, what do you know?" he said.

"As a rule, very little. Explain yourself, Montrose."

"You have a dampening effect on the Holders' vampire detectors."

"Nuh-uh. I never had that effect before."

Breas lifted one eyebrow. "You sure?"

"No. Come on. We've got a burglary to commit."

No moon flew in the sky, but the complex was well lit. We opted for the straight forward, march up the stairs as though you belong, approach.

"He has a negative unlock spell on the door. Pretty strong." Lex sounded suitably impressed.

"Yeah, well, fortunately we've got ourselves an old fashioned, lock picking, no magic required, kind of thief."

Smiling coldly, Breas bent to work on the door. "You do realize this is gonna cost you?"

"Send the bill to Argus, along with your rent payment," I snapped. The door clicked open and Lex waltzed right in. "Come in." I hauled Breas into the residence with me. Breas and I gave the living room and kitchen a quick once over and then headed into the bedroom. The laptop, along with research papers, was now in the closet.

Lex flopped on the bed. "Mmmm. I smell yummy man."

"Lex," I warned, setting up the laptop and pulling a CD from my pocket. Breas, tasked with scanning, took the papers. Once the laptop was running, I inserted my CD full of handy hacking apps into the drive.

"Hmmm. I bet it would be really wonderful if he were here with me," Lex said, squirming on the bed. Breas watched her with a peculiar expression on his face.

"Lex!"

"It could be you, Regan. Under, on top—"

"A'LexKishal D'Aravian!" The name flowed off the vampire's tongue. "Out! Go keep watch. Now!" Without so much as a moment's hesitation, the fairy fluttered up and left the room.

The security on Jason's computer posed no challenges and it didn't take long to access his email. The first email came from someone called Alison who used the word "darling" repeatedly.

"Ugh. Who says darling? *Daaahling*. Bleh." I scanned the message. "Alison. Bleh." My eyes traveled to Breas. *Asha, bleh.* "Bet she's blond. They're always blond."

The vampire watched me, his expression unreadable, so I moved on to non-Alison email. One email referenced a dossier on J. Ward. A little digging and I found the document on the hard drive. Nothing useful. Her real hair color was blond, so Joan's gothic dye job was a disguise. At this point, I probably knew more about Jeanine Ward. What was apparent was the absolute lack of useful information in the document. *Stupid, sneaky Holders.*

With a little more hacking, I got Jason's username and password and logged on to the Holder network as him. I looked up Juliet Lake. The car crash occurred on an icy road in Moscow. Now, it was possible the Brethren had found her activities and those of her partner, Roger Sidhu, threatening and eliminated her. She had been tailing my brother and Kadin's tolerance of humans only went so far. There was, however, no mention of that possibility in the file. The Holders usually made a fuss over people killed under those circumstances. Martyrs, essentially.

A lone photo of Juliet remained in the file. I stared at the picture of the dark-haired young woman, her features similar to Jason's but softer. I worship Kadin and Argus, but would I join an organization like the Holders if it was their dying wish? Probably.

Kadin and me. A query for Kadin Farahani drew up hundreds of entries. A second query for Farahani and Albuquerque returned a mention of his stop here three months ago. A third query using Boise as the location gave a cross link to Regan O'Connell. *Damn.* Apparently, we had been spotted in a diner. Fortunately, the operative mistook me for an ordinary human. *I wonder how many other times I've popped up on Holder radar?*

"Something interesting?" Breas asked.

I shuddered. "I'll tell you later. Done?"

We put everything, laptop and reports, back where we found them. Lex waited, sulking by the door. When we approached the car, Lex scurried over to the passenger door, shouting, "Shotgun."

Breas scowled, grumbling, "Damn, horny oompa-loompa," and I shrugged. I sank into the leather seats and closed my eyes.

As we neared the apartment complex exit, approaching car lights flashed through my eyelids. "The conquering hero returns," Breas observed. I cranked open my eyes in time to see an amiable wave.

"You *waved?*" I said, sliding down farther down into the seat.

"He recognized me. And he's following."

"I just wanna go home and go to sleep," I complained. We drove a few blocks before Breas slowed and pulled off the road. "What are you doing?"

"Would you rather he followed us home?"

"So lose him," I said, furious, and dropped to the floor.

"Relax. I'll get rid of him."

"Really?" Lex whined. "But he's so pretty."

"Not like that," Breas snapped, getting out of the car.

Lex started to get out and I said, "Stay. Let Breas handle this." Grumbling something in Fairy, she leaned out the window.

The car trembled as Breas assumed his customary slump on the back of the car. "Lake," he drawled.

"Dorian." Jason's footsteps approached at a slow pace. "Any particular reason you and a fairy are in my neighborhood?"

"Oh, wait, I know," Lex said.

"Lex," Breas snarled. "Came to see you actually," he said to Jason.

"Me. Really?"

"Because you are just dreamy," said Lex.

"Lex!" Breas's command was echoed by my own. Whatever looks the two men exchanged were then followed by Breas muttering, "Better you than me." After a pause, the vampire continued, "Rumor has it, a certain sheep, in addition to being black, is now missing and presumed insane."

Jason was silent for a few seconds and then agreed, "Yeah."

"And the sheep has developed a fierce hankering for chaotic magic."

With a slight edge, Jason asked, "And your interest would be?"

"Ah, you know. Chaotic magic wipes out all the tasty humans and all I'm left with are unpalatable fairies."

Lex let out a little huff, oblivious to the threat.

"Your people aren't telling you the truth, are they? Why she is doing this? They don't entirely trust you, do they?" Breas prodded.

"No."

"Don't take it too personal. Seems they are battening down the hatches, preparing for something big."

"What do you know, Dorian?"

"I can help you find your sheep."

"What do you know?"

I heard Breas laugh. "I know you've got a cute little girlfriend, Regan, right? I know Jeanine Ward knows you're in town. I know the bitch isn't above targeting people around you and Kyle. Eva found a vampire in her garage this evening. I wonder what Regan might find?"

That's low, Breas.

Jason took his time absorbing the information. "Is Eva—?"

"Eva is alive and well." The car shifted as Breas stood up. I heard a scratching cardboard sound and assumed he had given Jason his card. "Think about it. If you come up with anything useful, call me." His footfalls approached the driver's side. "I'm much safer than a Tracer spell."

"Why don't you just—?"

"Kill her?" Breas said. "Chaotic magic. That's where you come in. Maybe?" He reached for the door handle.

"Dorian." Jason spoke the name as a command. I saw amusement flicker on the vampire's face. "About Regan. Don't—"

"I assure you," Breas said, frowning down at me through the car window, "I couldn't hurt her if I wanted to."

He got in the car and I stayed on the floor, scowling daggers at him. "What the hell was that all about? Why'd you have to bring up my name?"

"Irony. Exploiting a weak spot."

After we had driven a few blocks, I crawled up on the seat and fell asleep.

Chapter Twenty-Nine

My mouth tasted like metal and something dug a painful trench in my side. I shifted position and sunlight glowed orange through my eyelids. Sprawled out, fully clothed on my bed where Breas had dumped me, I was lying on my cell phone. Rolling over, I pulled it out of my sweatshirt's pocket and fumbled with the buttons. Seven o'clock. "Stupid sun." I staggered into the bathroom. Then, freshly showered, some hair goop pushed through my hair in an attempt to tame its spikiness, and dressed in clothes I found on the bedroom floor, I faced the morning.

I apologized to Bill for the lack of attention he'd been receiving lately and he forgave me over breakfast. Like me, Bill is a food whore.

Ignoring the chirping of my cell phone, I put water on for tea and stuffed some bread in the toaster. With my luck, it was Joan, or worse yet, Eva had found the rest of my workplace, undead, in her garage. "In a pinch, a wooden pitchfork handle works wonders," I suggested through a mouthful of toast.

Munching on my sorry excuse for breakfast, I pulled out my laptop and began to upload and process the scanned files. Uncharacteristic guilt showed up to tweak my conscience. Thinking of the randy fairy nearly doing the self-love thing on his bed and the vampire I'd *invited* into his home, I said, "Sorry, Jason."

I squelched my guilt by assuring myself that I was doing this for him. If I could figure out a way to counter chaotic magic I could—what? Call him and say, "Guess what? I've got the solution to all your troubles?"

Send him a singing gorilla-gram who would croon out the answer to the tune of "Camptown Races?" This is how you cast the spell, doo-dah, doo-dah.

My plan needed work.

A while later, I sat at the kitchen table, poring over the reports, trying to make sense of Alec Gagnon's writing. Like my knowledge of Fairy, my French was limited to the more colorful expressions. Breas, genuinely fluent in French, was sound asleep and I wasn't about to wake him. I was flipping though a French/English dictionary when my cell phone rang a second time.

"Anyone important will call me on my land line," I said and kept translating.

Alec Gagnon spoke of the briefest of moments, before being swept away by an evanescence of possibilities, when the outcome of a chaotic magic spell could be controlled. "What the hell does that mean? Stupid French Holder."

I pulled out pen and paper and estimated the amount of energy that Joan might have created to date. "Now, thatsa lotta zeros." I whistled. My phone rang again. Frustrated by Gagnon's techno-French, I answered it.

"Yeah?"

"Regan, hello."

"Jason? Hi." According to caller-ID, he had already called twice. "Something wrong? It seems you've been persistent."

"Well, yes, actually. Sorry."

"You know you're giving off a pretty hefty stalker vibe." *Okay. That's mean.* I knew why he was calling.

"Really? I'm sorry—"

Deflecting a bit, I said, "Well, I guess you really can't be a stalker unless you have a proper Regan shrine, with candles and creepy photos and suchlike. Have one of those yet?"

"Er...no." He paused, considering. "Not yet. I'm waiting to get the photos back from the developer." The beginning of a smile crept into his voice. "Again. I'm sorry. It's a bit of a long story. Sorry, long night."

"Must have been one hell of a night, what with all the stammering. Should I be jealous?"

He laughed. "No. Definitely not. Work—"

"You need a new job. I'm thinking of quitting mine, by the way." *On account of my boss turning up undead.*

"Really? The bloodless coup a failure, then?"

Bloodless, ugh. "Yeah. You could say that."

"Have you ever considered doing something else?"

"Something less mundane?" I asked, testing.

"Or at least, something less Dilbert?"

"Management, the verbal whetstone against which I hone my razor sharp wit." I rubbed my wrist. "Mundane is okay." *Mundane is the vanilla to the crazy chocolate in the rest of my life.*

Redirecting, I asked, "You all right? You sound frazzled."

I could hear the expression on his face. "Well, yes. You know how you sometimes find yourself allied with the most unlikely of persons?"

I glared sharp wooden spikes at the spare bedroom. "Yeah. Sometimes you have to take help where you can, Jason."

"Hmmm. The enemy of my enemy is my friend." He changed the subject. "And you? Are *you* all right? I called at work—"

"I called in sick of management." I doodled a fanged happy face on Alec Gagnon's report. "Not to be an ingrate, but why the concern?"

The epitome of a pregnant pause followed. "Some of the persons I deal with are, em, less than savory. I just hope I haven't put you—"

"In danger? Sounds exciting." Sensing a protest, I asked, "Do you know where I live, Jason?"

"No," he replied, his voice heavy with the surprise of realization. "I don't."

"Exactly. And neither does anyone else." I couldn't help grinning. "I'm...elusive."

Jason didn't say much for a second, apparently trying to assimilate my admission. "Good, because—"

"I'll be fine, Jason."

"I'd really like to see you, but until this case wraps up—"

"Yeah. I understand." I hoped he hadn't run the Tracer spell to find Joan, yet. "In the meantime, get to work on my shrine. A digital camera, the tool of the twenty-first century stalker."

"How about I use Christmas lights rather than candles? Green lights, like your eyes."

The heat of a blush rolled down my neck and pooled between my legs. I swallowed and said, "Okay."

"In light of my new status, stalker, I think it would be appropriate if I called you later today."

"I'm counting on it."

After we said goodbye, I struggled with the flowery French for about twenty more minutes before my attention span dissipated like New Mexico rain clouds. I was staring at a crack in the ceiling when a cell phone rang, Beethoven bleating out of a small speaker. Scrambling up, I hurried to the recliner where Breas had left his coat. I recognized the number instantly. *Jason. Wow.*

I put the cell phone back in the coat pocket and walked over to the spare bedroom door. The vampire slept, totally unaware. I shut the door and then got out my violin.

After forty-five minutes and some bow and finger work that nearly had the strings smoking like the devil's instrument, the iron fireplace tools had not moved from their stand and my innate magic remained dormant. Nothing, not even the deep booming notes, ground out by hard pressure on the bow, worked. It felt as though magic, realizing I'd found a loophole in the words-make-spells part of the contract, had slapped an injunction on my musical sorcery. So much for progress.

Before I could really sulk, my phone rang.

"Regan," the voice said.

I really needed to make better use of the caller-id. "Joan. Hey?"

"Still playing with fire?"

"Still a few beers short of a case?"

Predictably, silence followed. Joan just doesn't get me.

"I need to talk to you."

"Yep. That would be what we are doin' now. Unless I got psychic powers to go with my pet vampire. K-Mart Blue Light Preternatural Special."

"I mean in person," Joan replied, a tad bit of annoyance melting through her cold exterior.

"Um. No. You're even more unnerving in person. Thanks."

"Regan. I need your help."

I sat down on the overstuffed arm of the sofa and stared at the spare bedroom door. "Help with what?" I asked. *What you got, only shock therapy can help.*

"I'm at the warehouse. I'll be here for the next two hours." As a sort of afterthought, she added, "Please, Regan."

The phone clicked and I was left staring sightless across the room. My fingers mechanically pressed Cypher's number and I was greeted by her answering service. I walked over to the spare bedroom door, opened it and stared at my snoozing house pest. Two o'clock in the afternoon, sun all yellowy bright, and Breas Montrose was pretty damn useless, even if he were awake.

I do my job flying solo about ninety-nine percent of the time. Breas is out of my life more than in, disappearing for months, years, and once, even a solid decade, at a time. I picked up my keys and gagged the warning voice in my head. I'm fast, so fast I make vampires look like sloths on sedatives, and I'm fully capable of dodging the occasional spell. I marched out the door.

Chapter Thirty

The warehouse was located in a commercial/industrial zone on the northern edge of Albuquerque. The Koar warehouse, dull orange and trimmed in turquoise around the roof and doors, sat far back on a corner lot, buffered on either side by parking lots.

In addition to the work she did on my projects, Joan had also been assigned to assist David, the warehouse manager, with the company inventory system. I had my doubts she needed my help sorting paper clips by type and color.

I turned down the stereo—blasting corrosive music that came with parental advisories—and studied the building. Like any warehouse, it was architecturally challenged and unworthy of study. A few scattered windows, a large garage door and a smaller entrance toward the front. I had only been there once before, to pilfer office supplies.

The only car in the parking lot was Joan's hatchback. David, fortunately, was on vacation this week.

Standing before the smaller door, I wrapped my hand cautiously around the doorknob and pushed the door open a few inches. The air smelled mostly of office supplies: the sharp chemical tang of printer toner and bleached white paper. A faint magical haze hung in the air, along with the raw smell of vampire. Pushing the door all the way open, I stood in the daylight, listening to the dimly lit interior. Joan stood menacingly several yards down the hallway, her outline edged by a reddish-glow.

"Clint Eastwood called. He wants his scowl back," I said.

"Your boyfriend, Jason, works for an organization known as Holders of the True Light." There was just enough light to catch a glint of the cross, gold and gaudy, around her neck.

"Sounds like a cult. So?"

"In some ways, it is."

Trying to pinpoint the location of the vampire, I listened, splitting my focus between Joan and the rest of the building. "So what? Is Jason gonna go all Mormon missionary and try to convert me?"

Joan's eyes widened. "You are an innate magic user. Yes."

"No, I'm not. And how do you know all this? About Holders and suchlike?"

"I was once a member of their organization." She stopped talking, lapsing into a grating silence.

"Yeah and you were deprogrammed or what?"

"I was...betrayed," she said, with enough magic force to make me very nervous.

Unconsciously, I took a step towards her. "How?" I asked.

"They took him. They killed Roger." Magical energy simmered.

"Your boyfriend? Why?" *Roger Sidhu—Jeanine's boyfriend, d'oh!*

"He'll betray you, too, Regan."

"Who? Jason?" I moved closer to her. "Why, Joan? Why did the Holders kill Roger?"

"It ends, tonight," she declared, and I realized I had stepped a tad too much into the building.

Dodging the first spell proved a little more difficult than I imagined, because it was highly dispersed, spreading around the room like campfire sparks. She wasn't expecting me to have any magical abilities, so my weak counter spell pushed most of it away. A few threads wiggled through my defense and made my brain feel like lumpy pudding. My feet lost contact with my head. I stumbled and landed on my butt.

Lifting a Rubik's cube-sized black wooden box, she repeated the spell. Power streamed from the cube, fortifying by chaotic energy. My legs ignored my brain the way I ignored Barry Stanton's emails. I put up another counter spell. Parts, important structural parts, of the building shuddered in complaint, and the chaos-strengthened spell hurtled at me, burning through my spell as though it were tissue paper.

My vision turned as black as the Maram'ro wood box.

Didn't I say she'd kick my butt? I thought, peeling my eyelids off my eyes. Sitting up and sniffing in the direction of the brand spanking, newly-turned vampire who lay motionless on the other side of the room, I rotated my head, popping out neck kinks. I was in a small room, containing, in addition to the vampire, various parts and pieces of computer hardware. A quick glance at my wrist confirmed that at least one unintended outcome of Joan's spell was the death of my watch. My cell phone had gone missing.

Sparing the vampire a quick look—he was out cold and the least of my concerns—I wobbled over to a section of empty wall. Even I could feel the arcane power running up and down the wall like termites on crack. The lock spell, originating at the door, must have been woven with chaotic and ordinary magic. I stared at the door, wondering if my simple lock picking skills could get around the problem.

On cue, the magic wavered and the door opened a few inches. Joan's angry-eyed visage peered in the room. "You're awake."

"Yeah. And thanks for checking. Mighty hospitable." I rubbed a hard knot in my neck. "What are you doing, Joan? All this…?" I pointed at the vampire.

"You are better off—"

"As a vampire beverage?" My eyebrows crawled toward my scalp. "Er, sorry, don't think so." I took a slow step in her direction. "What's going on, Joan?" I said, feeling like a recording.

Joan's right hand lifted. Thinking she held the little box of chaotic tricks, I staggered back, only to realize the thing in her hand was my cell phone. The phone held high so she could dart her eyes from it to me, she pressed a few buttons. "He's not in your phone book."

"He who?"

I think she frowned, although it's hard to tell with Joan. "What is his number, Regan? Jason Lake's number?"

"Oh. Got it. I'm Holder bait."

"What. Is. His. Number?" She *could* look angrier.

"I forget."

Joan's left hand rose. The box, constructed of matte-black Maram'ro wood and capped with a red oak top, sat primly on her palm. "What is his number?"

Lifting both hands, palm skyward, I raised and lowered them, weighing my options. "Hmmm. Zapped by powerful mojo versus vampire libation. How to go? How to go?" Joan opened her mouth to begin a spell and I held up my hands in defeat. "Okay, okay, Vampire Draft it is," I said, spilling Jason's cell phone number.

"He's not a bad person." I said, not comfortable with my own words. "Is that why you're doing all this? To get back at Jason for some reason?"

Her eyes, fathomless and scary, studied me. "They all will suffer. All, every last one, every last Holder."

Chaotic magical energy drifted in the air and mingled with Joan's angry force, making my knees shaky. I sat down before I fell down.

"They killed Roger." The beginning of tears glimmered in her eyes. "And then they tried to take him away. All that was left. Out of my memories."

Oh. The Holders must have hit her with a memory trim and it fried her brain. Poor Joan. "W-why, Joan? Why would they kill—?"

"Roger was expendable. They wanted Jason. Back in the Holders. Compared to Jason, even his own sister was expendable. It's all about power, Regan. Power at any cost." Her eyes, sad and human, met mine. "Compared to you, even Jason is expendable. Power. Greedy for power."

I saw Cara's face clearly for the first time in decades. Cyrus Purcell's data ran with blood. "I know," I said softly. "But revenge, Joan?" Clawing hair out of my eyes, I stared at her face. "It really won't bring anybody back. Roger will still be dead, Joan." Startled by the realization, I said. "They can't all be bad. Jason's not."

The phantom of humanity evaporated and her expression hardened. With one last knife-hard glare, she slammed the door, the locking spell humming in my bones.

♬

ALBUQUERQUE, TUESDAY NIGHT

The vampire was late. Jason frowned at the display on his cell phone. 7:20 p.m. He dialed Regan's number for the tenth time and received the same response as the previous nine tries. *Cellular customer unavailable.*

Jason leaned against his vehicle, a little seed of worry growing into a shrub and pressing thorny limbs into his consciousness.

He closed his eyes. New Mexico had a magic that went far beyond picture book sunsets and harshly beautiful scenery. Real magic, tangible and strong, flowed throughout the region. Even here, in the asphalt-covered parking lot, he could feel energy bubbling below his feet.

Yet another car's headlights flared and he raised his head. The car, a silvery gray Mercedes, slid into a parking place one row back from his SUV. The lights winked off and Dorian stepped out of the car.

There was nothing extraordinary about the physical appearance of the creature that approached him. Jason, whose experience to date was limited to Lesser vampires, had never met a member of the Grey Brethren. Dressed in a gray T-shirt emblazoned with a World Cup emblem, over a white sweatshirt, jeans, and hiking boots, the only truly outstanding aspect of the vampire's appearance was his eye color. Elf gray, a color rare even among the Fey. From what Jason understood, the Brethren coveted humans with elf bloodlines. *Like the Holders*, he thought, smiling at the irony.

"Lake," Dorian said. The vampire's gaze swept the strip mall's parking lot. At this time of night, people drifted in and out of the two restaurants and the one bar that occupied space in the mall.

"Dorian," Jason said, not quite able to disguise his irritation.

Amusement darted in the vampire's dark eyes and he handed Jason an envelope. "Jeanine Ward's local contact information as well as other background data," he said, scanning the parking lot with predatory wariness.

"I didn't bring Kyle," Jason said, opening the envelope and pulling out its contents. Ignoring the psychic buzzing of the vampire detector on his wrist, he perused the documents. "Shit," he said. "Koar Industries?" After Edward Aguirre's disappearance, he had conducted a thorough background check on all Koar employees. Joan Wallace's, a.k.a. Jeanine Ward's, fake identity had held up to scrutiny.

"Yeah. Lying in wait, like a rattlesnake in the wood pile," Dorian said, still studying his surroundings. "You people really have those things cranked up, don't you?" His gaze fell on Jason's detector masquerading as a watch. "I can hear it."

Jason paused from his scrutiny of the documents. The signal hadn't seemed so shrill the night before. "Really?"

"It's screaming in my head. I wouldn't expect to be able to creep up on any Greater vampires wearing that thing."

"That's comforting," said Jason, returning to the information at hand. "Roger Sidhu? He was my sister's field partner."

"Yeah. And Jeanine's Ward's boy toy." Jason looked up, startled. "I pulled his info on account of his relationship with Ward." The vampire turned and leaned on the SUV a few feet away from Jason. "Sounds like it wasn't a Holder sanctioned relationship."

"You are Grey Brethren, then," Jason stated, studying the picture of his sister, whose dossier was also included.

"I have contacts in the Brethren and access to their intelligence. But, I am not Brethren," the vampire replied. At Jason's dubious expression, he redirected, asking, "If you don't mind my asking, have you seen Regan today?"

"Yes. I do mind your asking."

Dorian's mouth broke in a dark smile.

"No," Jason answered after a moment's hesitation, his concern slipping through his words.

The vampire studied him with a disturbing intensity. "Call her."

"What?"

"Call—her—now."

Suddenly sharply aware that he was unarmed, his bolt launcher tossed in the back seat, Jason dialed Regan's number, only to receive the same message. "Her phone says she's unavailable. It's been that way all afternoon."

One of the vampire's eyebrows crept upwards and he pulled out his own cell phone, hit a couple of buttons and held it to his ear. "Same on my phone," he said. "It's my business to know things, phone numbers," he said with a condescending smirk. He pressed a couple more buttons on the phone. "Yeah. Have you seen Regan? Today? Don't lie to me. No? Thanks." He hung up and met Jason's eyes for a second. "Mutual friend," he explained, pulling a face.

Jason scrutinized Dorian, certain he saw a fleeting hint of emotion on the vampire's youthful face. He couldn't have been more than twenty when he was turned.

Jason's phone rang and not recognizing the number on the caller-ID, he said, "This is Lake." Even if she had told him he had just won the lottery, the woman's voice would have chilled him to the bone. Dorian watched, obviously listening in on the conversation.

"It's a trap, Lake. She's after you," Dorian said after Jason hung up.

"Well, obviously." *Why?*

"Grudge?"

Jason shook his head. "I don't think we've ever met."

"Or maybe she's just threatened by you. Your people apparently know what she is capable of. That's why they sent you. A strong innate to counter—"

"If I knew how, but I don't," Jason admitted, bitterness in his voice. He pushed the papers back in the envelope. "The irony is Regan is stronger, a stronger innate, than I am."

Dorian frowned, staring hard at Jason. "But I don't get the impression O'Connell's willing to admit that."

Jason returned the vampire's stare, wondering just how much contact he had made with Regan, experiencing a sudden, irrational twinge of jealousy. "No. I don't think she does." He stood up. "I have to go. Regan...."

"Back-up?"

Jason's expression turned incredulous. "You?"

"At this point, you're the only sorcerer with the potential to stand up to Jeanine Ward. It's in everybody's best interest to keep you alive."

His eyes narrowed, Jason said, "What about you? I suspect you were a strong innate even *before* you were turned."

The vampire shrugged. "Let's just say I don't go out of my way lookin' for trouble."

Something nagged at Jason's memories, but he was too concerned about Regan to explore it much. "Right." *The enemy of my enemy.* In this situation, another sorcerer was better back-up than Kyle.

Chapter Thirty-One

Having nothing better to do than kill the vampire, which hardly seemed fair since he was comatose, I climbed to my feet and stared at the wall the way people who know nothing about cars stare under the hood. Joan's crazy spell was disrupting my ability to *hear* what was going on beyond the door. Another bonus outcome, no doubt. The beginnings of despair hovered around my thoughts.

After a few minutes, the vampire shuffled and I absently summoned a dagger. Hearing the word, "Regan-O," I froze.

"Sean?" I gulped, turning. *Dammit. That bitch!*

Sean's familiar face regarded me with a combination of friendly interest and the typical raging thirst of an unstable vampire. Even at their hungriest, Greater Generation vampires like Kadin or Breas have granite-strong control over their cravings. Unstable Lesser Generation vampires, even the most coherent, lack that control, and are the origin of stories of drooling mindless bloodsuckers.

Standing without so much as a wobble, despite being out cold a few minutes ago, he stretched, and then glided two steps in my direction.

Completely unsettled, I didn't move right away when he lunged at me. Allowing him to get too close, I skirted his grasp and clocked him on the side of the head with the dagger's pommel. Athletic when breathing, Sean was an impressive newbie vampire. Though thrown off balance, he whirled back in my direction. Still reeling from shock, I lashed out three times with the business end of the weapon, driving him back.

"Ow! Damn, Regan," he said, as though my defense was unprovoked.

Skittering back to just before the door, I said, with as stern a tone as I could muster, "Sean, you've got to control yourself."

Confusion marred his handsome features. "I feel, I am so thirsty. And—"

"Hey," I said, willing him to listen. "You remember last spring, when I first came to town? Yeah? And you invited me to your parents' house? Your Mom was so cool. She made tacos with rice and beans and didn't hassle me about being a vegetarian. Do you remember that?"

With depressing normalcy, he nodded. "Yeah. My mom, she still loves you, Regan-O." His hunger drilled itself into my brain. "I can hear your heart beat," he said, his tone two parts menace and one part wonder.

"Yeah. That's vampire senses for you."

"Vampire."

"Uh-huh. Sean. Do me a favor. See this dagger?" I raised the weapon so he could see it. I began to twitch it back and forth, faster and faster. "Can you hear it? The noise it makes when it cuts the air?"

"Yeah. Wow! It sounds like movie special effects."

"Okay. So now try to picture your senses, hearing and smell, as though they were a bubble. You can expand the bubble or contract it." Sean, his concentration fading, watched me, annoyance showing on his face. "Come on, Sean, stay with me. Out there, beyond these walls, there are so many sounds and smells, it'll drive you crazy." I slowed the movement of the dagger. "Try it again." Once he focused, I continued, "Try pulling your senses back, contracting them away from the dagger. Pull 'em back so you can no longer hear the sound, the whooshing sound."

Amazement split his face into a small smile. "Wow, it worked."

"Okay. Now try to contract it back as close to your body as you can, away from me." His eyes filled with astonishment, he obviously was working at it.

Keeping an eye on Sean, I returned part of my attention to escape. "Where did Joan take you, Sean?" I rattled the doorknob, grinding my teeth in pain, as the biting energy of the magic vibrated through my hands.

"I'm not sure. Somewhere in the East Mountains, I think. Up high, past the juniper and piñon, up with the tall pines."

"Concentrate, Sean. Keep your senses away from me," I said, seeing the dangerous need growing in his eyes.

"It was really strange. She did something like hypnosis and I had to follow. I had to go with her."

"The spell is called Mesmer," I said.

"She took blood, from me."

Blood. "Establish a link with the human to be turned. Force a vampire to *turn* rather than simply dine," I said, mostly to myself. That explains some of the blood found at Edward's place. I turned and faced Sean.

My little Vampire 101 tangent had muddled his concentration and he watched me, eyes unfocused. "The damn cleaning lady vacuumed up more of my green army men," I said. He blinked. "Their ranks are thinning and they won't hold out much longer against the cranes. Think you could get me some more?"

"Yeah." He laughed.

Backing along the wall and away from the door, I pointed at the place where I had just been. "Hey, Sean? Do me a favor. Come stand in front of the door." Little flashes of hunger pinged off my senses and I whirled the dagger through my fingers. "Control, Sean. Control." He nodded and watched me. "Look at the door, use your *senses* if you have to. Can you see anything, like glowy energy trails?"

Sean examined the door and shook his head. "Nah. Nothing." Then he froze, every muscle in his body rigid. "Yes! It's like a circuit board, only with light or—"

"Magic," I said.

"No shit."

"Uh, yeah, shit." Noting his fascination with the discovery, I edged closer. "All that light, intertwined magic, that's what's keeping the door locked. Undo that mess and the door opens."

"Yeah. So, do it," he said, still fixated on the door, a dangerous ring in his voice.

"Not so good with orders, Sean. You know that." He grinned. "This isn't a computer. It's beyond anything I can do. But you might be able to see something, a pattern, anything?"

"Pattern. No way, Regan. Always changing, it's like—"

"Chaos. It's a really weird kind of magic. But there is order in everything, right? There must be—" His eyes glazed over and I took a step back. "The door, Sean, focus on the door. I'm not on the menu and besides, you owe me an army in a bag." Sean turned back to the locked door and I waited, wary and eager. Vampirism almost always provides, to varying degrees, innate magic.

Sean took an awkward step backwards. "You're right, Regan-O," he said. "Drums, like a drum group. Not a pattern, exactly. There's a *rhythm*."

"Really?" I chanced a step closer. Rhythm, harmony, even? I raised my hand and tried to follow the channels of energy.

"Yeah." Following my lead, he moved closer to the door and coasted his hand inches over its surface. "I got it." He gasped.

I pushed my senses at him, finding the psychic beat the magic drummed through his body. "Damn." I was awed. *Now what?* Find a harmony and then run another in counterpoint? A complex version of "a tune in my head." Setting the rhythm Sean had found as tempo, I mentally sang a simple five-note tune. In no time, the beginning of resonance shuddered through my head and started to work its way down my spine. Magic, energy, and power surged through my skin, my skeleton, every cell and I felt wonderful and sick all at once.

Remembering the "feel" of the deep notes on my violin, I pushed the powerful vibrations toward the door. The oscillating energy clashed with Joan's wild magic, and then the spell collapsed into harsh dissonance.

The door opened with a loud screech. Severing my connection with Sean, I scrambled away from the doorway as the newborn vampire rushed it in an irrational fit of rage. Jason's face appeared in the doorway and he lifted his arm, firing a small bolt launcher. Jumping back to avoid the result, I watched Sean's demise in dazed silence.

Mostly to fill the abrupt silence, or maybe to smooth over the painful lump in my throat, I said, "He saw it. The patterning, the rhythm. There is a kind of order...." My voice trailed off, suddenly aware of the unlikely pair who stood staring at me in the doorway. "Joan. She killed Sean," I muttered, staring stupidly at the pile of hot dust.

"Technically," Breas said, "he killed Sean." He inclined his head toward Jason.

"No." *He only did what I couldn't.*

Chapter Thirty-Two

"*R*egan. Are you all right?" Jason closed the distance between us and touched my face. I tried to ignore Breas.

"Yeah. I'm fine." No, I wasn't fine. But until I dealt with Joan, crying my eyes dry wasn't an option.

Jason tilted his head to the side, eyes on my neck. "But the vampire—" He shut his mouth, looking like a kid who'd just said the "F" word in front of Grandma. The emotions coming off him were overpowering.

"Really," I said. "I have a pulse. I still don't eat meat or the red stuff that flows through it."

Jason started to say something but Breas interrupted him. "How'd you open the door, O'Connell?"

Gulp. "I don't know what you mean," I said.

"Really?" Breas said, oozing disbelief.

"Sean. The vampire, he did it, the magic stuff," I answered, glaring at Breas.

"Do you two know each other?" Jason asked. I glanced up at his face. Something sinister—jealousy?—lurked under the surface.

"She's done some work for me. Computers," Breas answered.

Jason asked, "Are you aware that he—?"

"Hasn't had a tan in centuries?" I said. "Yeah. I know."

Jason frowned. "Are you in the habit of working for vampires?"

Saving me from the lie that ate Tokyo, Breas asked, "What happened here, O'Connell?"

The account I gave was pretty close to the truth. I left off stuff like my ill-fated magical duel with Joan and using a Wolfe's dagger to defend myself.

"A memory trim," Breas said to Jason. "Is that part of the Holder retirement plan? A pension and a gold watch, in exchange for all your marbles?"

Jason ignored the vampire. "She said, 'tonight'"— his eyes searched mine—"tonight, she would...." He fell silent.

"Revenge at a global scale," I said.

"Why'd the Holders kill Roger? And your sister?" Breas asked.

Jason's head turned to meet the vampire's gaze. "My sister and her partner were killed in a car accident. *Accident.*"

"Right," said Breas with a smirk. "Your people must have been covering something up. Why the memory trim?"

"There was nothing—"

"Don't be such a Boy Scout. You know what your people are capable of—"

"A lecture on ethics from a vampire?" A muscle twitched in Jason's jaw. "We are not the Grey Brethren. We do not—"

"Yeah. Tell that to Talis."

Jason face fell. "I-I, that wasn't my choice and when—"

"Hey!" I said. "Cell phone." I snapped my hand out to Breas. He handed me his phone. "I missed a meeting," I said in weak explanation. My fingers punching the number, I turned and walked out the door.

I knew I was setting myself up for a lecture, but I made the call anyway. Rabbits, little reddish blobs to my eyes, hopped around in the dark, snacking on a nearby lawn. According to Breas's phone, it was eight-thirty.

"Hello?" Kadin answered, surprised, even a little angry.

"Hey. It's me." I wondered what his caller-ID was telling him, feeling a guilty twinge for Breas. Kadin and Breas weren't exactly on each other's Christmas lists.

"Regan?"

"Yeah. I need to know something. Did the Brethren issue an

Eliminate order on Juliet Lake or Roger Sidhu?"

"No," replied Kadin. "Juliet was often persistent, but generally, quite pleasant."

"You *knew* her?"

"I met with her and Roger just two weeks before the accident. Trade negotiations. A Sharet demon had set up an unauthorized syndicate in Bangladesh. The Holders were hoping we could assert our influence."

"Oh."

"Why? What's going on, kid?"

I told him pretty much everything that had transpired, leaving off anything too squishy about Jason and me.

"If the secrecy they've accorded the matter is any indication, then Ms. Ward's claim may have some merit," said Kadin.

I shivered. "They're trying to hide their screw-up."

"And they're testing Lake." After a beat, Kadin said, "What are you planning?" The beginning of an authoritative tone laced his voice.

"Er, I didn't exactly do very well in my first confrontation, so—"

"You went in blind. Very stupid, Morrigan."

I sighed. If Kadin was getting this snippy, the same conversation with Dad would be absolutely hideous. At least Dad wouldn't call me Morrigan.

"I take it *he* is there."

Beating back the need to say, "He who?" with a big thorny stick, I answered, "Yes. Joan, er, Jeanine stole my cell phone." I fumbled in my pockets. *And apparently, my damn car keys as well.* The silence made me squirm.

"Now is not the time for absurd notions of self-preservation. If anything... *anything* happens to you, I will find him and I will take him apart over several centuries." Kadin carefully enunciated every word. "Understand?"

"Um, yeah?" I tried, knowing the statement was meant for Breas, not me.

"Plan this time, kid," Kadin said, his tone softening. "The sooner Ward is stopped, the better."

"But Kadin, isn't this the Holders' mess? Why not let them mop up their own—?"

"Regan," he said. "The family is running out of excuses. Please don't fail us this time." There was a note of desperation in his voice.

"I won't." Jeez. Who'd of thought a vampire would be so good at generating guilt?

Jason and Breas emerged from the building seconds after I hung up. I watched them approach, my thoughts on Cara, Sean, Edward, Talis, and even Joan.

Joan had murdered Sean and a part of me burned with a desire for revenge, the same feeling I'd had when Cyrus had killed Cara. The very same emotion that drove poor demented Joan.

The two men walked up to where I leaned on my car. The two sides of my life suddenly swirled together. Chocolate and vanilla. I had no idea which was which.

I pointed at the crusty dark stripe that ran down the left side of Jason's face, just along the hairline. "What happened?"

"I-I was—"

Breas laughed. "He got hit by a chunk of ceiling tile." His gray eyes panned back to the building. "Chaotic magic is hell on building integrity."

"Do you mind?" Jason said, almost amused. "I was trying to come up with something a bit more heroic."

"Battling legions of wise-cracking undead?" I said, pointing at Breas. The vampire gave me a cheeky wink.

Fortunately, Jason missed the wink. "Him?" Jason jerked his chin in Breas's direction. "He came with me."

"Ah, the vampire lease program. Don't leave home without one," I said, trying to smile.

"Beware the small print," said Breas.

"Speaking of which, maybe you should do something about the vampire marinara sauce." I ran my eyes up and down the blood trail on Jason's face. "In light of the company you're keeping." I pointed at the building. "The bathroom is the third door on the right."

Jason put his hand to his face, hesitating.

"She's hardly a snack," Breas said, understanding Jason's reluctance.

"I'll scream like a banshee if his stomach so much as growls," I said.

Shooting Breas one last warning look, Jason brushed past me and headed toward the building.

Chapter Thirty-Three

To complement my familiar state of sleep deprivation, I was starving. All I'd had to eat were a couple of slices of toast and a cup of tea. I wanted to go home, eat Bill's weight in food, and go to bed. At the distant squeak of the bathroom faucet, Breas moved closer to me.

"What's going on with you two?" I asked.

The vampire winked. "Jealous?"

"Should I be?"

"Well, I am prettier than you. And blond. 'They're always blond,'" he said, quoting me. Embarrassed, I found something fascinating on his shoes.

"Go home."

I frowned and lifted my head. "What?"

"Go home. You know Lake isn't going to want you along. As far as he's concerned, you're just the woman who"—he leaned in close to my face—"keeps my system running."

I groaned. "Breas, enough." I clunked my forehead against his chest and closed my eyes. "This is my party. Jihad Joan invited me. She made my tolerable boss and my friend Sean dead. And not in a good way." I straightened and rubbed my eyes. "You *heard* what Kadin said. You're just trying to save your skin. Same old Breas."

"My own skin? By throwing it in the line of fire? Skin's the first thing that gets burned."

"By my reckoning, even a chaotic magic user is preferable to Kadin Farahani."

"You know me well. At any rate, you are going home."

"Really? What's in it for me?" My eyes fell to the T-shirt he was wearing. *Cool. World Cup Logo.* "Your shirt. I want this shirt."

"This shirt?" he asked, surprised. "Shirt, pants, you can have it all. You know that," he said dropping his face near mine. "In fact, according to our deal—"

"Nope," I said, "just the shirt."

"I like this shirt," he whined.

"Me, too."

He paused, thinking. "No." The hard planes of his face softened. "Let me take care of this."

"No." I released his shirt and took a step back. "This is my job! I'm not going to—" *Oh, crap!*

At precisely nine-thirty, not a minute before or after, I was supposed to initiate the proceedings that would put an end to Teile and Sharet war. The location for the historic meeting was Nelly's, about thirty-five minutes away. Clamping my hand around Breas's left wrist, I lifted it to eye level and pushed his watch's little light switch. Eight-forty.

"I've got a scheduling conflict," I said, releasing his arm. I told him about the meeting.

"So the war will be over by ten o'clock?" he asked, his tone too uninterested.

"You're wondering if you can contact your bookie on the Fey plane, aren't you?" I asked. Breas shrugged and I punched him in the arm.

Jason's cell phone rang, and Breas and I pricked our ears in the direction of the bathroom.

"Lake's gonna have to bring that idiot in eventually," Breas said, referring to Kyle.

"Yeah, about that..." I said. "I don't suppose I could get you to, um, keep an eye on Jason?"

"I don't protect humans, I eat them." He crossed his arms over his chest and frowned down at me. "And what about me? Who'll keep an eye on me?" he asked, a flirtatious smirk replacing the frown.

"You? You don't need looking after. In the event of a nuclear war, vampires and cockroaches will rule the world."

With tremendous sincerity he said, "In the event of a nuclear war, I hope I'm at ground zero."

A minute later, Jason emerged, smelling of wet blood. The gash needed stitches.

Before I could mention the first aid kit in my trunk, he asked, "Did you say Jeanine had stolen your phone?"

"Yeah. My car and house keys, too."

"Tracer spell," Breas said.

Jason nodded and motioned us over to his SUV.

Since there are no other souls or consciousness involved, besides mine, using a tracer to retrieve stolen property is safe and easy. As we walked over to Jason's vehicle, I snuck another look at Breas's watch. *Eight forty-five. Damn, damn, damn.*

One component of the Tracer spell, various maps of the Metro area, was in Jason's vehicle.

"You really meant to go through with a Tracer for Jeanine?" Breas asked.

Jason frowned and answered, "All I had to work with was a name." Glancing uneasily at me, he continued, "It isn't as bad as it sounds. The Tracer spell. All Holders are bound magically."

"Induction Rites," Breas said, probably for my benefit. "Still sounds like trading a long leash for handcuffs."

I shuddered and studied the magical framework of the map Jason had unfolded in the back of his SUV.

"Er, em, Regan," Jason began. "The best way, I mean, in order for, well, see, you are—"

"She knows she's an innate, Lake," Breas said.

Startled, Jason eyes widened and then narrowed. "And how do *you* know?" he asked the vampire.

"It's a long and dismal story," said Breas.

Jason's turned to me, his expression wary. "So you can run a Tracer spell, then?"

"Um, no. See, I'm not so good with the magic thing."

"Oh yeah. By the way. She has a hang-up," said Breas.

Jason's eyes flicked to the vampire and back to me. "In this capacity, stolen objects, a Tracer is an easy spell," he said with no inflection.

My eyes widened. "Really. I don't do magic. Thanks."

"Like I said, a magical hang-up," Breas muttered.

I heard Jason's sigh. "Please," he tried, the suspicion in his eyes replaced with something warmer.

Aw hell. My eyes got all tangled up in his and my knees got rubbery. "Okay. I'll try."

Mostly, I wanted to avoid anything that involved touching, at least in Breas's presence. That turned out to be impossible. By the time we had finished the spell, my brain was buzzing so loudly from the effect of our combined magic, I felt like a frequent shopper at Talis's pharmacy.

Breas slumped on the back of the vehicle, his familiar smirk in place. "Darling, you really need to go home, or hero boy is gonna be rendered useless." I scowled, and he added, "Either that or the two of you should get a hotel room, and make the blissful beast with two backs."

I flipped him the bird. "I think he's right, though," I said to Jason, and my face got hot. "I-I mean about me going home." Jason nodded, his face devoid of emotion. "Bye." I spun and hurried over to my car.

Not wanting to waste time going about it the conventional way, I supplemented the unlock spell words with a harmony in my head. The lock, resisting on account of the car's iron alloys, shivered and clunked open. I pulled open the door and turned to regard Jason, who had followed me.

"Any chance you two might avoid getting yourselves dead?" I smirked at Breas. "Or more dead?"

Jason didn't bother to answer, instead leaning in and kissing me, and ultimately making it hard to remember how to hot-wire a car.

Chapter Thirty-Four

*I*n exchange for a permanent cessation of the slaughter of their neighbors, the Teile and Sharet demons were going to get an exclusive right to export chile off Earth plane—a demon chile pepper cartel.

I had run all the necessary Brethren authorizations through Cypher, rather than Kadin. Kadin, betting man that he was, might not have viewed the outbreak of peace on the Teile/Sharet plane in a favorable light.

Since Talis had helped me work up the paperwork, in the correct languages with all the appropriate cultural niceties, I cut him in as a third partner in the cartel. Maybe if he were busy being a legitimate or semi-legitimate businessman, he'd have no time to do drugs. Unlikely, but a girl can dream.

Even though it felt as though I had hit every possible red light on the way to Nelly's, I made it with five minutes to spare. As I entered the restaurant, Talis spotted me and waved. He and Angry were sitting at a large table at the rear of the restaurant.

A bean burrito, smothered in green chile sauce, sat on the table next to Talis. "That's yours," he said, "I had a feeling you'd be hungry."

"Hurray for your 'feelings.'" I sat down and dug into the meal. "Where's everybody else?" I asked, gesturing at the empty chairs.

"They should be here soon. I will go and wait at the door," Angry said. He got up and headed for the entrance.

I inhaled several more bites and then asked Talis, "You never answered my question. What's with these guys, anyhow? Why can't they just…" I grimaced, "get along?"

Talis blinked and then stared at me, dead-on, his expression unreadable. "Chaotic—magic," he said slowly, as though the words caused him pain.

After a couple of chews, I swallowed and said, "That day…the day Kyle hurt you, you said somebody had messed with chaotic magic in the past. Who?"

Talis flinched and then spoke. "The Sharet. They turned their plane into a parking lot. The survivors were relocated to the Teile plane."

"Which, from the Teile point of view, took 'There goes the neighborhood' to a new level," I said, after gulping down half the glass of iced tea that Talis had also anticipated me needing.

"And they've been angry ever since," Talis said, smiling at his pun.

Speak of the devil. Angry, along with two other Teile demons and three Sharet demons, had returned. Standing side by side, Teile and Sharet demons have a Mutt and Jeff kind of quality. Teile demons are short and blocky; the Sharet are tall with broad shoulders that taper down to narrow hips giving them a triangular geometry. Both races believe three is a lucky number.

Introductions were made and after a literal countdown to the nine-thirty, we began the negotiations. "Negotiations" was just a fancy way of saying, "signing the stack of paperwork." The process was reminiscent of closing on a house purchase, signatures to authenticate signatures and authorize other signatures.

Ten minutes and a forest's worth of paper later, we were done. Reasoning that prolonged exposure to either race of demons increased the chances I might say something stupid and undo all the good I'd done, I made my excuses and left, Talis in tow.

Just when I thought I'd made a clean escape, a voice called out, "Ms. O'Connell!"

We spun around and saw that Angry was rushing after us. Uh-oh. Now what'd I do?

As soon as Angry reached us, he held out his hand.

"Thank you," he said, baring a set of pointy white teeth.

I shook his hand. "Er, sure, okay."

He released my hand, drew himself up and lifted his chin. "Your eyes are the vibrant green of an egg-bearing Yahtet dragoness."

Talis squeezed my arm. Oh. I guess Angry had just paid me a compliment.

I fished around in the slimy recesses of my mind and came up with, "Er, yeah, and you are a magnificent monument to man meat."

Talis made a noise that sounded like a cat hacking up a fur ball. Angry showed more teeth, bowed and said, "It has been a pleasure, Ms. O'Connell." With a nod in Talis's direction, he headed back to Nelly's. Talis and I crossed the street and moved across the parking lot.

Once we were out of earshot of the demon, Talis said with poorly suppressed laughter, "Man meat?"

"Uh-huh. I've mastered the art of lewd compliments. Won't my father be proud?" I muttered, my mind already racing towards the East Mountains.

Talis put an arm around my shoulder. "And you've ended a war."

I cut a glance at his arm, noting a watch. The big hand and the little hand said nine-forty. According to Eva, Kyle lived somewhere in Westside Albuquerque. It would have taken Jason at least twenty minutes to go collect his partner. Factoring in at least forty-minutes to drive out to the other side of mountains, Jason and Kyle could still be on route. If I left now, I might get to Joan's place just after they did.

"Time to cap off the evening by saving the world," I said, "and my job."

"Huh?"

In the streetlight, the reminders of Talis's encounter with Kyle were black slashes on his smooth dark skin.

"I've got business with the Holders. Wanna come with? Maybe you'll get a chance for some kind of payback."

"No. I don't do payback," he said. "But if you want company...?"

I nodded, slightly chastened. My conscience bore a striking resemblance to a dark elf with a drug habit.

Joan had fled to her factory of the undead in the East Mountains. The Tracer spell disclosed a location in what I recalled was a rather nice subdivision, tucked away high in the towering pine trees. "East Mountain" is a generic term used for anything on the eastern side of the Sandia and Manzanito Mountains. The mountains wall off Albuquerque's attempts to sprawl eastward. They have a Janus-like quality; their western face, Albuquerque's side is largely treeless, while the eastern slopes are thick with conifers—piñon, juniper, and at higher elevations, Ponderosa pine and blue spruce.

Joan's house of horror appeared as a bright pinpoint of color on the map. The nearer the user got to the site, the brighter the spot would glow. It would turn deep midnight blue when the target was very close.

Of course, I didn't have the map and was operating off my memory of the site's approximate location. Keeping an eye out for Jason or Breas's car, I cruised up a mountain road.

"Jason came by my place, a couple days after..." Talis said, the first words he'd spoken since I'd filled him in on Joan. After my explanation of the day's events, he had lapsed into a strange silence.

"Jason? Why? What'd he do to you?" I asked, instantly suspicious. "Did he hurt you?"

"No," Talis said, hair flopping as he shook his head. "He apologized for what Kyle did."

I bit my lip. "Do you think he was, um, sincere?"

"Yes," Talis replied without hesitation.

In lieu of thinking too much about Talis's revelation, I pulled the window down and tested the chilly air. Jason had shoved his vehicle up high off the roadway and I nearly missed it when we drove by. As the vampire had pointed out, Jason would have had to involve Kyle. If Breas was around, he came by himself. I drove on up the road for a few tenths of a mile, before spotting his Mercedes.

Envying Jason's taste in vehicles, I pulled my car as far over as possible without four-wheel drive.

I shut down the car and smiled at Talis. "Ready?"

He shot me a guilty look. After a deep whooshing breath, he said, "I didn't do you any favors, helping you cheat."

"Uh, yeah, you did. I can't do magic." Why this, now?

He turned and faced me, dropping his chin toward his chest, pale eyes peering through black hair. He spoke two words. "Harmonic magic." Cutting off my protest, he said, "That heal spell you ran on me—"

"I fixed a broken rib, no big deal," I said, horrified that he had noticed.

"Four broken ribs and a small tear in my lung, actually."

"So what are you saying?"

"You know I'd do anything for you. But-but, I think that is the problem. I, uh, hold you back." He offered a sad closed-mouth smile. "I think you need to do this on your own."

I stared at my gentle friend. The darkness stripped away the harsh evidence of drug abuse, revealing the handsome playboy I knew long ago. "Harmonic magic is the answer," he said. His lips parted, showing a dazzling smile. "Trust me."

The trouble is, I did trust Talis. But trusting him in this matter meant letting go of my dream of "normal." Normal by human estimations might be a job, two kids, a spouse and a house in the suburbs. For me it is speaking a few words and making magic.

I nodded agreeably, all the while resolving not to so much as think about music.

"Okay. You stay here," I said. "I need a getaway driver." I reached under the wheel and resparked the wires, making a mental to get one of those hide-a-key things to stash under the car's fender. I climbed out of the car, crossed the road and moved into the cover of the trees. Straight ahead, shrouded by pines, was a large cabin. A quick check revealed nothing more unusual than the charred smell of a dinner gone awry. Assuming Breas would park farther beyond the site than Jason and Kyle, I headed down the roadway. I passed two driveways before coming to a third that was marked with a broken placard, proclaiming it to be the home of the SonShine Christian Day School. Who'da thunk it? Joan had a sense of irony.

Frozen in place by a sudden craving for raw cookie dough, I peered up through the trees and saw the constellation Orion flying totem-like in the Eastern sky. A touch of Breas's obsessive self-preservation itched along my spine.

Dull thuds and cries, the sounds of fighting, woke me from my attack of cowardice and I jogged toward the building.

Chapter Thirty-Five

Halfway to the house, I walked through a huge spider web. Spitting and blowing away sticky threads, I stopped, realizing it wasn't truly a web. Magical perimeter alarm.

There wasn't any doubt what kind of guard dogs Joan was using. The sooty airborne remains of Jason and Kyle's encounter with her security force tickled my nose. Feet crunched the gravel driveway and human-shaped shadows separated from the school's hulking form and progressed toward me.

There were an awful lot of them. Twenty at least. Does she send out a bigger group each time the alarm is triggered? I had a hard time believing even Jason and Kyle could handle more than a half dozen vampires.

I summoned both daggers and felt for my speed. Icy-hot speed is always there, in my blood, waiting to fuel a pace not even vampires can match. Against a few opponents, I don't need much. Against a small army...well, that was a situation I usually avoided.

Outlined in blue ghost light, the Lesser vampires converged on me, some muttering inanities to themselves, most silent, emanating stark thirst. I scanned the gathering horde, detecting no true unity in the group.

"In the immortal words of a friend, 'I'm hardly a snack,'" I said, saluting them with a dagger.

They surged forward in an inelegant mass. Passing through an opening created when two of them met my daggers, I spun, daggers gone, short sword in hand, and decapitated two more. Three lunged at me. Speed fizzing in my bloodstream, I dove under and between legs, lashing out at tendons. Rolling to my feet and directly in front of a scrawny blond vampire, I called a dagger and jammed it into his heart. The collected scrape of feet on ground alerted me to another group pounce. I jumped, rewarded by disappointed growls when the vampires dog-piled the place I had just been.

I don't like killing, but with enough speed active in my system, I start to forget that. There's an indescribable joy in moving that fast and the knowledge that I am good at something. My arms, legs and body cut through the cold mountain air, icy friction dragging against my skin. Like clever tentacles, my senses whipped around. I smelled intentions and heard the gooey flex of muscles. Halfway through the fight, it occurred to me that there were a few more than twenty vampires—thirty?—but I was having too much fun to care.

And then it was over. The last two vampires, showing remarkable intelligence, came at me low and high. The first, a stocky white male, dove for my legs like a ballplayer going for home. His partner, a tall black woman, leapt towards me at chest level. I jumped, pulling my legs out of reach and twisting in the air. Without me to stop their momentum, both ended up face down in the gravel. I gave each the opportunity to get up and face me before I killed them.

With the ashy sigh of a burnt out fireplace log, the last vampire collapsed. The orange embers in her remains hadn't yet dimmed, when the first signs of weakness manifested.

I took two steps toward the old school, and the muscles in my legs gave out. My knees hit the gravel, sharp stones cut through denim, and the elation of battle fled. Running vampire speed in a partially human framework is akin to shoving a big block V8 engine into a tiny compact car—grossly overpowered. I sat in the gravel, taking a moment to comprehend the magnitude of chaotic energy represented by Joan's vampire guards. What did she need that much power for?

I listened to the building. Second floor floorboards squeak-ground against each other. Jason and Kyle were still alive. Where was Breas?

I asked my legs to work and they obeyed, but the dull ache in my muscles signaled an impending rebellion.

Two steps away from the door, I staggered back. The cause, another vampire, stepped through the opening, tripped, and righted himself. He held up his hands. "Wait. Please."

I think he had dark hair and light brown or hazel eyes. I got the impression he was cute, almost pretty. *"Pretty man with eyes like grass."* His scent had a kind of solidity; only one emotion poured from him. Fear.

"What am I waiting for?" I asked.

"This." He ducked as though expecting a dagger and then ran like hell. Away from me.

My hand twitched on the sword hilt, but I didn't move. I didn't waste my energy. He seemed sane; I doubted he was a willing participant in Joan's scheme. Once he was out of sight, I entered the building.

I stood in what had been an office or reception area. Lighter rectangles of carpet marked the location of long gone office furniture. Overhead the pallid, white cover on a sputtering fluorescent light hung open. Doors on the left and right side of the room opened to what had been classrooms. A subdued aroma of vampire came from the classrooms, but I opted for the staircase at the back of the room.

Totally evading my sneaky skills, the stairs creaked as I climbed to the second story. Hot and jumping with possibilities, the taint of chaotic magic twisted in the air; light from light fixtures and lamps flickered, fighting its influence. Stepping over grimy piles of vampire remains, I headed down the hallway at the top, following the sound of heartbeats.

"Dorian," I heard Jason say.

Peeking around the corner of a doorway, the door itself long gone, I stared at the backs of Kyle and Jason. A bleary-eyed Breas leaned heavy on the far wall.

"Like candy from a baby," Kyle said, pointing a bolt launcher at Breas.

Jason turned, his mouth half open, debating. "I don't think that would be wise, Kyle," he said.

I traded the short sword for a dagger. Breas's scent was odd, muddled and lacking coherence. The dagger hung in my hand and with a flip, it switched to throwing position. In that brief moment, I stared at the back of Kyle's thick neck and remembered Cyrus Purcell. Then Kyle's finger tightened on the trigger. I calculated and sent the ebony dagger spinning in his direction.

The pommel, rather than the pointy end, hammered the back of Kyle's head. Kyle's finger jerked reflexively even as he fell. Proving my concerns, Breas didn't even flinch when the bolt smacked into the wall next to him.

"Kyle?" Jason spun, his weapon aimed straight at me. I lifted my now empty hands—the dagger banished—and tried smiling.

"Regan?"

"Hey." I took a few steps into the room, trying to ignore the weapon that was still pointed at me. "What's wrong with him?" I asked. Breas had slumped to the floor.

Jason lowered the weapon. "I think Jeanine is using a yew-derived tranquilizer." He moved to my side. "Why are you here?" he asked, glancing at the vampire detector on his wrist. "There are still vampires in this building."

"Warm and tasty, right?" I pointed at him and me. "So why aren't they attacking? It's not like they've been snacking on people in the neighborhood, either." I frowned at Breas, who wasn't conscious.

"Again. The tranquilizer. It seems she set up a magical alarm system. Step too far onto the property, and an antidote is delivered—"

"Oh. Cry havoc and let slip the dogs, er, vampires of war."

"What did you do to Kyle?"

"Hit him with a rock. It's not cool to shoot a guy when he's down," I answered, and moved over to Breas. "Hey." I kicked his foot.

"Regan, perhaps you shouldn't...."

My foot shoved Breas's harder and his eyelids twitched. "Hey. What happened?"

Peeling his eyes open, the vampire regarded me with open irritation. "I'm just fine. Thanks for asking, Florence Nightmare." His eyes closed. "If you're gonna quote Shakespeare, does it have to be Julius Caesar?"

"What happened?"

"Like the Holder said, yew-sap tranqs. And a Bane, powerful Bane." Breas let out an exasperated hiss. "There's a door, somewhere along that wall...heavily warded and obscured. She went that-a-way."

Jason walked over to the wall, searching for an opening. I joined him.

"See anything?" Jason asked.

"Wall's a-crawling with magic," I said, shrugging.

His greenish eyes met mine. "But you deny having any magical ability?" He smiled.

"Seeing is not the same as doing." I studied the dull white wall. "The door's here, by the way." Stopping any comment he was about to make, I explained, "The plaster is cracking. I can see the outline of the header. Basic, non-magical, construction knowledge." Jason chuckled and shifted position to stand in front of the blocked doorway.

Waiting until Jason was immersed in spell casting, I returned to Breas, and crouched before him. "Where'd she shoot you?" He ignored me, so I sniffed, detected blood, and located two small darts. I examined the second dart, which resembled something from a nature show. The device worked on a time delay, pumping in additional yew poison and circumventing the normally quick vampire detox mechanisms.

"Thanks," he said, uncharacteristically.

His eyes were closed and he still felt distant. "You think you can get up?" I asked, getting a twinge of unpleasant feelings. Breas Montrose irritates the shit out of me, but I'm sort of accustomed to the irritation. After a moment, his gray eyes met mine and something passed between us, something that wasn't my ongoing desire to turn him into potting soil and something that wasn't his ongoing desire to—

Then he smirked, squashing any warm-fuzzies I was harboring.

"You got bloodstains on my shirt," I said, helping him stand. Still unsteady, he kept his back to the wall.

"Here," he said and I suppressed a yelp at the sensation of cold metal, Icarus's gun, in my hand. "Put all those hours on the firing range to use."

"No—"

"Yes." His hands were suddenly around my neck, thumbs pressed to my pulse. "You smell weak, like prey. How long before your body shuts down? Ten, fifteen minutes?"

Less, I thought. Speed pain was building in all my joints; a nice long nap beckoned. Breas released me. I wrinkled my nose at the weapon, checked the safety, and stuffed it in my waistband.

Jason's spell reacted with Joan's, making my sore bones vibrate. Then a dull green light defined the outline of the door. Another series of spells, triggered by the door opening, ran in a rattling train, releasing the vampires downstairs.

"Back at you," I whispered, wrapping his hand around the hilt of the Wolfe short sword. He was armed, but I knew he wasn't about to turn down a superior vampire-killing weapon.

I scurried back several steps before Jason turned around. The staircase's protestations, loud groans and cracks, announced Joan's pack of guard dogs as they scampered up to the second floor.

Jason's head whipped around as he surveyed the door, his detector, and finally Breas. Eyes silvery-gold, Breas spun the sword and straightened, his gaze on the door. "Take the brat with you," he said to Jason.

Jason gave the Wolfe's weapon and the vampire a dark scowl, took my hand and pulled me in the direction of the un-spelled door. "Liar," he said to the vampire, drawing the door open and dragging me with him.

Chapter Thirty-Six

*A*ny lingering, squishy, worried thoughts I might have had about Breas were swept away by the stomach churning concoction of chaotic and ordinary magic that filled the room. My knees buckled and Jason steadied me before I fell. Wow. My original goals had been to avoid doing any harmonic magic and, of course, keep everybody alive. I added "Don't throw up on cute guy's shoes" to the list.

A "Reading is Magic" banner hung above a white dry erase board, alluding to the room's former life as a classroom. The room was luminous with the cast light of Joan's intricate spell structure. Joan stood in the middle of a hemisphere of light, the Maram'ro wood box a shimmering core near her feet. The fog-like aura of a warding spell covered the structure making the details hard to see. Obviously confident in the strength of her fortifications, Joan gave us only one perfunctory glance. Caught up in spell casting, her hands and arms danced in an elaborate pattern.

"What is it you mean to do, Jeanine?" Jason asked. She ignored him and he examined the structure. "Jeanine? I met Roger. He was a decent man, not the kind who'd approve—"

"Does he know, Regan?" she said. Her eyes moved back and forth like a tennis ball, from Jason to me. Magic sloshed around in my head; I was too sick to respond. "You and the blond vampire are lovers?"

The bean burrito made a leap for daylight and I battled the urge to throw up. I shrugged off Jason's help, throwing a glance in his direction.

There was no indication that he had heard Joan's comment. Concentration rendered his face expressionless; I could feel the electric tension of his gathering power.

"Vampires don't sleep with humans, Joan." To me, she was still Joan. "Any more than humans sleep with livestock. Except hillbillies, and Jerry Springer talk show guests." I sat down.

"Oh, of course. 'Dorian's just a friend.' Your words, Regan."

I'm too damn quotable. The air thickened with Jason's impending spell. To keep her focus on me, I said, "Funny. I thought you and I were friends." Her face transformed by shock, she paused her work for a second.

The power behind Jason's spell was amazing. It spewed forward, tearing at her protective spells. This is it, I thought, he's in. He could take apart Joan's spell and—

A few wispy sections of the protective spell curled away like smoke, but the majority of Joan's defenses held. The influence of chaotic magic was just too great and only a small portion of her protective armor was damaged.

She retaliated by throwing a fireball in my direction. Jason, anticipating the attack, spoke several short Elvish words. Hot magic splattered against the Wall he constructed before me. I cringed, half expecting his spell to evaporate. It held, the force of her spell drumming on its surface for several seconds. I squinted through the glare of magic and watched Joan speed through a repair.

The fireball died and Jason helped me to my feet. "Have you ever channeled magical energy?" he asked.

"I know how, the mechanics, but I can't—" Jason tried to catch my eyes, but I dropped my gaze to stare at his chest.

"Yes, you can. With your level of power, it should be easy." He wrapped my hand in his, pressing energy through my skin. Grinding my teeth together, I tried shoving it back. Nothing happened and in desperation, I resorted to the stupid tune in my head trick.

He shivered as my power surged past his and penetrated his palm. "That's it. When I say 'now,' do it again." He turned toward Joan and I felt energy building in his body. I brushed away the influences of Joan's magic by latching onto the throbbing of blood in his veins.

"Now," he whispered. My power was snagged like a small boat in his current. I bit my tongue, overcome by the sensation of pins and needles through veins and arteries.

The spell roared through the wards. Joan's eyes nearly popped out of her head with surprise. I shook free of Jason and staggered a few feet away. Separated from the protection of Jason's power, the nausea returned and I fell to my knees. Overcome, I stared at the floor, noting the Seventies green carpet and white patterning.

Jason's harsh gasp echoed in the small room. I looked up. Shields blown away, the full extent of Joan's spell lay before us. A crystalline lattice wrapped in ever-changing spiraling marks and sigils. It was quite beautiful.

"Good God." Jason's face was frozen in shock. "It's a Soul Binder."

Joan spared him a fraction of a glance and said, "To all Holders, all who have undergone the Rites of Induction." She reached into the lattice, peeled away a thread of light and twined it around her finger. Jason wavered; his eyes glazed over. She muttered a few words and swirled her other hand at him.

He crumpled and fell hard on the grubby carpet.

Shit!

Stunned, I just sat on the floor, forgotten for the time being and more than a little befuddled. Almost nonchalant, Joan returned to her preparations. She didn't even gloat at the ease at which she dispatched Jason.

Get up. Get up. I struggled to my feet and over to Jason. He was still alive and breathing, his heart rate regular. "Jason. Wake up." I shook him lightly. "Come on. You're the hero. Wake up!" No response.

I threw a heal spell at him, carried by, of course, a clever ditty. Within seconds, the gash on his forehead closed to a thin scar. But he didn't wake up.

"Grrrreat. He'll die nice and pretty. Bloody worthless." I stood up and shuffled closer to Joan's lovely spell framework, trying to push away the effects of sickening harmonics.

With my limited magical knowledge, the construct resembled a holographic map of space in a sci-fi movie, a half circle covered in an odd grid. Moving closer, something else was apparent. Sharp edges. Cutting surfaces.

Surprised, I took a step back. "You mean to take their souls?" Joan lifted her gaze to me for an instant. "But doing that to someone who isn't near death...." I gulped. "It-it will shred their spirit forms, leave 'em like a zombie. If they live through it at all."

Joan's hand spun and another layer of twitching symbols fell on the structure.

"What do you care, Tara?" she asked, and I couldn't hide my shock. "You don't set off vampire detectors, but you can't be human."

Lost for words, I stared at her, the picture of a slack-jawed yokel.

"You're Tara Kane, aren't you?" she asked. "Tara Kane, black-haired, green-eyed vampire, implicated in the murder of Cyrus Purcell."

"He deserved it," I said dully.

"They all do," she responded.

"No, Joan," I said, with surprising conviction, "they don't. Not all–"

Two fireballs, raced at me. Icarus's Bane. The remnants of speed and some old fashioned adrenaline got me moving. I dodged both, darting down and to the left. She hurled two more. I jumped over the first and watched the next hiss by to my left.

"No human can move that fast," she said.

"Yeah. No vampire, either," I said with stupid pride. Overworked and bitter, the muscles in my legs started to tremble, threatening mutiny.

"You're letting sentiment get in the way of the big picture," she said, giving a Jason a long look.

"You're zombie-fying an entire organization over sentiment," I replied.

The black box, connected to the lattice by a delicate thread, quivered and the thread swelled thick, dazzling power coursing in a broad river. The hemisphere responded by growing brighter, the symbols running and stopping quicker. Jason moaned and convulsed. I dropped to his side and cradled his head in my lap. I could hear the swish of her hands as she re-fortified her wards.

"It would be best to kill him now. If you really care," Joan said. Jason, his innate energy surging in wild patterns, squirmed, blood trickling from his mouth.

The thing is, she was right. My fingers encircled the weapon at my waist; my thumb flicked the safety. A silly thought occurred to me.

If Breas and his lock picks could get around a lock spell, maybe I could chip away at her protections with bullets? I lifted the gun, squeezed the trigger and the recoil rattled down my arm.

Just before I got off two shots, Joan launched a barrage of vampire darts in my direction. I threw myself over Jason, cringing from the swarm of biting darts. The horrid realization hit me as the bullets struck her.

She had assumed that her primary threats would be from magical, rather than conventional weaponry.

I straightened, pulling out the half dozen darts that burned like wasp stings. I rotated the last dart in the sparkly light of the lattice, sensing the remains of electrical impulses that jerked useless through Joan's body.

Jason moaned and I stared disbelieving at the Soul Cleaver. Up and running, it no longer needed Joan. I had killed her, accomplishing nothing more than saving her from the effects of her own evil spell. Jason shuddered, and lapsed into tooth chattering shivers. I held his head, horrified, as his energy flowed in all directions at once and nowhere at all.

"No," I moaned and reached out, trying to sense Breas, but the magic blocked my efforts. Just touching Jason was unbearable; the sensation of near ripping and ferocious stretching of his ethereal energy took my breath away. I picked up the gun, popped out the clip and snapped it back. Four more bullets. It would be best. Rough stubble scraped the back of my fingers as I ran them along his jaw, studying his face. I wondered who Allison was. Would she miss him? I would.

"I had a human best friend once. Her name was Cara," I told Jason. "Even if Cyrus hadn't killed her, she'd be dead by now. It's that way with humans." Jason gave no sign he heard me. "Talis is my best friend, now. I know he has bad habits, but that doesn't give anyone the right to treat him unkindly." Jason shuddered and I spoke quickly. "Thanks for apologizing to him." I kissed him, set the gun down, and eased his head to the floor.

Three of the darts had hit my right leg and it was going numb. Limping, I lurched toward the Soul Cleaver.

Joan's remaining magical protections sizzled against my skin. I hummed a simplified version of a Paganini caprice, setting the bright energetic notes against the wards. Like tissue paper set on fire, they hissed and evaporated.

The Maram'ro box sat on the floor emanating waves of energy, light pouring out of the oak top, channeled neatly by spiraled inlays. Separating the lattice from the energy source would be the most logical approach. I lifted my hand, palm down and lowered it over the structure. Ow! The edges existed both in ethereal and real space. Three bright red stripes marked my palm.

I had to unravel the structure. Except, then the power source might still be spewing wild energy everywhere. Jason groaned, a thick wrenching sound, and I wondered if I could find the link, his alone, and nick him away from the massive structure. But the pattern was ever changing and meaningless. I'd never find his link.

All or nothing. Not much of a choice. I reached out with my senses, felt the room and beyond, tasted gritty crumbling plaster, smelled moldy carpet and fireplace smoke. I heard insects scurrying, trapped in patterns they didn't understand, and Jason's heartbeat. It still had a certain regularity, but the effects of the spell were slowly breeding the shadow of asymmetry.

Vampire senses questing, threatening to extend too far, I placed my hand over the lattice. Razor edges sliced into my palms. The pain held my focus on Jason and added the echoes of other beating hearts. Other Holders? All linked, all drumming in time. The thought made me ill.

Just as I had done back in the room with Sean, I used the heartbeats as a tempo, and began building an inner melody, something in D-Minor, because I think best in that key. The numbness from the darts spread up my side. My blood is a whole lot vampire without the lightening-fast detox ability.

Keeping the tune pure and improvisational and avoiding repetition, I began searching for a point of origin, the place that first seeded the Soul Cleaver. Minutes passed, and the location eluded me. Jason's heartbeat got more and more erratic.

It wasn't working.

Singing is not my forte; my fiddle is my voice. But the notes in my head clearly weren't enough. When I was a kid, I used to make up songs, the words in an imaginary language based on the Elvish and Gaelic my father spoke.

Harkening back to long ago voice lessons, I took a diaphragm expanding breath, and started to sing.

Funny how something can take you back. Eight notes into the song,

I was back in my childhood home in Ireland, ten years old and giving an impromptu parlor concert for Dad and Kadin. I guess in the absence of televised sports, watching your kid sing weird songs was a hoot. I warbled in my squeaky little girl's voice, perfectly in tune. Dad and Kadin watched me, bemused smiles on their face. And Dad's eyes were filled with something else—pride.

Better than the summer sun in New Mexico, the memory warmed me. And my power responded, running down my arms and enveloping the Soul Cleaver. Like a bright stain, my magic seeped into the structure, exposing seams and joints. And the point of origin suddenly materialized.

It was a line, really, like the impossible-to-find end of a roll of clear packing tape. I can do this. Before it could shimmer away, I used the music like an appendage, snagging the edge and skimming the magical corner away from the primary structure.

The structure fought back. The entire lattice vibrated with grating resonance and pain rattled through every bone in my body. Again, I wondered if I could free Jason, and Jason alone. But the spell's substance was rubbery, waiting to snap right back to form the second I released it. Blood from my palms ran warm down my arms, but the rest of my body hurt too much to notice my hands.

Outcomes and possibilities. I'd forgotten more about statistics than I'd ever learned. I continued to unwrap the spell, searching, hoping to see the possibility that all the magic and power would, could slide back into the Maram'ro box. Modulating my tune from D-minor to a haunting Middle Eastern key, I kept searching.

I was getting frustrated and even a little panicked. Speed exhaustion waited in the wings. Even the pain in my hands wouldn't keep me conscious for long. The sharp edges drove into Jason's spirit forms and connected to him, and my own soul struggled like a moth in a spider's web.

My voice broke, and several notes dropped out of tune. Both to stay upright and remain conscious, I shifted more weight onto my hands. White-hot pain shot up my arms. My song was now hopelessly out of tune, each note flat of the one I was aiming for. The weird dissonance between the notes I was thinking and what actually came out created tooth chattering vibrations that blurred my vision.

I blinked hard and then the possibilities were laid bare before me.

Wow!

The possibilities were similar to reflections on a television screen. As a rule, the brightest and most colorful image, the television show itself, is what the eye focuses on. But shift your focus a little and you see the reflection of the surrounding room. In this case, there were hundreds of reflections, all dominated by Joan's original purpose.

As the structure peeled away, the source energy now started to jump from the box and around the room. Adrenaline—all my speed was gone—filled my blood, and my song quickened, filled with rapid staccato nonsense words.

There it was! The "possible image" of the energy shrinking and folding back into the little black box. Grabbing it before it was swept away, I bound it with music and innate power. My bones protested in rheumatic pain.

For a moment, nothing happened and then the lattice expanded, seeming to reconstruct. "No," I protested, but all my energy, physical and magic, was gone.

And then, the power and light snapped into the box, so fast it seemed as though it had not been real. Obediently following the laws of science, the equal and opposite reaction reached out and hurled me across the room.

I curled in flight, trying to land on my feet. Like a baseball bat, a wall thwacked into my back. Air whooshed out of my lungs and something cracked. The floor came up hard and fast and I lay there for some time, trying to remember how to breathe. Then I remembered and regretted my mortal need for oxygen. My diaphragm convulsed and air rushed down my windpipe, expanding lungs against broken ribs.

The sound of Jason's breathing and now regular heartbeat got me to my feet. The gun lay nearby and I picked it up and dropped it—my hands were slippery with blood—and scooped it up, without a glance in Joan's direction. After going through the usual checks, I stuffed it back in my waistband.

"Jason. Lake!" He didn't respond but otherwise seemed healthy. Since carrying him was out of the question, even without cracked ribs, I grabbed his arms and managed to drag him out of the room.

The floor in the next room was flecked with pigeon shit, but my body ignored my revulsion. I passed out next to Jason.

Chapter Thirty-Seven

On Friday, I was finally able to walk erect, like Homo sapiens, without crashing to Earth in a bruised heap. In honor of the occasion, I took a long hot shower, dressed in clean jeans and a T-shirt, and then investigated my refrigerator, hoping Lex had left anything edible. Three take-away cartons, a trace of Talis still on the Styrofoam, sat on the top shelf. I ate a breakfast of cheese enchiladas at the kitchen table, in the late morning sunshine, and then moved to the living room.

Even with the satellite-enhanced legion of television stations, there was nothing on. I settled on a talk show. "You're My Baby's Father" was today's topic. A girl barely old enough to vote confronted four sullen young men, all possible fathers of her child, fatherhood to be determined by a paternity test.

Breas emerged from his room, kerplunked next to me, and put an arm around my shoulders. "What's on ESPN?" he asked.

"Bowling championships," I lied. If I told him the truth—NASCAR —he might tackle me for the remote. My freshly healed ribs weren't up to it.

His fingers squeezed my shoulder. "Liar." He took in the televised dysfunction. "Little Miss Panties at Her Ankles," he observed.

"She's been with twice as many men as I have. All in a span of one week, apparently."

"Because you choose quality over quantity."

I did the world-weary look thing, but it was wasted. Rather than a smirk, the vampire watched me with a fond smile.

"Who are you?" I asked. "You're not my vampire. My vampire doesn't do mushy smiles."

"No," he replied, "I'm not your vampire." His cool lips brush my cheek. "But not for lack of trying on my part."

I tried not to laugh and failed. "Ow, stupid ribs." The bones were intact, but sore.

"Careful, Humpty Dumpty. I wasted a lot of energy putting you back together."

I let the comparison to an egg slide and leaned against his shoulder. Because Breas specializes in harm, not heal, Talis contributed the majority of the magic necessary to patch me back together. But the vampire still took the opportunity to "play doctor." In the past two days, I'd been felt up more than a teenage prom queen. Nevertheless, in his own warped way, Breas had tried to come to my rescue.

In his version of things, Breas cast himself in the role of hero, battling legions of Lesser vampires and a Baccalshi demon, buying Jason and me the time to deal with Joan's Soul Cleaver. The more likely scenario went like this: he easily eliminated the vampires, started to snoop around downstairs, looking for something worth stealing and was interrupted by the untimely arrival of a ten-foot tall Baccalshi demon.

Pete Tanaka's prediction had been correct; an extra outcome of Joan's spell had been a brand new interPlanar fold, located high in the scenic Sandia Mountains. The transport of a ten-foot demon through that fold was an added bonus. Rather than enjoying its unexpected holiday, the demon vented its frustrations by attempting to disembowel Breas.

After dealing with the demon, Breas had rushed upstairs, where he found Jason and me unconscious, but alive. He embellished this part of the story as well, claiming he tried to take me away before Jason woke up, but alas, the human awoke and found me in the vampire's arms. Huh. I wouldn't be surprised if Breas shook Jason awake. Breas wasn't likely to miss an opportunity to establish his territory.

I don't know what transpired between the Holder and the vampire. All Breas would say was this: "Lake will take credit for what you did. The Holders will never know you were there."

Breas leaned his head against mine and we watched television in silence. The show ended, followed by another with the very same topic.

Breas's phone rang. I switched the station to car racing and he mouthed "liar" at me before answering the phone.

I wasn't eavesdropping, but I realized who it was instantly.

"Yeah," Breas said. "I think her phone's off. Try her at home. No, I guess you can't." He cocked a questioning eyebrow at me.

I hesitated and then said, "Give me the phone."

Even without chile, Albuquerque isn't half bad—the weather, at any rate. Despite a cool breeze, it was an otherwise nice sunny winter day, the kind of day that makes time spent indoors feel like a cardinal sin. If Kadin asked, I would have said that I chose the Albuquerque Botanic Garden because it was strategically safe—people around, ample escape routes. Honestly, I just wanted a nice setting to do what I had to do.

He was sitting at an umbrella-shaded patio table, in the area that separated the Botanical Gardens from the Aquarium building. Spotting me, he stood with athletic ease. My eyes cut a line down his body, noting the iron gray turtleneck under a black leather jacket, lean muscled thighs under blue jeans. The scar on his forehead, revealed when wind puffed his hair aside, added an appealing mix of danger and vulnerability.

I gulped. Yep. No doubt about it. I wanted this human.

"Hey," I said, stopping several feet before him.

"Regan." Jason closed the distance and took my hands, turning them palm upward. "Healed," he observed. "Dorian?"

"He did the initial healing. Talis did the rest and removed the scars."

"Talis," he muttered, thumbs rubbing my palms.

"Yeah. Maybe he can help you with the one on your forehead."

Jason shrugged and said, "I'm told scars are sexy." I stared at his shoes to hide my blush.

"I need to sit down," I said, because it was true. We moved to the table he had just vacated. Jason sat across from me, one leg bent at the knee, the other stretched out, thick soles of a hiking boot inches from my leg.

"Mind if I ask exactly what happened with you and Jeanine? How did you stop her?" he asked mildly. My car and house keys jingled as he set them on the table's metal surface.

"Thanks." I scooped up the keys and jammed them in a pocket. "I don't remember much about that night. Really." I took a deep breath, smelled Jason's clean musky masculinity, and the gardens beyond—rich soil, chemical fertilizer and other garden chemicals. "Joan, the shooting. It was an accident. I didn't want to—I was just trying to break—" I swallowed twice, pushing down guilt. "There is a sort of order to it all, chaotic magic, just like Sean said. Almost rhythmic, musical. For a second, I saw it."

"Harmonic magic," he said, and I flinched. "The ability is largely unknown outside of the Sh'ree. Demons."

I looked in his eyes, expecting disgust and seeing only mild curiosity. Yeah, demon magic, I thought, feeling a hint of pride. My memories are sketchy and getting sketchier—the more I try to remember what happened, the more details slip away—but I know I did the near impossible.

"Normally," I said, "I have a hard time with the simplest of spells. I don't know why it worked that night."

"Really? Someone must have trained you."

"Yes. Attempts have been made, unsuccessfully. I'm just not all that good at magic."

"Dorian?"

Recognizing the tone in his voice, I sneered. "No, not Dorian." Maneuvering away from the subject of the vampire, I said, "Joan, er, Jeanine was convinced the Holders were responsible for Roger's death."

"Well, yes. But it doesn't make any sense, Regan. Why would they kill him? He, along with Juliet, was one of their most highly regarded operatives. Juliet was in line for a promotion, possibly to Tactical Command." His mouth closed, realizing he was saying too much. "Assuming it wasn't an accident, it's more likely that the Grey Brethren, vampires, are responsible."

Ignoring his last statement, I said, "Kyle's spying on you. He's been charged with reporting any 'odd' behavior on your part."

"I expected as much." Following my lead, he changed the subject. "And Dorian? How did you come to be associated with a vampire?"

His jealously smelled like hot metal. "You know, scowling like that, it'll give you wrinkles." I pointed at the angry creases between his eyebrows. In response, he worked on his smile lines.

"I met Dorian when I was sixteen. And I've never been free of him since."

"So you are his familiar, then." Jason gaze dipped down to my neck.

"I'm nobody's damn Renfield," I said. "I'm not his servant or his walking blood bank." I sighed. "Mostly, we're just friends. If the definition of friendship is drifting in and out of each other's lives and mutual aggravation."

"Friend?" he said, doubt evident in his voice. "In all this time, he's never taken blood from you or—"

Worn down by lies, I squirmed and he nodded knowingly.

"I was young, younger, astonishingly stupid, and even a little insecure. He knew all the right words, three words specifically. 'I love you.'" I shook my head in disgust. "One night. First time and last time." My eyes met his. "You've never done anything stupid?"

He forced a thin smile. "Well, yes, but—"

"But you haven't done the naked naughty with a blood-loving creature of the night?"

"No." He winced. "But, I've done my share of stupid." He shrugged. "You didn't know what he was. He obviously has...power."

"He didn't use Mesmer and I was well acquainted with vampires," I said. "Look," I began, pausing to check our surroundings, "do me a favor. Put an obscure around us. Please."

Jason's mouth opened, started a question, and then closed. Concentration smoothed the lines from his handsome face; his hands moved with the elegance of someone speaking fluent sign language.

"Done," he said. The spell surrounded us, invisible, but humming like a tiny electric motor.

He obviously didn't rely on verbal crutches to cast simple spells. "Wow. You are good." I summoned a dagger and placed it on the table.

"Why couldn't—?" His voice faded as he stared at the weapon. "Is that what I think...?"

"Yeah. Pick it up. It won't bite."

His long fingers folded around the hilt and he lifted the dagger, supporting its tip with his other hand. "Dorian's?" he asked.

Repressing my snort was impossible. "Hardly. It's mine." I summoned its mate. "Wolfe's weapons only respond to one master." When he saw the second dagger, I sent it away.

"But, you're human. That's not possible."

"Nothing is impossible, Jason. Highly improbable, yes, but not impossible." My Wolfe confession was a high enough dose of honesty; I didn't correct his species assumption.

He tilted the weapon in the spell-muted light, studying the workmanship. The blade cut air as he whirled the dagger, turned the hilt toward me and handed it back. "What does this mean?" he asked.

Despite the hard set of his mouth, I found myself remembering the taste of his lips. I spun the dagger and set it on the tabletop. "It means I'm a danger to you. If your people learn you've been, um, associating with a Wolfe, one with my unique attributes—"

"They won't. I won't let them—"

"And Kyle? And-and the Brethren? The Brethren keep their secrets." I placed my hand, palm down over the dagger, and stared at the silvery metal interleaved with black wood. "I can't protect you. Not if you make yourself a target."

"Really?" he asked, blunt anger in his voice. "Is that what you are doing now? Protecting me? Regan, I care—"

Oh heck, don't say that. "At this point, all the Brethren know is that you're a Holder I was using to get information."

"Information." I looked up in time to see pain transform his face. "You were using me?"

His face blurred crystalline before my eyes and I looked away, grateful for my sunglasses. I blinked and said, "I'm sorry." I banished the dagger but kept my hand on the table. With my other hand, I pulled an envelope out of my jacket pocket and dropped it on the table. All the information Cypher had dug up on Jason Astin-Lake. I looked at him one last time.

As evenly as possible, I said, "I checked. The Brethren, Kadin Farahani, did not order a hit on your sister or Roger. Whatever happened, the vampires had no part in your sister's death." I cut off the argument I saw in his eyes by saying, "You can remove the obscure spell now." I stood up fast, probably too fast. As he undid the spell, his magic brushed my skin. "Bye, Jason. Be careful. Please."

I turned and walked away, fleeing the park before the urge to increase my men-I've-been-with tally to three overrode the wise voice in my head.

Chapter Thirty-Eight

The night was chilly and comforting, the air yummy with the smell of fireplaces. I stared at him, feeling guilty, like a neglectful mother. His blond mane was a mess.

I switched on the barn light, grabbed the tack box and then opened the gate. "Hey, Bill." I grabbed the conditioner and dumped globs in his mane and tail. While the conditioner did its magic, I buried my fingers in his fuzzy coat, scratching my short fingernails over his skin. "Sorry, buddy, I was off saving the world, if you can believe that." I found an itchy spot and Bill stretched his long neck, nose skyward, an expression of horsy ecstasy on his face.

When the itchy patch played out, I reached for the hoof pick. Bill obediently lifted his front left hoof so I could scrape out the clods of accumulated dirt. Behind me came the sound of my door opening and a car's trunk opening and shutting. I set Bill's hoof down and continued on to the other three. Only when I heard his approaching footsteps, did I look up.

Un-invite and other spells, fortified by Lex, are slathered on Bill's little home like chile and cheese on huevos rancheros. Not even my father could pass through the gate without an invite.

Breas opened the gate, strolled through, and shut it behind him. Bill's ears pricked forward and he offered up a throaty nicker.

"Hey, Bill," said Breas. The vampire snapped a carrot into small pieces and Bill bobbed his head up and down in a ridiculous "yes" motion. The poor horse resembled one of those little bobbing red birds that used to be sold in the back of comic books.

Breas handed him a piece of carrot.

"Why'd you have to teach him that?" I said. "It's undignified."

Bill finished his treat and bobbed his head. Breas handed him another carrot bit and said, "He has a mane full of girly hair goo. You've already stripped him of any dignity."

"He looks like a blond Rastafarian," I protested weakly.

"Real men don't condition, do they, Bill?" Breas's fingers scratched Bill high along the top of his thick neck. I squinted at Breas's far from product-free hair and withheld comment.

"You leavin'?"

"Yeah," he answered, handing Bill another carrot. "I've got business to attend to." At my raised eyebrows, his teeth flashed and he added, "Legitimate business."

"Right." In Breas's dictionary "legitimate" means, "Nobody dies, but otherwise terribly illegal."

I used a stiff brush to work the dirt off Bill's coat and Breas continued stuffing him with carrots. Something gray was draped over one of Breas's shoulders.

"All gone, mate. Sorry." Out of the corner of my eyes, I saw Breas show Bill his empty hands. Bill, who hides his brilliance under a toasty blanket of lazy, sighed and accepted scratches as compensation. After a few minutes, Breas came to stand next to me.

We faced each other, Breas absently scratching Bill's withers and me just standing there. He pulled the gray material off his shoulder and dropped it in place on mine. I grabbed the thing, it was a T-shirt, and examined it in the light. World Cup T-shirt. "Cool. Thanks."

"You still owe me—"

"Nope. I did your laundry. The debt is paid."

"If I wanted a valet, I'd—"

"Valet. That's me." Much preferable and a lot less complicated than anything else.

He smiled. "Next time, no sweet-smelling fabric softener."

"Spring fresh vampire." I returned his smile.

"Stay out of trouble, huh?" He hesitated and then gave me a brother-chaste kiss. Turning on his heel, he walked away.

Pausing briefly at Bill's head, he dropped his face to the horse's hairy ears. "When a human named Jason drops by...kick him in the nuts." I grinned at the vampire's departing back.

My grin faded. "When?" I hadn't seen or heard from Jason in a week and I'd pretty much come to terms with "never."

"Yeah," Breas returned, mildly glum, still walking away. I sighed.

"Bye, Regan."

"Bye, Breas."

Looping an arm over his broad back, I leaned on Bill, watching Breas's lanky silhouette. Breas isn't much for goodbye and usually just slips away when my back is turned.

Feeling irritatingly amused, I started working the knots out of Bill's mane.

~About The Author~

A lifelong resident of the desert southwest, P. Kirby grew up in El Paso, Texas and is a graduate of New Mexico State University. Though an avid reader, she only started writing fiction in 2003. She prefers to recast familiar villainous archetypes—dark elves, vampires—in a more heroic light and avoids traditiona; "big-bad out to destroy the world" storylines.

Home is a tiny house in the desert, shared with her long-suffering husband. She is co-owned by an Arabian horse and a greyhound. She has never owned or been owned by a cat.

The latest incarnation of her blog is here:
www.patriciakirby.com/blog

Immerse Yourself in Fantasy
with
Decadent Publishing

ॐ

www.decadentpublishing.com

www.ingramcontent.com/pod-product-compliance
Lightning Source LLC
Chambersburg PA
CBHW031305170626
46807CB00001B/313

* 9 7 8 1 6 1 3 3 3 0 6 0 9 *